The Last Days of Draden

The Last Days of Draden

A Post-Apocalyptic Saga

RJ Wolfe

ISBN-13: 9781543006018
ISBN-10: 1543006019
Library of Congress Control Number: 2017911427
CreateSpace Independent Publishing Platform
North Charleston, South Carolina

Table of Contents

The Ten Sectors
of the World

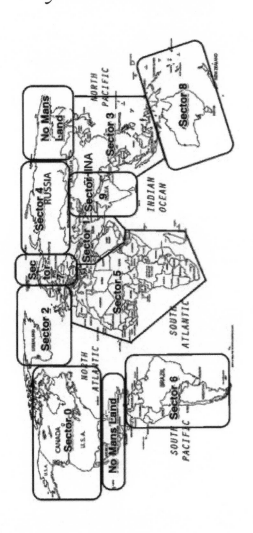

CHAPTER 1

Chronicles

"And I saw the beast, and the kings of the earth, and their armies, gathered together to make war against him that sat on the horse, and against his army."

REVELATION 19:19

"SO IT BEGINS..." says General Samuel Draden, Commander of the Seventh Resistance. He stares down the peak of the Golan Heights. The approaching army is two times larger than his own. He turns to his second in command, "Instruct our soldiers to prepare, Lieutenant General."

General Draden's army of two hundred and fifty thousand strong appeared suddenly and without warning atop the peak of the Golan Heights six days ago. They are camped approximately one hundred and seventy miles to the south of Damascus, Syria, in Sector 1. The capital of the new world.

The strategy to arrive undetected inside the borders of the capital city began on the westernmost side of Sector 5, the area once known as Morocco. Two hundred and fifty thousand warriors were hand-picked by Draden and his commanders then divided into fifty groups of five thousand soldiers each. They were ordered to move covertly across the northern-most perimeter of Sector 5 and freely through Sector 2 and Sector 7, formerly western and eastern Europe. A journey of nearly four months came to a head upon the 6,500 foot peak of the Golan Heights in Sector 1 to begin the invasion of the capital city of Damascus. The global-imperial army scrambles to answer the Resistance threat.

⚓

Draden's forces are completing their preparations to the land beneath them and to the terrain ahead. Tomorrow, for the first time in 30 years, the deserts of Damascus will decide the fate of humankind once more.

Scouts return. "General, the global-imperial army has nearly five hundred thousand troops. Another two hundred fifty thousand are still holed up in Damascus."

Draden nods, "I see." He looks to his Lieutenant General who appears surprised by the numbers, "they are a little lighter than we calculated aren't they?" exclaims Draden.

Lieutenant General Alvarez looks toward the northern horizon in the direction of the global-imperial forces, scoffs, "well, this will be over before noon tomorrow, won't it?" With a broad grin he says. "Just in time for lunch."

Draden smiles slightly, nods then sees to the final preparations of his army.

⊹⊱⊰⊹

As night envelops the sun scorched sands of Syria, a cool October wind carries with it the scent of jasmine throughout the camp. Draden's mind drifts to happier days. A large, silvery moon is suspended overhead and illuminates a clear autumn sky.

Draden asks the artillery corps of engineers. "Do you have everything you need ladies and gentlemen?" Inquires Draden.

"Aie General." they respond enthusiastically.

"Tens of thousands are relying on you to make the skies and the sands fight alongside us tomorrow. You all got us covered?" asks Draden.

"Yes General. Count on it." Answers the lead engineer.

"Excellent." Draden looks up and good-humoredly points toward the hundreds of pigs wallowing a short distance away. "I think one of your pigs is escaping," He smiles, clicks twice to his horse, and rides off.

The engineer looks anxiously over his shoulder. Nothing is the matter with his pigs. They have been in order all along. The engineer turns back to Draden and starts in with a reply but the General is already engaged in other matters. He looks at his netting on the ground and laughs. Amused and inspired by his commander returns to his task.

⊹⊱⊰⊹

3

The brisk twilight breeze gives way to the dawn of tomorrow. The global-imperialist generals pushed their march on through the night. Their soldiers are tired but determined to put an end to the Resistance once and for all.

Scouts hurry to Draden's tent, "General, the global-imperial army is less than seven miles away." Draden grabs his sword and fastens his brown leather and silver plate armor to his body. Mounting his horse, he makes his way to his vantage point.

Though the enemy army is still a few miles away, the rumbling of the horses proclaims to be much closer. Pounding of hooves intensifies the drubbing of the pulse in the temples, resonating like an ominous rainstorm in the ears. Beats of drum once declared to be faint noise in the distance replace the sounds of heartbeat. Blood curdling howls of the eager soldiers in the distance send ripples of fear through the body. Dust from the march, while still far, can almost be tasted in the throats of the men and women who await to receive them on the other side of the heights.

The phase of action has begun.

"Positions!" shouts Draden.

He gallops toward Lieutenant Commander Katsumi Nakano, Commander of the infantry. From his horse, he fixes his gaze squarely into hers and speaks to her but directs his dialogue to the body infantry so they can hear, "Lieutenant Commander Nakano," he asks, "our infantry has entrusted you with their lives. What say you to that honor?"

Lieutenant Commander Nakano replies with a subtle hint of her homeland, "as I have entrusted them with mine, General." Nakano's infantry reply with clamors on their shields by spear and sword.

Draden looks on for a moment. Satisfied, he rides to the cavalry troop. His light blue cape flaps behind him with each stride.

Commander Ezra Yver, a former British cavalry officer before England was annihilated and absorbed into Sector 2, answers the same question with the same reply as Nakano. Yver's knights knell upon their shields with sword and lance.

Mansour Haddad, Commander of the archer and artillery division responds with inflections in his voice from one born and raised in the Middle East. He answers as have the two before him.

Draden stops before Lieutenant General Alvarez and asks for his reply. General Alvarez compels his horse to hind legs, proudly unsheathes his sword from scabbard and hoists it above his head. He addresses the army directly; and declares, "As I have entrusted them with mine General. Victory awaits! The time has come to finally sever the serpent's head."

As if the sky split to the heavens - an eruption in the wind carries with it the pounding of metal on metal. Enlivened spirits boom forth hoorahs and hussahs. The first rays of dawn gleam and dance upon swords raised up high. The Seventh Resistance prepare to meet the opposing army.

Mangonels and trebuchets creak and scrape along the sand and stones beneath them as they are placed into position at the top of the Golan. Once arrived, soldiers hurry to fill tremendous metal spheres with poisonous snakes, scorpions and scalding sand. One by one, Egyptian cobras, Levant vipers, Palestinian vipers, and Saw Scaled vipers are expertly handled and placed inside their temporary holding vessels. A single bite from any one of these serpents is enough to induce paralysis and death within minutes. Once the large steel bowls are filled with as many killers as they will hold, they are locked loosely so as to shatter quickly and break open easily.

Yellow death-stalker scorpions are the most dangerous species of scorpions in the world and are found in abundance in the sands of the middle east. They are loaded into separate canisters in preparation for their flight behind enemy lines. While many humans have been known to survive a sting from the death-stalker, the pain inflicted can be immobilizing and last for hours. They are large enough to carry an excruciating dose of venom, yet small enough to crawl into the spaces between the gaps in armor and tear into victims with their poison. In some cases, the sheer volume of stings dispensed by the death-stalker at one time can lead to fluid build-up in the lungs and eventual death.

Sand is placed into copper and iron containers then heated over a searing fire until white-hot. Once the sand reaches intense temperatures it is carefully shoveled from the heated container into siege engine vessels. The transport carriers are perforated so as to shower the enemy from above with blistering grains before making final impact, shattering, then inflicting an excruciating punishment. The sands will seep into the smallest openings in armor and slowly eat away at the flesh underneath. Death is common.

Spread out across the high points of the Golan, archers plant their arrows in the ground and prepare to let loose their arsenal.

Carefully eyeing the natural mile markers buried in the earth by his spies, Draden coolly anticipates giving the signal to begin. He is approached by Commander Yver. "General, I have an idea. Their flanks are weak. We can make it to their artillery and back before they can stop us."

Draden listens. He is not one to implement sudden changes in plans without sufficient calculation, nor does he initially take to what Yver argues. "Commander, what you're proposing is too dangerous. You would be giving up the high ground before its time. Our defenses are strongly in place."

"I understand General. But we agree, their artillery is their biggest threat to us. Our defenses are strong, yes, but only while they are acting in unison. More and more will die the thinner our defenses get. Besides...," he shrugs, "Nakano will be here. She can certainly handle matters in the area until we get back."

While not yet convinced about Yver's proposal, Draden concedes the point regarding Lieutenant Commander Nakano. He scans his troops, assessing the potential loss of life from Yver's plan. After contemplating the risks thoroughly he decides that there is a chance of reducing overall casualties. He unenthusiastically agrees to Yver's plan. "Very well Commander. Don't make me regret it." He insists, "and I'll permit it on one condition…"

Yver awaits the demand, "What's that General?"

Draden instructs, "Alvarez goes with you."

"You know me General, I take regret very seriously." Yver nods assuringly and communicates the new battle plan to his warriors and the other commanders.

"Okay Alvarez," jokes Yver, "Don't steal my thunder now. Plenty of glory to go around."

Alvarez reassures him somewhat truthfully, "Of course not." He tightens his grip on the reins and pats his horse mischievously. Yver shakes his head. Alverez's forces join Yver's. All are aligned.

Resistance scouts report, "General, they are 2 miles away."

Draden raises his hand and awaits the right time to give the signal to begin the attack, his white horse stirs beneath him. Carefully he watches the mile markers. As soon as the first enemy boot crosses 1.5 miles Draden thrusts his arm down signaling to Commander Haddad to begin phase one.

At once the sound of catapult fills the air. From this height, lethal objects are hurled to substantial distances. Canisters of snakes and scorpions ascend into the sky, disappear in the sun then fall remorselessly upon the attackers. Steel spheres collide with soldiers killing them instantly. Metal crashes into the ground shattering. The deadly containers burst open, spilling their agitated contents on to unwilling hosts. The slithering assassins, now unrestrained, find their marks. Like a plague, they spread death. The cries and screams of the victims carry into the clouds. Once eager soldiers are reduced to paralyzed corpses. They hit the ground and seize uncontrollably. The neurotoxic venom is efficient in its work. Flesh melts away under the weight of the poison. A torment that slowly and agonizingly sends its victims away to a final journey out of this life. Disorder and panic descend.

The Global-Imperialist commanders eventually re-establish order, rally their soldiers, regain control and push on. Advancing troopers hack the heads off the reptiles and press forward.

Commander Haddad ushers in phase two. "On my signal…" he shouts. Waits patiently for the enemy to cross beyond mile marker 1.

They cross.

"Now!" roars Haddad launching the burning sand into flight.

Searing sand rains down on the imperialists bringing with it utter misery. There is no escape for anyone within range. The molten grains of sand sift down on to the soldiers of Damascus, scorching their skin with intense heat, inflicting terrible pain.

Victims writhe, try to shake off the sand, and shriek like those under torture. In excruciating agony, men and women wriggle mad with pain – collapse. Screaming and rolling on the ground they desperately try to remove their armor. Some die when they inhale the burning sand and burn their lungs.

Others pass on when the grains melt their skin. Some manage to remove their sweltering garments but their wounds will continue to smolder until death eventually finds them. The devastation is severe.

The global-imperialist army starts their counter-attack. Close enough to use their artillery, they begin an unrepenting bombardment into the wind against the Resistance. Ballistas combine with arrow, trebuchet and mangonel.

Commander Haddad thunders his response, "Release!"

Defensive catapults of the Seventh Resistance hurl large stones and projectiles directly at the incoming artillery assault. Medieval missiles crash violently into one another shattering above head. Debris and shrapnel from their collisions wound many below. Reinforced nets are sent flying through the air. Two melded stones on either side give them momentum to fly.

Manilla fibers, promanila, polydacron, nylon and kevlar are woven together to create a surface to air defense system reminiscent of the patriot defense and iron dome era. By scavenging materials from the wreckage of boats, boat yards, abandoned military posts, towing and rigging apparatuses, warehouses and factories, Draden's engineers found the materials they needed to create a formidable defensive netting that is capable of withstanding nearly any artillery attack.

Harnessing the kinetic energy of two projectiles to one, the global-imperialist attacks are deflected from their intended target and collapse directly upon their own soldiers killing them with falling stones, iron arrow and collision debris. Nevertheless, the imperialist artillery assault is relentless.

Commander Yver was correct. The Seventh is beginning to take heavy casualties.

Commander Haddad unveils the final phase of his opening opus. "Archers!" He yells. "Let loose!"

A canopy of arrows blacks out the morning sky above. None are left in flight. Thousands have impaled the imperialists, some have sunken into ground.

"Again!" Haddad orders. They release another furious volley. The clang of arrowheads into metal armor and shield echoes across the battlefield. Hundreds more perish.

"Firestorm ready!" Calls out Haddad. His aides hurry to ignite thousands of arrow tips. Bowstrings are pulled back and prepare to fire.

"Aim!" he continues. The archer corps direct their aim downward into the ground at the marshland below.

"Fire!" yells Haddad.

Flaming arrows take flight, they whir and whistle through the air. Striking the ground below, they set the marshland ablaze. Beneath the feet of the unwary is an incendiary fueled by hundreds of pounds of pig grease floating atop the wetland. A fire-marsh now engulfs the unwitting soldier. Those who are not set alight are consumed by smoke. Blurring vision and hindered breathing is now their misfortune.

In action upon their opportunity to strike, Commander Yver, and Lieutenant General Alvarez swarm down the hillside widening to the flanks of the disoriented enemy.

The horsemen break into three columns. They accelerate their surge, the first column is led by Yver. He takes the left flank. The second column is led by Alvarez. He takes the right flank. The third column follows closely behind in the center to defend their back. Their target is the enemy artillery that is disrupting the offensive of the Golan.

Engaging with swords drawn, a mighty fight follows. Pressing through, Yver and Alvarez cut down soldier by unlucky soldier. Dismantle siege engine by crumbling siege engine. A trail of destruction follows them. When the deed is done, they whorl their horses around to charge the enemy from rear and side.

"Charge!" orders Alvarez, pointing his sword straight ahead - squaring his attack toward the enemy. The horsemen form a wedge. Alvarez is in front. They race forward and divide the global-imperial army into two separate bodies from the rear.

Seeing her opening, Lieutenant Commander Nakano orders "Attack!" and sprints down the hillside ahead of her infantry. She grips katanas tightly in both hands as her toned arms pump backward and forward in rhythm with her stride. Her soldiers make haste to keep up.

An expert combatant, Lt. Com. Katsumi Nakano was raised and trained by underground remnants of a ninja clan, her martial prowess is unmatched. Orphaned by the global-imperial army when she was three years old, every battle is personal. At 28 years old she is the youngest of Draden's commanders. Standing at 5 feet 4 inches, she is a powerful force.

Moving with blistering speed Nakano dispatches multiple assailants. Her adversaries often see her sword for the first time after she has already pierced their armor and cut them through.

Thick in the fray, she mounts a ferocious assault with swift, well-placed blades, bone crushing kicks, jaw breaking strikes of hand, palm, elbow and fist. She zeroes in on an enemy officer, four rivals block her path. Nakano vaults into the air, summersaults behind one and plunges her blade into his back. She repurposes him as a human shield - fending off incoming blade - drops quickly to the ground - in one clean circling motion with her heel - knocks another off his feet. He falls. Before hitting the earth, Nakano's dagger tears into his jugular. He goes limp and is no more. Still horizontal to the earth, she reaches into her boot and slings two throwing stars just under the helmets of her assailants slicing their exposed necks. They drop to the ground and struggle to breathe with final dying gasps.

Nakano rises from the marsh, fury is fresh in her eyes. With a quick snapping motion flings the mud off her jerkin sending dirt and wet soil flying in every direction. She glares at the enemy officer. Anxiously he raises his sword overhead and charges. Approaching her at full gallop, he tightens his grip on the hilt of his weapon, ready to strike her down. Nakano dashes fearlessly toward the head of the charging colt. At the moment she is about to be trampled she pulls her dagger and throws herself forward to both knees arching her back so her hair touches the earth behind her as she glides underneath the animal through the mud. Swampy wetness sprays to her right and left. From below the horse's belly Nakano cuts the saddle from underneath. Once passed the steed's hind legs, she jumps upright to her feet with perfect balance. The enemy officer is tossed off his mount and splashes helmet first into the desert wetland. Disoriented, the officer finds his way to his feet. Nakano leaves no time for him to consider what to do next. With a swift blade strike to the back of his knee she cuts through the posterior cruciate ligament disconnecting his femur from his tibia. He drops to injured leg. In a flash, Nakano spins and cleanly severs head from shoulders.

Nakano scans the battlefield for Draden. She finds him. He is surrounded. Refusing to let harm come to him, she jumps on to the back of the deceased officer's horse and races to Draden's side. Urgently she battles through blade and steel to get to him, hastily riding over carnage. From behind Draden the glint of metal is seen raised in the sunlight. An axe is about to be plunged into the back of the General. Before the axe drops, Nakano flings her sword through the air. Her blade lodges firmly through the attacker's neck. Blood and steel shimmers in daylight from the other side. A clean throw through his larynx. He drops. His axe rings as it strikes the stones beneath.

⚜

The clash recedes. Remaining global-imperialist forces retreat to find refuge back in Damascus. Nakano pulls her sword from her victim's neck and casually wipes off the blood on the corpse's sleeve.

Nearly out of breath, she asks Draden with an understated Japanese accent, "How many times am I going to have to save your life before you realize the front line is no place for old men?"

Draden replies, "As often as it takes. You know how stubborn I can be."

Yver's cavalry and Alvarez's troop thunder across the terrain picking off what retreating stragglers remain until finally consolidating their victory at Draden's position.

What is left of the global-imperial army shrinks away as they fade into the distance. The whole of the Seventh Resistance celebrate their triumph.

Draden measures the time by the sun and directs his observation to Alvarez, "I'd say it's closer to three o'clock," referencing the statement Alvarez made earlier about the battle being over by noon. Alvarez laughs.

⚍

General Draden surveys the outcome. This victory is glorious, but it is only the first phase of a larger goal. He looks up to the heavens and takes in a fresh breath. The air is warm and is mixed with the scents of cactus, burning oil, blood and smoldering wood. He looks down the horizon in the direction of the capital city. It is still only a blurred mirage in the distance. He prepares himself to make an unreasonable request of his troops.

This campaign is to be the one that sends a message to the global-imperial army. It must be conveyed that the 7th Resistance is the final balancing force between good and evil. The resistance of the people who have been shut down, shut out and forgotten. The iron wall of valor that will prevent true and complete global domination by global-imperial despots and elites. The call to the good, fair, bold and courageous to strengthen their wills and reinforce their stance.

A successful completion of this campaign and a speedy conquest of the capital city will begin to restore momentum to the Resistance. It will reignite hope for those huddling in the shadows awaiting the right event, the right sign, the right victory to rise up and join the fight against oppression and tyranny. They are faced with a fresh opportunity to thrust forward against an under-powered and under-prepared enemy. They have vanquished an opponent with time to spare, but to see the plan through, Draden must press his army on without rest.

Draden draws his sword and circles it above-head. The attention of all is given. Commanders gather their forces around to hear what their general has to say.

Draden begins, "I know you are tired. I know you are bruised. I know your arms and legs ache though they carried us to victory today. I know your weapons have been dulled and your bellies rumble for a feast..." Draden's white horse stirs beneath him, "Aie, it is true, a rest and feast are well-deserved... but what I am about to ask, you also deserve." Draden raises his voice, "You have earned freedom from oppression, solace from tyranny, safety from cruelty, and an unshackling of your chains from the domination of an awful and unjust beast. The beast that serves only the self-serving and those in its service." His heart swells with conviction; he continues, "We serve no man but each other. We bend no knee to tyranny. We cannot and will not declare faithful obedience to bloody, merciless persecution by an evil and intolerant regime." He turns his horse and points his sword toward Damascus, "There..." he proclaims, "There is where we take back what is rightfully ours." Points to the landscape ahead, "Just beyond those hills we will break away our chains forever. Just beyond those hills, we will deliver a mighty and fateful blow. Just beyond those hills, is where, we reclaim our souls!"

The crowd cheers. Sensing that victory is nearer to them than has been for the last 50 years, they are eager to respond. The Seventh files into formation. Food, rest and shelter are put out of mind.

⚜

The Seventh Resistance has marched twenty miles. Only one hundred and fifty miles now separates them from their objective. The wetlands below the Golan Heights have given way to rough, windswept desert sand and a gleaming capital city in the distance.

The global-imperialists saw Damascus as an ideal capital because it was situated in the middle of a natural and seemingly inexhaustible fresh water supply. In the first seven years following the great black out, one-third of the earth ran dry. A drought had ravaged the earth. During the wars, bridges, roads, structures and buildings that decorated the landscape of Syria and Israel were destroyed. Dams that had sealed off the surrounding water supplies were broken. Water flooded the sands. For a time, the deserts of Syria and Israel had turned green again. Underground fresh water springs nurtured the rebirth of a lush, flourishing oasis. It was also strategically significant. It sat at the center of the entire world.

Over the next seven years, two thirds of the earth was without water. Little was left of many seas. All that remain as far as the eye could see are desolate, scarred basins that once thrived with marine life. Any remaining water was forcefully seized by the powerful to be rationed as they saw necessary. Mostly, they rationed water and resources to anyone who they felt could be useful in retaining control over the population. Anyone with a different ideology or who bore an unshared eye on replenishing the grip of the powerful over the people was left to struggle. These people usually died in short time thereafter from thirst or bandit, or beast.

The machinations for controlling the water supply extended east from Damascus to the easternmost borders of Iran dividing Turkmenestan through the middle, encompassing the Caspian Sea. To the south, the borders of the scheme enveloped Saudi Arabia and Yemen all the way to the shores of the Indian Ocean. The gambit stretched west to just passed the Nile river, and north, encircling the whole of the borders of Turkey and entire Black Sea, then back east cutting through the middle of Kazakhstan. What were once known as the paradise lands of the middle east, are now plainly known as Sector 1.

—※—

The Seventh Resistance comes upon a pocket of vegetation among a sea of sand. "Here," Draden instructs, "we rest for the night."

The soldiers get to work pitching their quarters. A detachment of five thousand go ahead a few miles to take forward guard. Children travelling with their parents begin building fires while shelters are erected. Lower ranking soldiers and travel companions prepare the meals.

—※—

For fourteen years, Lieutenant Commander Nakano habitually raised her sleeping quarters closest to Draden. She has been especially protective of him since he watched over her after she lost her father to the global-imperial army. Her father, Tomo Nakano, revered by his clan as the re-incarnation of Hattori Hanzo, was the head of the powerful Iga ninja clan that raised his daughter. When the Iga clan became displaced by the wars, he fought under Draden as commander of the infantry. He was killed in battle when Katsumi was just three years old.

As he lay dying he asked Draden to promise him he would look after his daughter. Draden agreed. He found her father's clan and sheltered her with them. True to his promise, he visited Katsumi every chance he got to tell her war

stories and impart on her the wisdoms of the old philoso-
phers and strategists. He spared no tales about her father's
heroism and they spent endless nights laughing at the funny
things her dad would do - even in the darkest of times. For
years, Katsumi Nakano was trained to be the next leader of
the Iga clan. This was her birthright. Though at 13 years old
she stowed away on Dradens convoy and showed up one day
undetected in his camp. When Draden tried to return her to
the Igas, he had found the clan had been discovered by the
global-imperialists and were forced to move once more. Not
knowing where they had fled, he kept her under his personal
protection ever since.

As soon as Kasumi turned 14, against Draden's wishes, she
threw herself into battle for the first time. General Draden
never left her side during that conflict. After the battle he
admonished her severely, pleading with her to let him keep his
promise to her father. His pleas fell on deaf ears. Katsumi was
too stubborn and consumed by rage. At the end, they reached a
compromise. The best way for her to honor her father and feed
her wrath was to be placed at the head of the infantry. This
way she could carry on her father's legacy. To fulfill her clan's
legacy, she was commissioned as the commander-in-charge
of spies and intelligence. Fourteen years later, she remains
Draden's most loyal and trusted commander.

Samuel Draden is a towering figure standing at 6'5 with
a broad athletic frame. His hair is thick and wavy; a darker
shade of brown. His eyes are the color of all the colors of the
earth with traces of the sea around the rims. He is not scruffy,
neither is he clean shaven. Somehow he maintains a steady five

o'clock shadow around the clock. The hair on his face is never too much yet is always apparent.

He has some words for Nakano, but approaches her with soft eyes, as a loving father does to a devoted daughter. He visits with her as he has done for over 25 years.

"You could have gotten yourself killed out there today looking after me Katsumi." He chides her.

"You *would* have gotten killed today if I wasn't looking after you, Godfather." She fires back.

"We don't know that for sure." Defends Draden.

"I'd be sewing you back up at the very least." Smiles Katsumi.

Draden shrugs and pats her head like he used to when she was three. "Thank you for having my back, Katsi."

She nods in assurance and shares her latest intelligence from the field, "The global-imperial reinforcements from the north-east quadrant of Sector 1 advance on our position. They are being supported by a full complement of mercenaries from the northwest quadrant of sector 9. They are 120 miles away from the capital city just beyond the northern mountains. The have been marching toward us since we landed on the Golan Heights."

Draden assesses her report, "What of Colonel Busellis? He is to hold them off until we complete our campaign into Damascus. How are they matched up?"

"With the addition of the mercenaries, the Chancellor's armies are three to one stronger than Busellis' forces. He has already engaged them once with little to show for it." She explains.

Draden looks skyward, rubs his chin, breathes out, "one and a half million reinforcements bearing down on us leaves little room for error and idleness. Thank you Katsumi."

He exits, walks outside to the smoke-filled night air. For some reason, the scent of fresh wood smoking on a campfire, the crackling sounds of timber on flame and the clanging metal of blacksmiths re-shoeing horses and repairing damaged weapons and armor helped Draden think through troublesome times.

Lieutenant General Alvarez joins him.

"General, what's on your mind?" inquires Alvarez.

Startled, but not showing it, Draden responds, "Diego," and pats him on the shoulder, "Colonel Busellis is in position to stall the reinforcements as planned."

"Well that's great news General, but what aren't you telling me?"

───※───

Lieutenant General Diego Alvarez's father, Silvio, was a Cuban government official who worked in the Ministry of the Interior of Cuba. His job was to monitor the Cuban population for signs of dissent and uprising. Political fidelity was monitored at workplaces and in schools in Cuba. Academic and labor files on each citizen were kept in archive. Recorded in their pages were actions or statements that may one day speak against a person's loyalty before they were allowed to advance to a new school or position. Poverty was rampant. Dissent was far-reaching - but fear and the Cuban Ministry of the Interior made certain, dissent never gained support. His mother, Maya was a music teacher. Teaching was a thankless job in Cuba, especially if one's Ministry of the Interior's archive bore witness against them. Most of the days Maya spent teaching she was in fact serving as a social worker for disillusioned and ill-fated children.

Having had enough, the Alvarez family smuggled themselves out of Cuba in hopes of starting a new life in America. The cost of smuggling one person from Cuba was a hefty eleven thousand United States dollars. With an average wage of not more than the equivalent of fifty United States dollars per month, leaving Cuba was an impossible idea for most. Silvio used his government and political connections to make the impossible idea of leaving Cuba possible for him and Maya. He diligently saved and amassed a small fortune of money through gratuitous payoffs he would regularly receive as a government official. Through combining his connections and financial resources, Silvio created the opportunity for he and Maya to find their way out of the vicious Cuban cycle. The journey was full of peril and penance.

Having secured passage from Cuba, Silvio and Maya were shipped under cover of night to Ecuador. Their orders were to move through the inhospitable jungles of Ecuador to a different location and await carriage to the next port. After ten days of staving off malaria carrying mosquitos and would-be kidnappers, they were transported to Panama. They spent three days and two nights in hostels for the homeless before transit to Haiti. They awaited their next orders in Haiti for two months. They could not seek work for fear of being discovered. Working off a list of names, vague addresses and tattered photos of people considered to be friendly human traffickers, they sought salvation in the shelters of strangers night after dreadful night.

Finally, after two grueling months, they were ordered to a quick stop-over in the Dominican Republic for a fortnight before embarking on the final leg of their journey to Puerto Rico where they stayed with more savory types of traffickers and eventually with family. From Puerto Rico, they freely booked travel into Florida. Without a diverse enough economy in Florida, Silvio and Maya made one final trek to the mountains of Colorado where they could live away from persecution in relative obscurity. Silvio at thirty years old, just about to turn thirty-one, and Maya at twenty-two, were finally ready to start a new life in America.

The next year, the first of the great wars broke out. Silvio and Maya joined the Colorado resistance militia. Diego was born nearly twenty years later into war and upheaval. Diego was taught field tactics by his father as soon as he was able to steady himself on a horse and wield a sword. With water in short supply, gun powder could no longer be made. Mechanization, firearms, and explosive weaponry were no longer possible.

Diego had heard of the legend of General Samuel Draden while fighting in the Colorado militia. Silvio would share stories he had heard of General Draden's adventures with him over the years while they sat next to campfires night after night. Diego was twenty-one years old when his father died cleanly of old age. Soon after his dad's death, he and his mother set out to find General Draden. Diego left the Colorado militia with the reputation of being one of the finest field tacticians ever to take part in the great wars on the North American continent.

Diego and Maya found General Draden ten years ago in the Blue Ridge Mountains of Virginia. Five years ago, Maya died peacefully on the trail.

The North American people and the region's landscape endured tremendous punishment since Silvio and Maya landed in Florida almost fifty years ago. The destruction there was unparalleled to any other continent in the world. The visage of North America would remain forever and permanently scarred, unrecognizable, torn asunder from unrelenting fight and devastation. So little remained of the once glorious American civilization that the entire land from Washington, DC to Sacramento, California is a virtual ground zero. Consequently, it came to be known as Sector 0.

Barren wastelands are all that remain of Mexico and the Carribbean Islands after the first wars. The entire mass separating north and south America is now a no man's land between sector 0 and sector 6.

Sector 6 is the former territories from Costa Rica to the Falkland Islands. Because of the fallout in North America, South America was spared no respite. The devastation was bad, though a few inconspicuous villages remain.

Draden answers Alvarez with a stiff upper lip, "Colonel Busellis is a fine commander but I fear he may be out of his league on this one."

Alvarez tries to express encouragement, "He knows what is at stake here. Capturing the capital city will turn the tide of this war. He won't let us down and we won't let the resistance down."

Draden nods his head and stands as the pillar of immovable strength, he curls his lips together briefly and pats Alvarez on the back, "We move at first light."

"Roger that General." Answers Alvarez. He heads off to convene with the troops and relays the General's orders.

General Draden stops by Commander Mansour Haddad's tent. "Am I interrupting Commander," asks Draden.

Draden's voice surprises Haddad and pushes him to accelerate his bite into his sandwich. Haddad hurries to a stand and turns toward the General in attention, crumbs of bread and mutton spray from his mouth as he answers with a Levantine accent, "No, not at all General." He coughs on his food and eagerly searches for his canteen to take a sip of water and rush the food down into his stomach. He continues, "what can I do for you?" Clears his throat and checks his mouth with his hand for any remaining morsels still stuck to his chin.

Amused, Draden replies, "at ease Commander. I just wanted to congratulate you on a job well-done today. Really, a fine job."

A humble man, Haddad feels embarrassed taking compliments but he responds, "Thank you General, we have great people with us. And we have the greatest of Generals leading us."

Draden, a humble man himself, answers, "You're always so gracious Commander. Thank you."

Mansour Haddad is three years younger than Draden at sixty years old. The paths of their lives could not have spawned at more opposite corners of existence. Draden is a simple man, without much education who was forced into war when he was twelve years old. He is also a spiritual man who never considered himself religious although he is fascinated by the power of religion and the contents of the scriptures. Haddad is a practicing Sufi Muslim, who, while growing up, spent days memorizing and learning the Qur'an and Hadeeth. Haddad was born into an aristocratic Syrian family, prays as often as he can, and is very religious. His father, Mounir was a well-known neurosurgeon in Syria, and his mother, Maryam was a generous, refined woman of noble birth.

Despite his father's urges to take up a meaningful profession and follow in his footsteps as a neurosurgeon, Mansour was entranced and awed by mysticism and the occult. Mansour's father was a religious man. He and his son would often debate the meanings of scripture passages. Yet he would always return to the point for Mansour to put the scriptures aside and re-direct the seemingly inexhaustible devotion he had to the study of mysticism into the study of medicine.

Ignoring his father's wishes, Mansour, instead spent years trying to reconcile the Bible, Qur'an, and Torah with one another. He spent yet more ages comparing Muslim Hadeeth with the Christian and Jewish gospels. Decades of isolation in study of philosophy, history and theology added layers of eccentricity to his already refined character.

When the wars began, Mounir and his family stayed out of any involvement whatsoever. However, because of his medical training, Mounir was called upon to tend to the sick and wounded on regular occasion. Mounir resisted getting further involved in the war at every opportunity. Yet, culture and common practice dictates that men and woman of means were automatically dragged into the politics of world affairs. After eight years of avoiding involvement in the wars, Mounir, Maryam and Mansour were thrust into the bowels of the conflict as members of the global-imperial movement. Thus, Mansour Haddad was on the opposite side of the wars as General Samuel Draden.

Mounir and Maryam died five years after being burdened with a war and a movement they did not believe in. They died within months of each other, first Mounir, then Maryam. As the years progressed since his parent's death, eight years in all, Mansour Haddad's awareness of the conflict reached new heights. His true emotions erupted uncontainably from his core. The lessons of his parents found no place among the actions of the global-imperialists. Maryam was a woman of pure gentleness, with inexhaustible compassion toward humankind. Mounir, was a man of learning and enlightenment, tolerance and acceptance. Traces of their teachings and what they stood for were absent from the tenants of the global-imperialist doctrine. Mansour followed his conscience and disappeared one day into the mountains. There he entrenched himself in the study of Solomonic magic, mysticism, religion, theology, philosophy and metaphysics. He became a master of the occult.

Trained in combat, he brandished a scimitar yet carried a bo staff on his back. He preferred the white robes of a mystic with armor concealed beneath rather than wearing the obvious metal, plated armor and leather for all to see. For several years Mansour Haddad lived peacefully in solitude, while occasionally fighting off the trespassing brigand, bandit or vagabond. He kept a pet wolf outside his cabin and his hawk nested nearby upon a cliff ledge. It is said, he can speak to animals and the unseen.

Draden and his army came upon his lodgings during expedition one day along the western Taurus mountains in southern Turkey. The Taurus system is a massive mountain system that extends along a curve from Lake Eğirdir in the west to the upper reaches of the Euphrates and Tigris rivers in the east. Haddad took his usual defensive posture when receiving outsiders, but Draden was intrigued by this hermit who spent his days in obscurity learning scripture and speaking to animals. After Haddad was satisfied that Draden meant him no harm, he invited him into his home for strawberry tea made from melted snow and fruit he harvested from the local strawberry tree. As the fruit of the strawberry tree was somewhat of an intoxicant, information and knowledge soon flowed freely between the two men who could not have begun their journeys further opposite than has been.

After three days camped in the mountains, Haddad and Draden agreed that the opportunity to fight together in a cause greater than themselves was sufficient enough reason for Haddad to abandon his lodgings and rejoin the war. Only this time, Haddad could be part of a cause that his consciousness could condone and his parents would approve of. His wolf and hawk came with him, but time and age sent them back into the earth. Haddad managed to captivate other animals to travel with him. A gray desert wolf and an eagle are his current companions.

⚏

After a brief discussion on scriptures and mysticism, Draden left Haddad's company and made one final stop.

Commander Ezra Yver was just returning from a meal with his troops. "Commander Yver." announced Draden.

"Yes General," answered Yver.

"I would like to acknowledge and congratulate you on a successful adjustment. You made a great difference in the outcome of the fight. Well done." Acknowledged Draden.

"Thank you General, I know how you hate to make last minute adjustments, but I saw the opening and had to act. Just like you taught me." Returned Yver.

"Indeed. A masterful stroke." He continues, "We move early in the morning tomorrow. Colonel Busellis has his hands full and we don't want to make him hold out any longer than he has to." Cautioned Draden.

"Understood General." Accepted Yver.

Early in the wars, Ezra Yver was a cavalry man in England under the command of various generals. At the prime of his years aged forty-four, he has lived a military life borne into war. Both of his parents were members of the British royal forces. His father Dominic was a Major in the British royal marines and his mother, Suzanna, was a Captain in the royal British army. Having descended from Jewish stock going all the way back to the biblical times of Israel, Dominic retained his dark-skinned complexion while Suzanna was a fair-haired, porcelain complected, green eyed Gael from northwestern England.

Ezra knew nothing else of the world but war, famine, suffering, and conflict. He learned duty and sacrifice from his father, while obtaining the qualities of care and understanding from his mother. Ezra was a thoughtful man and talented strategist. When the first wars broke out, Dominic instilled courage and discipline at extra measure to his son. He would take him on tours in the tanks he commanded. At times, Ezra would sit tight alongside his father in the fearsome British Challenger tank while Dominic was engaged in battle. Suzanna went out of her way to let her son know that there once was a life without war for their family. During breaks in combat, she would take him to the English countryside and tell him about all that once was in the earth before the global-imperial movement began to put the world in a vice, slowly dismantling everything they once knew and loved in existence.

Ezra was a man of the earth and a loyal soldier. When mechanized warfare disappeared he quickly became an expert horseman and gifted swordsman. He was unbeatable with a longsword and preferred the bulk of plate armor to the slightness of leather. Early in the years following the extinction of mechanization, gunpowder and firearms, Ezra and his family were dispatched to conflict in the Balkans on the border of Slovenia. Here, his battalion was ambushed and routed by a hardened global-imperial force. He lost his parents that day while almost acceding to become a casualty himself. He lay broken and bloodied on the field when Draden's reinforcement brigade reversed the fortunes of battle and pushed the global-imperial army back toward the sea. A marauding fleet of mercenary pirates finished off what remained of the imperialists that evening.

This is how Commander Ezra Yver came under the tutelage of General Draden fifteen years ago.

⚬

Draden retires restlessly for the evening. An unknown destiny beckons his arrival.

CHAPTER 2

Acts

DRADEN IS AWAKENED by the scuffling of soldiers, siege engines, horses and hogs moving outside his tent. It is not quite daybreak. He hurriedly leaves his quarters and is surprised to find that his entire army has been assembled while he slept and is prepared to march on Damascus. Lieutenant Commander Nakano stands at the head of her infantry battalion - her black tunic is coolly draped over hardened leather armor underneath. Two katanas cling to her back and two triple-pronged sais are secured on each side. Commander Haddad is poised at the front of the artillery division, attired as usual, donning the white robes of a cleric, draped over chain and plate armor underneath. His gray desert wolf stirs obediently next to him. Haddad aptly named him Sa'eed, for the unusual happy disposition he displays for a wolf of the wild. His great eagle, Nabila rests erect on a nearby cliff, one-third larger than a fully grown male eagle. True to her name, she is a noble and graceful creature. Commander Yver is mounted in front of his cavalry force, neatly armored in plate. Lieutenant General Alvarez sits proudly at the head of the great army, saddled - magnificently clad in shining armor. A midnight-blue cape hangs easily from his shoulders, gently swaying in the breeze.

Draden exchanges knowing looks with his commanders then leaps onto his white horse without saying a word. He takes position at the lead. The army marches toward the capital of the global-empire.

⎯⚏⎯

They march for 4 days and arrive but a short distance from the moat surrounding Damascus.

The majesty of the ruling city was at once an ominous and awe inspiring sight. When the global-imperial council rebuilt Damascus to represent their government body, they agreed that it would be fitting to embed shimmering jewels into its walls to give it an air of divinity, power and opulence. A misguided appeasement to those who would claim to be men of God. In distorted accordance with their scriptures, they decreed that a city of global rule ordained by God should be one appropriated in opulence and mired in decadence.

The glint of jewel reflected the sun's rays and conveyed a message of superiority, invincibility, and arrogance. Twelve of the earths most precious stones decorated twelve levels of the wall surrounding the ruling city. At the foundation was jasper, it spanned the length of the front wall. Sapphire above, next was chalcedony, then emerald, followed by sardonix, then sardius, chrysolyte, beryl, topaz, chrysoprasus, jacinth, and at the very top of the wall, amethyst glistened like a purple beacon to the unwary.

Draden eyes the moat and scorns, "Such a waste of water. Thousands of people die every day from thirst and they just spill it all around their walls making mud."

He turns to Nakano, "What news of Busellis?"

"He is holding," she responds.

With no time to spare, Draden orders his army to immediately begin the assault on the great, jeweled city. At once, Haddad launches his arsenal and smashes rock, boulder and fire into the walls. Debris is flung into the sky and to all corners. The crushing sound of stone, wood and metal rumbles in the ears.

Haddad's artillery barrage offers a worthy distraction for Draden's engineers to get to work bridging the moat and dislodging the city's gates from their hinges. The assailants use rollers, levers, ropes, pulleys, and winches to maneuver their tools into place at the base of the castle wall at the foot of the barricaded entry way. Once the machines are in position they remove the wheels and stabilize them against the great structure. Now pressed upon stone fortifications, they batter the corners of the aperture, expertly chiseling away the stone mounting that holds the iron hinges in place. The immense doors creak and scrape under their own weight as their support is gradually deteriorated by the incessant carving. Morale in the Seventh Resistance is high. Soldiers are eager and fresh.

The defenders open fire from the city towers and from behind the city walls. Springald defenses swing into action, smacking tremendous boulders at the sieging Seventh. Haddad returns suppressive fire. The warriors assume defensive positions. Damascus loads and unloads their terrifying ballistas into the body of the Resistance. Massive iron and wooden arrows are flung into the besiegers. Every missile impales dozens. Casualties mount.

"Breach!" cries Alvarez, "Breach!" The fortifications crumble on the southeastern wall. First into the breach is Nakano with her infantry, they are passed by the rush of Yver and his knights. Alvarez joins the fray with his company. Defenses at the breach are heavy. The earliest waves are denied immediate entry.

"Fall back," orders Draden, "Fall back!" While his troops are still eager to break the city they return obediently beyond the moat. Each battalion does their best to guard the other from harm.

"Regroup!" shouts Draden. He understands that the siege is the least desirable road to victory for any competent commander. It exacts the heaviest tolls while yielding the fewest immediate results. He would never allow his soldiers to be unnecessarily battered by failing to pull back from a fruitless assault directly into a city's defenses. "Regroup," he hails again.

He knows quietly within himself that he needs more time. His uncertainty about Busellis's ability to confront an enemy three times his size limits his options. Without even enough time to construct a belfry to scale the capital walls he is forced to resort to the most primitive siege strategy. Direct assault. He curses the circumstance. He cannot break the siege off and wait for reinforcements. He cannot order a halt for the night without conceding precious moments to lost eternity. He pulls his force back beyond harm and remains careful to keep the city's walls just within range of his artillery. The Seventh Resistance continues to pound away at the capital, destroying walls and provisions and crushing the siege engines defending the city.

Hours later, into the early morning, with the dawn still hours away, splintered wood and distorted metal tears away from the stone heralding the collapse of the city's western gate.

Draden inquires about Busellis, Nakano has no word.

"Dammit." He whispers to himself.

"What was that General," asks Nakano.

"Nothing," returns Draden, cloaking his concern he continues, "move your company to the western wall, let's see if we can spread their defenses throughout the city."

"Yes sir, General." Complies Nakano and moves to the western wall.

Yver is assigned to the eastern wall, Alvarez to the southern. Draden moves his battalion in proximity to Nakano. From his position, he is able to react to developments in the southern and western wall with equal command. Haddad's archers and trebuchets are divided among the divisions while he maintains a few mangonels at center behind Alvarez. The barrage of the global-imperial stronghold continues. Every wall of the city is pummeled by Resistance batteries.

The main gate to the heart of Damascus breaks off its hinges and falls, supported only by the adjacent wall. A well-placed shot from Haddad's center catapult bursts into the wood and metal frame, shattering it into several pieces and blowing it inwards into the city as if shot from a cannon.

"Into the city!" yells Draden. All divisions of the Seventh Resistance surge into the walls from every broken corner of Damascus like water erupting from a chasm 2,000 fathoms deep. A furious battle for control of sector 1 is full-fledged.

One hour later, the struggle still rages when upon the horizon a single, shadowy image emerges and moves toward Draden's army. Unable to make out the wavy, silhouette under the desert sun, Draden becomes uneasy. His battle-hardened senses become leery with apprehension. His heart sinks inside his chest. The shadow approaching may as well be the grim reaper beckoning death to follow behind him. He recognizes the riderless horse that comes his way. It was the horse that carried Nakano's spy to Busellis's position. A dust-cloud forming behind the steed and battle drums urging on the songs of the warriors of the global-empire confirm Draden's worst suspicions. The blue-black flag of the global-imperialists sways triumphantly in the wind. Busellis has been defeated. Draden and his force are about to be pinned down and surrounded by their enemies.

An object is hurled from behind the riderless horse and lands at Draden's feet. The already broken and headless body of Nakano's spy is pulverized further when it hits the rocks and sand. Lifeless bones crack and disjointed limbs shatter. The deceased spy was severely tortured before finally being put out of her misery. There was no telling what tales she told while being ravaged and torn apart. Burn marks, lashings, and severed digits were all that remained of the naked, mangled corpse.

The all too familiar snap of tens of thousands of bows ushers in a cloud of arrows that block out the sun. Thousands of missiles sail through the sky toward Draden's army.

"Retreat!" cries Draden! "Retreat!" His aides sound the horns to retreat. Unaware of Draden's realizations, confusion descends upon the Seventh Resistance. Yet, they obey the call and gradually disengaged from the enemy. "Retreat!" yells Draden, the horn sounds again with greater urgency. 1,800 of Draden's warriors succumb to the perforation of arrows flung from the edges of the horizon.

The horn sounds several times more until disengagement is complete. All companies but one fall back to Draden's position. Alvarez refuses to let glory go. Not heeding the call of the horn he implores his warriors to fight on until the last man. Many follow the calls to retreat. Some remain entranced by their commander and fight on.

"Alvarez, I said retreat!" calls out Draden behind hard, pressing eyes.

Alvarez continues to swing his sword recklessly, with little regard for his survival or for the survival of the men and women under his command. He does not disengage. Yver takes 50 horsemen and plunges back into danger to pull Alvarez out of the melee. Several of Yver's men carry Alvarez to the ground. He challenges them the entire way down. Once dismounted, Alvarez's horse runs back across the moat to safety.

Recognizing that death was only a fleeting blow or arrow away, Alvarez's group promptly fall back to Draden's position. Yver and his troops follow with the lieutenant general in tow. He wrestles with them to return to the fight. Yver restrains him under cover of shield. Sixteen are killed protecting the two officers. After a time Alvarez regains his senses and moves voluntarily with them.

The edge of the desert is no longer bare. Hundreds of thousands of global-imperial soldiers now stretch across the horizon. They move swiftly toward the smoking and broken city of Damascus. Panic falls on the Resistance.

The global-imperial army pick up the pace of their march. Rhythmic steps steadily gain momentum. Momentum accelerates into an all-out rush. Their mission is to destroy every man and woman standing in opposition. They thirst for blood.

Draden circles his horse in place, raises sword above head and points toward the mountains. He desperately orders his army, "Into the mountains! Into the mountains!"

The Seventh move northwest through the mountains toward the Mediterranean Sea. The ridge will give them cover while making it impossible for an army of 1.1 million to follow closely behind. The Resistance gather their bearings in all haste and move quickly northwest. 15,000 are killed before they are able to get far enough into the mountains and under the protection of the earth.

Encamped, the weary Seventh settle into their respective duties. Several shrug off the pains of defeat in drink, others in song by the fire, some share their dejection in the affection of another. Officers carry on. Preparations are made for tomorrow. There is much to be done. Many more miles to go, supply lines to arrange, recovery for the un-injured, care for the wounded, provisioning for the sick, food and water for the healthy, topography, reports from the spy grid, weapon status, prisoners, horses, weather and diplomacy.

⁓

Lieutenant General Alvarez appears at the entrance to Draden's tent. The toll of the near 1,300 mile long retreat into the ruins of Sofia, Bulgaria steadily gnaws at his body.

Draden acknowledges Alvarez standing patiently for permission, "Permission to enter sir?" asks the lieutenant general.

"Permission granted, lieutenant general." Answers Draden. "What can I do for you young man?"

Alvarez ponders how to best open the subject, "I made a fool of myself back in Damascus, General."

Draden listens without passing judgement, "Mhm," allowing him to go on.

"I lost my senses, I ignored the retreat, I endangered myself, but more importantly I risked the lives of our troops and got our people killed trying to save me." He looks down ashamed.

Draden starts with a story about a pirate he once knew, "Many years ago when I was in England, I delivered supplies to resistance fighters preparing to move across the sea. All of a sudden, out of nowhere a mighty pirate fleet from Norway appeared and sailed on our position. You may better know these lands as south-eastern quadrant, Sector 2."

The borders of sector 2 surround what was once Greenland and extend down southeast across the Atlantic ocean until circling Portugal and Spain. Thereafter, the border turns directly east touching the shores of north Africa to just passed the boot of Italy and angling 90 degrees north carving Sweden in half, passing all the way to the north pole before turning sharply back west toward Greenland and completing the border.

Draden continues, "There was one very famous warrior among them. They called him Ivar the Magnificent. He was the king of the northern pirates."

Alvarez motions to a chair in the corner of the tent requesting permission to take a seat. Draden nods and continues, "he was a ruthless, brutal killer – large and powerful. Many times his army would win victories without shedding a drop of blood because nobody wanted to stand against him. His reputation for savagery and brutality spread far and wide!"

Alvarez sits captivated, Draden goes on, "Many thought that he was the devil in human flesh. They would say he was immortal and no man-made weapon could harm him. Until one day, he wanted to take our stronghold in northern England." Pressing the point, "He had never taken a prize so rich and so powerful despite his notorious reputation. He was overcome with a frenzy so consuming that he lost his grip on reality. Blinded by his own glory, his own ambition and by his own reputation, became unaware of what was happening around him. Then, a small, young and very brave warrior was able to move in close enough behind him and drove her sword into his back and through his heart. The fantastical legend of Ivar disappeared that day and the northern pirates fell into chaos without their king. Soon after, the great northern pirates were destroyed by rival factions, forever erased from history." Draden finishes and carves a piece of pear with his knife, guiding the fruit into his mouth with the blade.

Alvarez sits contritely unable to make eye contact. He understands the lesson behind the story. Draden avoids gazing directly at Alvarez preferring to leave him to his own reflections for a time.

Alvarez's voice breaks, "I'm sorry General. I let you down. I let the Seventh Resistance down."

Draden nods, acknowledging the place that Alvarez had gone to in his own mind and heart. "Thank you for recognizing that Lieutenant General."

A moments' pause passes, "How do you do it General?" prays Alvarez.

Draden asks what he means with a look.

"I mean, how do you never make a mistake? How do you guide millions of people into harm and pull most them out of harm time and again?" pleads Alvarez.

"I've made plenty of mistakes Alvarez. People just seem to ignore them because they create this supreme image of me. An image that I will never endorse, and one that I will never acknowledge that I deserve. It is a dangerous thing to paint a man as supreme; whether painted by others of him or of him to others." Draden cuts another piece of pear.

Alvarez returns, "How can you say that? You are the greatest, most brilliant General the Resistance has ever seen. It's like you know what the enemy is going to do before they do it. Where they're going to move next, where they will be after and where they would never go. I do not know anyone more deserving of admiration than you, General."

Draden exhales, "I could not accomplish anything I accomplish without others accomplishing them with me." He chides. "You would do well to understand and embrace that Lieutenant General."

Alvarez shakes his head side to side, "Damascus has made me realize much. Unfortunately, for what I have realized, there is not much for me to be proud of. The wars in Sector 0 were different - they were more physical and improvised. Somehow it seems like the wars here are fought mainly behind the scenes in strategy and politics before any army ever takes the field."

Draden nods, "The global-imperial rulers have more to lose by losing on this side of the globe, Lieutenant General. Like meerkats defending their burrows, they will fight like hell to protect the ruling clan and preserve their own power."

Alvarez sits in reflection.

Draden interrupts, "Sometimes, I do know what they will do in advance, Lieutenant General." He confides. "Sometimes I don't know. Sometimes I think I do and take a calculated chance. And sometimes I just guess."

"What do you mean sometimes you do know?" He asks, gesturing with his right hand, palm upward.

Draden raises his eyes toward the night sky, head slightly tilts to the left, points upward with his right index finger, then moves both hands in a manner that expresses, I am not sure how to explain it and sighs, bewildered how to answer the curious Lieutenant General.

"What is it General?" He posits. "Does God talk to you?" Alvarez asks, half-way hoping and expecting him to say yes.

Draden dispels, "Hah, no. Well..., at least not directly and not just to me. But to anyone willing to explore the meaning of the world around us. The good and the bad."

"What do you mean General?" inquires Alvarez.

Draden walks toward a solid oak chest, in the corner of his tent, just beside his bed. With a key he removes from his pocket, unlocks the equivalent of a modern day safe. "Try to keep an open mind." Draden requests.

He opens the chest removing several large volumes of literature and numerous loose papers held together only by a sharpened piece of metal pointed on both sides, thrust through the sheets and bent around the corners to keep the pages together. A make-shift military staple. Though noticeably worn and withered, Draden delivers them to the center table in otherwise immaculate condition.

He points to the collection while looking at his second, "In here." Draden ponders a moment, "I don't think there are any more copies left in the world. I haven't seen any besides the volumes Haddad carries with him."

Curiously and with tremendous care, Alvarez handles the books and reads the titles out loud. With each recitation his confusion increases, "Torah, Bible, Qur'an, Gospels, Hadeeth, Zoroaster, Zohar, Mesopotamians, Sumerians, Babylonians, Mayans, Aztecs...What are these?"

He looks up from the tomes, with a subtle shake of his head and shrug of his shoulders communicates, "I still don't get it."

With an indistinct smile, Draden responds, "These?" "These books and papers are in a way, history lessons with propositions for the future. I collected them from the ruins of temples, universities and libraries around the world."

"er...propositions for the future?" queries Alvarez.

"I know. It's a hard thing for me to wrap my head around too." Considering what to say next, "But everything that's happened up to this point in the world was written at some point thousands of years ago in one of these books." Draden grabs the bible, gently carrying it to the other side of the table so Alvarez can see.

Draden places an open hand on the surface of the book and explains, "There is a lot of history in these books," gesturing to the bible and the other tomes laying on the table, "there is also a lot of future as well." Thoughtfully sharing, "Just as much of what has transpired in this world was proclaimed in these pages long ago. There is still much that I believe will happen according to their predictions."

He pauses deciding how to continue sharing his premonition, "even the last remaining strongholds for our people. It's all in there."

He stops to consider if he's given the young commander too much to think about.

Alvarez displaces the silence with a sudden realization, "This march, this retreat, it's not random at all then, is it?

You're taking us to a stronghold described in one of those books, or those papers aren't you?" He exclaims. Gladdened by the discovery.

Draden appreciates Alvarez's awareness, "Mhm."

Diego places his hands on his hips and chuckles in disbelief yet somehow believes. "Will you tell me where we are headed General?"

"Soon. Somethings I need to keep to myself until the time is right." Cued by this statement, Draden imparts wisdom, "That's another mark of an effective leader, preservation of information and concealment of intention. Sharing information when the information needs to be shared. Not a moment sooner, not a moment later."

"I see." Acknowledges Alvarez. "Have you ever used the information in those manuscripts to win a battle?"

"Sure I have." Answers Draden, "but the answers aren't always clear. There is a lot of room for interpretation...and misinterpretation."

"Can you give me an example, General?"

Draden puffs his cheeks and breathes out, searching for a time and a tale to tell. He recalls, "We were just dealt a crushing blow losing the armies of Sector 2. We were pushed east, in between Armenia and Azerbaijan." Draden Points east where these countries used to be.

"We had mountains at our back and mountains on either side of us. We were trapped." Once again he walks over to the center table and exchanges the Bible for the Qur'an, "We were outnumbered 5 to 1. I only had one night to figure out how to save what was left of the western division. We were so vulnerable and so exposed that even one night was too long for me to wait." Alvarez stands at once captivated and concerned for the fate of his compatriots and brothers and sisters in arms.

"I was out of options and out of time." He reflects. Still in disbelief about his decision to trust prophecy and folklore over hard military strategy. "I read what was in there," placing his hand on the Qur'an, then turning to chapter 18 and directing Alvarez's attention to verses 89 through 94. The story of The Cave illustrates what he did next, "It gave me an idea for a way out."

Alvarez reads the passage as if reading it to Draden himself, "Then he followed a means till he reached the place of the rising sun. He found it rising over a people for whom we had not made any shelter from it. This it was and we encompassed that which lay before him in awareness".

When Alvarez finishes reading the passage, Draden continues, "I sent my scouts through the mountain pass into the direction of the rising sun to look for a *means*," he explains the meaning of the word *means* to Alvarez, "a path," he continues, "a path that leads to the other side of the mountains until we were behind the enemy. A path that gave us the power of the sun to blind them as we descended upon them to clear our way out of the indefensible position we were in."

Draden continues, "When the scouts returned I could hardly believe what they found. They confirmed that such a *means* existed. We hurried into the passage until we were in position to deliver a surprise offensive. When the sun was brightly in the sky, we descended from the mountains and hit them hard. Unrelenting." Animating the decent with his left hand.

"The imperialist army was paralyzed by our attack. When they were blinded by the sun, we had every advantage and took the day." He affirms, "we brought such carnage upon them that day, they took months to replenish what we destroyed." Curiously he evokes, "but, there was something else on the battlefield with us. A force that surrounded the global-imperialists and helped us carry the day. I can't explain it, but I accept it." He continues as if asking a question, but not actually asking, "I couldn't see it, yet I felt it's presence all around." Draden circles with his hand to show what he means.

Silence deafens the tent.

Silence breaks after a moment's time. "My father told me about this battle, the battle of Armenia. It was then that I decided I had to join the Resistance." Proclaimed Alvarez. "It was the reason I sought you out, to serve under you ahead of all other commanders. Who else knows about this? These books. The stories in here? How it's going to happen?"

"My son knew." Draden looks away remorsefully and exhales acknowledging the burden he carries over his son's loss.

Alvarez softens at the realization, "What do you mean, *knew?*"

"Once upon a time, I had a son." Declares Draden.

"I'm sorry General." Not knowing what to say or how to relieve the burden. Believing that in Draden's reaction, he is calling for solitude, Alvarez rises from his seat to exit the tent.

"It was early October," starts Draden. Alvarez turns away from the exit and starts back to a nearby chair. Listening with genuine empathy.

"We fought together in the early wars. Both he and his mother battled by my side" he recalled while fighting to keep his voice from losing its ever-certain and calming inflection.

"I was a young man, 43, years old. I was travelling with a small company of 1,000. Our mission was to escort displaced people and refugees to our outpost in Richmond, Virginia. We had just celebrated our son's sixteenth birthday the night before. My wife reminded me that I had also just passed my 20th year as General of the resistance." He pauses, "we were ambushed not far south of Richmond…" He continues, placing himself back at that moment…

Draden and Aurelia lay awake in their tent and take time to enjoy a quiet day. They wanted to celebrate Nuriel's sixteenth birthday in peace, a day away from war. Nuriel was outside his parent's quarters training with the rest of the army. Faint screams carry not far from where Nuriel is training. Screams grow louder and more frequent. He quickly runs into his parent's tent.

"Father, father," cries Nuriel, "something is happening."

Samuel and Aurelia grab their weapons and rush outside. They do not have time to put on any protective coverings.

Nuriel, takes up his position to his father's left. He is dressed in training gear and has slightly more protection than his parents, but remains mostly vulnerable. Aurelia stands ready to her husband's right, her sword and shield in hand.

Aurelia Draden is the embodiment of a Viking shield maiden. Standing only 4 inches above five feet, she makes up for height with her ferocity in battle. Aurelia is fleet-footed and well-balanced. She knows how to use both sword and shield as lethal weapons of attack and deadly instruments of defense. Before the wars broke out she had grown up looking after horses on a ranch with her parents in Arizona and was an excellent rider. She spent her childhood training for the Olympics as a gymnast and managed to bring every ounce of dexterity from her gymnastics training into her motions and movements on the battlefield. Her hair is honey-gold and her eyes are a mystical blend of turquoise and sage, azure and gray. The blue calm of her eyes turn icy and piercing when she is thrust amidst the flames of war.

The attack is an assassination attempt. A horde of global-imperialist mercenaries are dispatched to kill Samuel Draden and his family. Draden is the most dangerous of all resistance generals winning the most battles of any other commander on his side of the conflict. His brilliance as an expert strategist and masterful tactician was evident early on and this made his name feared by his enemies. Over his career, Draden had struck a series of devastating blows to the global-imperial fabric and their ruse to subdue the world under their regime. He and his entire line had to be dealt with or the global-imperialists would lose their grip over the population.

The camp is thrown into madness. It is a free-for-all. Hysteria dominates the field. Samuel, Aurelia and Nuriel stand together to form a deadly defensive triangle against the attacks. Aurelia moves gracefully on the battlefield, her swift motions and strikes are elegantly destructive and fatal to the opposition. Nuriel defends with the agility of his mother and the cleverness of his father. He delivers 20 hardened troops from this life into the next. Samuel exacts maximum death and struggles to create any opportunity for his family to escape. The horde keeps coming.

Aurelia briefly breaks her mind from battle and at the top of her voice calls over at her husband, "Samuel, get out of here. You have to make it out of here. If you are lost, the resistance is lost."

Nuriel shouts in support of his mother's plea. "Father, please, you have to go. Mother and I will draw them away from you."

"I am not going to leave you two here, better I die and you live to carry on what I taught you. Go. Go now." Draden fires back.

"Samuel please, you have to save yourself." cries Aurelia.

"No." replies Draden.

"Father, you have to get out of here. Mother and I will look after each other. You don't owe us anything. You told me once that I owe the world my service, now I tell you what you once told me. It is you who owes the world your service, you who owes the world your survival, and you who owes the earth your leadership. It was written for you, not for me. Please father, live on. We will see you again in the next life." Nuriel says in his final appeal.

Two large horsemen of the resistance speed toward the General. With a mighty heave together, they pull his 6 foot 5 frame off the ground and carry him into the protection of the nearby foliage against his will and over his screaming protests. Nuriel and Aurelia breathe an approving sigh of relief and battle on for as long as they can.

Still in the powerful clutches of the horsemen, Draden clings to the hopes that his family's wisdom and supplications were not made in vain.

The globalist horde kill everybody in sight and set fire to anything that will ignite. The cries of battle die away, all is now nothing. The horsemen release their grip on their general. He drops to his knees covered in the blood of his enemies. Guilt, remorse, regret, anger, sadness ooze into Draden's mind. His hands grip each other over the hilt of his sword. He draws his limbs close to his body - looks into the earth with an empty, forlorn stare. His chest aches with grief. Places his forehead upon his hands. Hands rest on the hilt of his sword and releases suppressed tears through clenched jaw.

Sadness transforms into rage. Anger into conviction. Conviction into faith. Upon him arrives the possibility that perhaps he was not forsaken, but beckoned. He was not cast away, but cast forth. His wife and son are gone, but he and the Resistance yet remain.

⚜

His memory fades to blackness, he turns to Alvarez, "I went back for them as soon as it was safe and the fires had died down. All that was left from them was this."

He shows him a beautifully kept moonstone bracelet that he had given Aurelia for her birthday during their second year of marriage. It still held a brilliant white hue on its surface, permeated slightly by a suggestion of blue shine while rays of black and red radiate boldly through its center as if the blood that connects him to his family is frozen in time forever.

"Oh my God! I'm so sorry, General. How did the world get this way?" pleaded Alvarez

While pondering how to respond, and where to start, Draden drops a spoonful of ground, dried coffee in his cup, pours water from a pot boiling over the fire and stirs in the center. He struggles to push the memories away while offering Alvarez a cup of the rare and sought after commodity. Alvarez politely refuses.

Draden starts, "In many ways, the world situation today is not much different than it was 55 years ago. The greatest difference is that long ago, world governments and our so-called leaders were much more discreet about their aims to bring the world under one all powerful, ruling body." Draden recounts the events leading up to the present...

Before global conflict erupted, there was a coalition of 20 countries that made decisions that impacted the entire world. They maintained that their objective was to promote financial stability on the planet. Their true goals however were more nefarious. The leaders of those countries masked their intentions behind flowery speeches filled with empty promises, false narratives and lies until they achieved the one-world order they wanted under one supreme ruler.

Slowly and gradually, people were pacified and narcotized until they became oblivious to the ruse that was being played against them. Members of a productive and flourishing society became disillusioned and demotivated by the political process. Unable and unwilling to make a difference in who represents them in government, they withdrew in frustration preferring to be left alone. The condition of the world became so dire after the mass withdrawal that 10 countries out of the group of 20 countries who were allegedly committed to financial stability on the planet went bankrupt. The remaining 10 countries quickly re-drew their borders to absorb the failed states and promptly placed them under their control. A massive redistribution of power and wealth followed.

A few years later, the first resistance arose from the ashes. It was a loose alliance between a lost generation of individuals, private corporations, independent states and religious leaders who tried to recapture the freedoms that were quickly dwindling away. They banded together to protest rampant government corruption and the increasing power of the ruling elite. They used cyber-tech, information networks, and television broadcasts to challenge the evolving centralized government structure. Their efforts were short-lived.

Governments making laws to seize the technological airways. Increasingly the governments asserted immense control over the internet and cyber communication. The information network began to backfire against anyone speaking out against a single, supreme government. Enhanced digital forensics were used to identify and silence dissidents. The most powerful opposition leaders were dealt with first. Heads of religious movements presented the largest threats and were handled accordingly. They were told to indoctrinate their followers to the premise that all that was happening was in accordance with God's will here on earth. If they refused, they would be persecuted. Laws were passed that limited funding to churches, mosques and synagogues – religion was branded and marketed as an abhorred obstruction to freedom of expression. Unable to keep the doors open for their congregations, religious organizations faded into obscurity. Millions still practiced their faiths secretly. To remain undetected believers destroyed their holy books and resorted to traditional oral learning across generations.

Political leaders, business leaders, academics, journalists, radio personalities, television personalities, writers, artists, community organizers, and any powerful individuals who did not fade away or readily accept the new regime were smeared, shamed, shunned, set up and cast out from society by falsely concocted conspiracies and untrue accusations. They became unable to make a living or share their warnings with those who were seeking the truth. The truth became whatever the ruling elite told the people it was. In order to stay in business or simply survive, the population obediently complied. Freedom of speech and freedom of the press turned into *only free if you agree.*

The Last Days of Draden

Not long after the governments consolidated power over the cyber waves and squashed their opponents, did the economy of many developed countries really start to melt down. Cyber-attacks were rampant. Attacks on financial institutions created chaos by altering online payment accounts. Retailers shut down all digital transactions. Global markets were sent into a free-fall before the exchanges halted trading altogether. Criminal gangs, religious extremists, and warlords flourished amidst a thriving black market for water, food, drugs, weapons, forced prostitution, and human trafficking. Even faith and redemption was bartered secretly underground like heroine or hashish.

Disease spread. There were not enough medicines. Without enough diversity between business leaders, academic leaders, political leaders, religious leaders and accurate information to keep a balance in society, the most powerful countries, needed to turn their attention inward. Their societies were collapsing. They were forced to face their own domestic crises and address their growing poverty, crime and rioting problems. Food and water shortages were commonplace. Civil war erupted in many countries across the world. On the one hand, this outcome was exactly what the politicians and power brokers wanted, a destruction of the existing social structure, consolidation of their own power and more reliance on them by the people for survival. On the other hand, they made a grave error by not accurately considering that people would still resist their rule and that they would never run out of money to care for their populations. The governments and leaders were so ideologically blind that they could not separate reality from their fantasy.

The United States became increasingly occupied with maintaining order in its streets and turned away from what was happening in the rest of the world. Eventually the U.S. withdrew entirely from being involved in anything around the globe but its most important vital interests. What America's actual vital interests were at the time remained a mystery to all but a handful of unscrupulous autocrats. Isolation became simply an accepted American position. Other world powers began to feel the stress of not having sufficient water to supply their populations and, without the United States around to keep order, foreign powers made tactical decisions to improve their own influence in surrounding regions. Russia made the first move by diverting major rivers away from its neighbors to quench the needs of its own people.

As a result of Russia's subversion of the region's water reserves, China, India and Pakistan's vital interests in their nation's water supplies were threatened. They appealed to the European Union for help. The EU, could not help, they had their own internal problems much like the US. Consequently, for fear of appearing weak, and to address their deteriorating irrigation situation, China fired the first shots against European financial centers with cyber-attacks in hopes that Russia would see a mutual benefit to crippling the west and come to a water-sharing agreement. It worked. Russia and China cooperated and sustained their water repositories. India and Pakistan were left out of the deal and were too weak to assert themselves against China and Russia. Incidentally, they attacked each other hoping a victory would yield access to more water for their own people. The first attacks were cyber-attacks on one another's financial infrastructure. When these efforts claimed little in the way of a decisive victory over the other, they resorted to long-range ballistic missiles. Ultimately, tensions came to a head and nuclear weapons were launched. Full war between the two countries ensued. India prevailed.

Water reservoirs in and around the earth continued to recede. Religious tensions between Sunni Muslims and Shi'ite Muslim reached an historic high. Iran fired nuclear missiles into Saudi Arabia. Without the United States protecting the Arabian kingdom, the ancestral lands of Muhammad were easy prey. With the help of China, Russia and India, Iran followed their missile strikes with ground offensives from the borders of Iraq to Yemen and Oman all the way to the Indian Ocean hoping to secure an alternative water source. The holy cities of Mecca and Medina fell into ruin.

With the world situation getting out of control, the U.S. needed to retaliate swiftly and strongly to restore order. They answered with long-range precision guided strike systems, nuclear weapons and boots on the ground. America and its allies reclaimed Arabia, Indonesia, the Philippines and had complete control over the territories between Sri Lanka and Islamabad. But with drained resources, empty treasuries and their own water supply issues, the U.S. led coalition did not have a complete strategy to subdue and contain the four powers who have by now consolidated the eastern water supplies. The coalition fell apart and America was forced to stand alone.

The integrated forces of Iran, China, Russia and India proved too much for the U.S. positions. Sensing an unraveling, they responded by launching a series of devastating Electro-Magnetic Pulse missiles at American armies in their lands. When they saw that the U.S. was weakened and unprepared for an EMP, they pounded the American forces unlike ever before and set their sights on Israel. The US could not effectively defend Israel and Israel was no match for the combined powers of the four new rulers of the region. Israel was taken. Jerusalem was divided between China and Russia with the reasoning that since both countries boasted a sizable population of Christians, Muslims and Jews neither country was exclusively entitled to its rule.

When Israel fell and the allied coalition unraveled, Europe was overwhelmed. The United States suffered punishing attacks almost daily. A constant barrage of EMPs' and nuclear missiles wrought havoc on American defenses and civilization.

When the first EMP exploded above the United States, the sky erupted into a dizzying blaze. With their circuits and navigations fried, airplanes in transit across the country plummeted helplessly from the sky ending their descents with fiery crashes into dozens of schools, buildings, roads, fields and houses killing thousands. Fire caught the brush where the land was driest. Many were forced to abandon their homes or die. Immediately, Americans were once more in the dreadful clutches of terror when structures crumbled and collapsed in every major city - collided by aircrafts that tumbled power-lessly into the earth.

Fires sparked from the surge of powerlines. Cities darkened. Plumes of thick constricting smoke enveloped the nation and blotted out the sun. Anyone riding an elevator was stuck. Anyone in a car was stranded. Anyone holding a key or metal object was scorched by the pulse. Every unprotected battery and electric device was rendered useless. People on life support were no longer sustained. Many in hospitals died. Prisoners escaped when the electric power to their cell doors was interrupted. The worst of whom carried out attacks on the weak; raping and pillaging along the way. Nuclear plants that could no longer be kept cool detonated. Absolute mayhem ensued. Stores were looted. Food spoiled. Water could not be accessed. Loved ones could not be contacted. The ruination of the American civilization was under way.

Following the bedlam consuming the U.S., enemy ground troops landed simultaneously on the shores of Annapolis, Maryland just east of Washington, DC and Monterey, California. The American military, along with Canada, Australia, and what was left of the English, French, and German forces fought desperately to stop their advance into the United States. The distressed conglomerate was known as the Second Resistance. Despite their best efforts, California and the west coast of Mexico still went to China. Oregon, Washington state, British Columbia, the Yukon and Alaska went to Russia. New Hampshire, Maine, New York and Pennsylvania fell to Iran. North Carolina, South Carolina, Georgia and Florida were taken by India. Washington DC and Virginia remained under Resistance control. Over time, electronics and technologies on both sides were decimated. Even when they were repaired and brought back online, the exchange of assaults was too much to keep up with.

Slowly the information network infrastructure on both sides would be pulverized out of existence. Without enough water, people and resources to recreate the lost infrastructure - sophisticated long range, mechanized, computerized and cyber weaponry became a thing of the past, replaced with machinations of primitive wars come and gone.

The Third Resistance rose out of the new era of warfare. A different breed of soldier was needed to face the horrors of close, personal combat with crude steel and wooden arrow. After 19 years of non-stop global devastation, a balance of power was restored and a line was drawn directly through the center of Syria, culminating at the North and South poles. The world reached an icy standoff between the eastern and western hemispheres.

<hr>

Alvarez processes the events, "If the world is divided in half at that point...how did the 10 sectors form?"

Draden takes a deep breath in, puffs his cheeks and breathes out wistfully, "This is where the Chancellor enters the story."

The Chancellor is an extremely charismatic and enigmatic figure despite having major physical imperfections and rising to power from mysterious and shrouded circumstances. His hair is black, twisted and cropped. It falls in shiny curls down the side and front of his face. He is not tall, standing at five feet seven inches. He displays an average physique. His right eye is sewn permanently shut; a consequence of his many battles. At times he wears an eye patch when allaying the nerves of a jittery audience too frightened to gaze upon him or when he addresses the citizenry in public. He has use of his left eye though a scar runs from his forehead above his right eye, across the bridge of his nose to just under his left eye. Time has lightened the color of his eye that when the sun reflected off it from certain angles, the shade took on a crimson tint rather than a deep brown. He walks with an unsteady limp favoring his left leg, the result of multiple traumas sustained on the battlefield.

The exact nature and location of his birth remains a mystery. It is said that he was born in a cave system somewhere along the borders between Iraq, Syria and Turkey to a nomadic tribe of mystics. He was educated in the traditional manner of his tribe and learned to bend man, woman, and nature to his will using science and other-worldly techniques. His true name remains unknown. He offered his name simply as Darius when confronted about his origins.

A master of combat, he was a ruthless and pitiless warrior. In the aftermath of the US invasion by the 4 eastern powers, he was among the first to join the Second Resistance despite having been born a citizen of the east. It was widely known that his commanding officers feared him though they commanded him into the throws of battle. In fact, legend spread that some of the higher ranks wished for his quick demise during the fighting. They were left wanting. As a young officer, Darius never protested an opportunity to spill the blood of his enemies and relished in being ordered to so. His enemies feared any battle in which his name was cast among the combatants. When victorious, he engaged in the gruesome ritual of capturing the enemy commander, securing him to wooden posts and carving him or her into two equal halves from crown to torso. He would then nail the halves to targets on opposite sides of his camp and encourage his bow and javelin divisions to use them as target practice.

His bloodlust gained him support from the west and obedience from the east. He used his infamy to wage a global campaign against the world. He justified his motives by claiming he will stop the bloodshed, restore order and unite the nations in peace. Upon hearing his declaration and seeing the Resistance multiply under him, the opposing armies of the world quaked beneath his advance. When the carnage was complete, he divided the world into 10 sectors and appointed 10 governors to each sector. This is the council.

Draden directs Alvarez's attention to a passage in the bible, revelations 17:12 *"The ten horns that you saw are ten kings who have received no kingdom as yet, but they receive authority as kings, with the beast, for one hour."*

Alvarez nods, bemoaning the history lesson.

Draden clenches his teeth together then speaks, "He was hailed by many as a savior. The Messiah in some people's minds. At the end - all of it, the fighting, the conflict, the bloodshed, all of it, was one, great, big, unholy ruse to consolidate his power."

In response to Darius' deception and the deteriorating human condition by war, drought, disease and famine, several war veterans and generals rebelled. The Fourth Resistance was launched in the fifth year of his reign and extended into the sixth. It was the first open uprising against the Chancellor. More notably it was the first insurrection that was not completely annihilated within the first few weeks following its emergence. The troop of the Fourth were disorganized and inadequate however. The hammer of the global-imperial army fell heavy on the Resistance, shattering the movement before it took hold of its second year.

"You were already a General by then." Recognized Alvarez

"I was. I stood against him along with the others." Draden replied despondently.

"How did you survive?" asked Alvarez.

"I knew the terrain of the Americas far better than him. I used the mountains and caves, rivers and ruins. I was a hunted man and my family was hunted along with me." Despondence gives way to indignation.

CHAPTER 3

Salvation

HORNS BELLOW OUTSIDE Draden's tent. Alarmed, Draden and Alvarez hurry outside. They are met by Nakano and Yver. "Blue-black flags spotted marching toward us," exclaims Yver.

"It was only a matter of time," confirmed Draden. "How far off?"

Nakano replies, "3 days march."

The once noble blue-black flag of the third resistance has been transformed from a hero's calling to reclaim the eastern hemisphere to a symbol of terror and destruction across the entire globe. The flag was originally designed to symbolize the clash between good and evil. One half of the flag was colored light blue to communicate divinity and celestial power. The other half was shaded black to emulate the darkness humanity was facing. The two colors were contrasted by a bold white line diagonally dividing the colors bottom left to top right. The bold boundary represented the dividing line drawn between the hemispheres. After rising to power, Darius darkened the light blue to more resemble a shade of night, contrasted still by the white line separating the black from bottom left to top right. Both pallets were then infused with a subtle, shimmering crimson thread that gives the flag an eerie blood-sheen when it is met by the light.

The Last Days of Draden

"Gather everyone." Orders Draden.

Simultaneously Yver and Alvarez ask, "Which direction general?"

"North, Northwest gentleman, full haste." He instructs.

Earnestly, the Seventh Resistance makes its way through the mountains. The chills of a February frost have rung in one of the most severe blizzards to hit the continent in nearly a decade. Snow and mud make the mountain passes treacherous and deadly. The wind is biting and blinding. There is a shortage of provisions, food, and medicine. Some supplies cannot be navigated through narrow ridges. Tons of much needed supplies fall hundreds of feet from the slopes to the ground below taking people with them. Many become ill on the journey, several die. Draden's mighty force of two hundred fifty thousand elite souls has dwindled to a mere ninety thousand. Many remain sick with winter afflictions. An urgent 1,100 mile long trek through peaks and valleys comes at great cost to life, time and resources.

At last, after a month and a week of death-defying travel they reach their destination.

The plains of Hanover were once home to the capital city of lower Saxony. Long ago, the region was revered for its thriving trade, commerce and finance. Decades of warfare have left little to remind the wayfarer of the rich, proud and royal history it boasted. Towns in the region of Sector 2 are scattered miles apart and traffic through the area is minimal. Though as one looks upon the field with the February frost settling on the land, a strange serenity is to be had. The land is wide and peaceful. The white glimmer of undisturbed snow on the ground is beautiful and rejuvenating.

"We can stop here for a few days before we press on." Says Draden. "We need wood for our fires and a foraging party to bring back whatever we can find."

Mansour Haddad volunteers to lead the expedition for food. He takes twenty five of the Seventh Resistance's most formidable hunters and gatherers with him. Sa'eed readily accompanies him and Nabila glides along with them through the air. Haddad instructs one hundred people to start bringing back firewood. The rest of the Seventh begin erecting their camps for the days ahead.

Sa'eed runs at the head of the foraging party. He sniffs at the ground. His tongue extends slightly over his lower jaw. Short, quick breaths fuel his powerful lungs. He is a massive animal with forelegs that ripple with muscle at every stride and hind legs that move with determination and equally muscular form. Haddad and his twenty five foragers follow on horseback. Passage is slow because of the snow, but they are resolute. Sa'eed is unperturbed. Following his canine instincts he presses on in a north-westerly direction. Occasionally the curiously cheerful wolf will glance up to Nabila to confirm his instincts. He calls to her with slight, quick, shrill yaps. She returns his calls with rapid pipes and short peals. They have attained conversant proficiency with one another over the months. They are a harmonious duo intent on serving and protecting their master.

Nabila calls out with an extended peal. Sa'eed growls and stops abruptly. He takes measure of his surroundings. His ears perk up and move back and forth. He senses that something may be amiss. Nabila circles above head. Sa'eed growls. Haddad holds steady on his steed. The horse breaths. The cool crisp air reveals the brisk breaths of every living thing in the foraging party. The rapidity of breathing is heightened by increased adrenaline and palpitations. Silence.

Haddad looks to Nabila and presses all five fingers of his right hand to his temple, palm not touching, inhales deeply and closes his eyes – breathes out slowly. Nabila tilts her head to the left and looks at her keeper. There is an exchange. He releases her from his conscious stream.

Haddad explains, "She saw rustling in the trees ahead. Snow was disturbed. She could not see any humans." Haddad looks at Sa'eed, presses his fingers to his temple, inhales and closes his eyes – breathes out slowly. A connection is made. He removes his hand, "There is a different scent ahead," he shares and compels his troop to move cautiously into the woods. Nabila lands at a nearby branch.

Slowly and undeterred the hungry band of rummagers make their way through the dense woodland. The forest maintains some trees without leaves and some remain evergreen. Snow hangs on and weighs down branches. One hour later, Sa'eed snarls. Takes a defensive posture. He barks and growls exposing deadly fangs. Nabila lands nearby. Haddad hears the rustling in the trees, "Whoah," he urges his mount, draws his bow and secures an arrow. The remaining party draw their weapons. Each listens intently to the other's breath. All scan the forest with sidelong glances careful to limit their movements. Hands on weapons, shields clutched tight.

An arrow whooshes by Haddad's ear and takes out the man to his right.

"Ambush!" Haddad cries out. Sa'eed plunges in the direction of the assailants, his full beast form takes to the bandits.

One hurls a spear at him but Sa'eed quickly tilts his shoulder out of the way. His fangs penetrate the throat of the spearman. In an instant, another victim is in the clutches of his jaws. So swift and precise are his movements that confusion quickly folds in on the rogues. Nabila soars down from the tree tops. Her razor sharp talons tear into the shoulder of the bowman and rip off a pound of flesh. He falls to the ground grimacing and writhing in blood-soaked pain. She sinks her talons into another and peels him to the floor.

Haddad and his party engage the highwaymen. He is knocked off his horse and drops his bow. He pulls his bo staff from between the blades of his back. In the form of an ancient druid master, Haddad wields his weapon with breaking and deadly accuracy. No sooner does he strike the neck of one enemy does he spin the staff behind his back and across his shoulders to take out the legs from underneath another. With a flip of his wrist and a twist in his hips he drives the end of his staff into the chest of the tumbled opponent. In one swift motion he crushes his chest and removes the life contained within it. The fight rages.

†

Defeated, the bandits flee. Haddad calls Sa'eed back from pursuing them and asks Nabila to stay close by. He assesses the damage. Five of his party are perished. Twenty three of the bandits bodies litter the landscape.

"We do not need any more casualties." Says Haddad out loud. He shakes his head, picks up his bow and returns his staff to its resting place between the blades of his back.

One of the party asks Haddad, "Commander, why do you use your staff and not your sword?"

He replies, "I hate wiping blood off the blade with my sleeve." The other chuckles as he wipes the blood off his blade with his sleeve.

Haddad adds behind cold breath, "And in the frost, sometimes, blades stick." He pats him on the back and continues, "Let's do what we came out here to do and get back to camp before it gets too dark."

A short distance ahead, Sa'eed draws the group's attention to a passel of boar. When they create a sufficient hunting circle around the swine, Sa'eed jumps into action and drives them in the direction of his human counterparts. Nabila joins with a squeal in a squall. Haddad lodges a well-placed arrow directly into the shoulder and through the heart of the largest one. The remaining troop follow and loose their own arrows into the hogs. Sa'eed rests his belly against the snow triumphantly clutching the neck of one in between his powerful jaws. Paws draped over the body to keep it steady. The warm blood trickles down from his mouth onto the forest floor. He looks like he is smiling. Pleased with himself. Nabila pulls her talons out of a freshly killed pig then darts into the sky.

A moment later at an icy nearby stream, Nabila swoops down to the water's surface with all her grace and plucks a full-sized salmon from the water. She flies over head of Haddad and drops it directly at his feet. She returns once more to the stream and extracts another. Once more delivering it to his feet. They jump and flop around until their breath is exhausted. When motionless, Haddad picks them up and puts them into his sack. Nabila returns a third time to feed herself.

"Wow!" reacted one of the party in amazement. "Why did she do that?" he asked.

Haddad replies, "I don't eat pork my friend. It's against my religion." He smiles, "Halal is healthy," and laughs.

Haddad continues, "Now let's get this meal back to camp. God knows we all need it." He says a quick prayer to himself in Arabic, kisses the first knuckle of his pointer finger, touches that knuckle to the center of his forehead and points above his head toward the sky as if releasing his prayer into the hands of listening angels. He follows this with thanks to God, *"Alhamdulilah."*

⚜

The army is exuberant at the sight of Haddad's foraging party returning from the hunt with nearly 7,000 pounds of meat.

The trail of the last month was brutal and exacted a heavy toll on life, provisions and morale. A bonfire is lit in the center of the camp. The subzero temperatures of February twilight in Hanover are unforgiving to body and mind without a large and steady fire. It is a challenge to ram the roasting spits into the hard, frozen ground. After some effort the spits stand steady to support the swine above the fire.

The trodden spirits of the soldiers slowly return to them with every morsel they take. Morale rises bit by bit to the surface. Almost instantaneously strength starts returning. Some break out into song, others leisurely sip their drink.

Relieved, Draden retires to his tent and reads. He falls asleep.

⚬

Two hours later, Draden re-enters a dream he has been having the last several months. He is in a prairie reunited with his wife and son. All is peaceful. Joy and laughter sound in his mind behind his resting eyes. Then the sky turns red, the clouds darken - blue lightning streaks through them breaking open the sky. The sun is displaced by darkness and laughter is displaced by shrilling screams of people in the distance. Hapless villagers are overrun by Darius and his army. Aurelia and Nuriel are sucked into the sky by their legs. They reach toward him for help as they get smaller and smaller in the distance. They cry out to him but don't make a sound. Voiceless are their pleas. Anguish and sorrow is their expression. Draden reaches helplessly toward them as they fade away into the clouds. He yells in despair, "No, No, not again!" and falls to his knees. In the distance, the prairie is on fire. The smoke suffocates his lungs. He resists death, wipes his tears and heads toward the fire. Still reeling with heartbreak he draws his sword.

⋙⋘

Nakano enters, she is angered by something. "General," she calls. Draden awakes and struggles to decipher whether he is still in the dream. Realizing he is no longer asleep replies, "Yes Katsumi, what is it?"

"Darius, his army..." she begins. Draden beckons her to continue. "They know we're here, how many of us remain and our condition."

"What do you mean Katsumi?" Urges Draden, "how?"

Nakano walks over to the entrance of the tent and with her sword draws open the entrance. She directs Yver to enter with their prisoner. Yver enters with a spy from Alvarez's cavalry. The spy is secured in chains. He is badly beaten and bruised. Alvarez hurries in shortly after.

Draden rubs his forehead, estimating the consequences stemming from the deceit. He looks furiously at the prisoner but maintains a calm voice, "What's your name?" he asks the spy.

Having difficulty speaking through a broken jaw he utters, "C-C-Cooper...," still a soldier he finishes, "G-General." Draden looks at Alvarez for clarification, Alvarez clarifies, "Corporal James Cooper, General." Draden studies him a moment.

"I recognize you from Damascus Corporal. You were one of those who remained in the breach with Alvarez, weren't you?" asks Draden.

Through restricted breath he answers, "Y-es, General."

"Why Corporal? Why would you turn on your brothers and sisters?" inquires Draden.

Cooper pauses to answer. Alvarez punches him in the back of the shoulder, "Your General asked you a question." Cooper answers belaboredly, "It is a lost cause General. The resistance is a lost cause. I don't want to die." He begins to cry.

"How?" asks Draden, "How did you communicate with Darius and his captains?"

Cooper struggles to stop crying, "I sent messages with the townspeople and by the birds," he confesses. Nakano steps out of the tent briefly and returns with a box filled with skewered birds and pigeons – freshly killed by her hand. Cooper looks at the box of dead fowl and quickly nods his head as tears roll down his swollen cheeks. He confirms those are all the birds he used.

"Do you have family travelling with you Corporal?" Asks Draden.

Cooper falls to his knees and wails as best he can through broken bone, "Please General, please, please don't hurt them. They had nothing to do with this. Please…" he begs.

"Bring them here." orders Draden. Alvarez leaves the tent to get them.

Cooper crawls toward Draden's feet sobbing, "no please General no," he cries. Nakano promptly drops a knee on his back and keeps him from getting any closer to Draden. He cannot move beneath her strength.

"No, no General, no, please..." pleads Cooper. Alvarez returns with Cooper's wife, sister and daughter.

Though enraged at Cooper's treachery, Draden looks kindly to his wife. When speaking to her, he feels genuine empathy and regret before asking, "What are your names?"

Cooper's wife replies, "Rebecca," pointing to herself. She is noticeably shaken and confused, "and this," she points to her daughter, "is Amalee."

Rebecca's hand trembles as she gestures with open palm. Amalee clutches her doll tightly in her hand. She is horrified and does not understand what is happening.

"How old are you?" Draden asks Amalee.

Her face long with worry, raises 8 fingers while still clutching her doll under her arm, "Eight," she says softly.

Draden smiles warmly at her, "That's a good age Amalee. You have your whole life ahead of you. Look after your mother and auntie okay?" Not knowing how else to respond Amalee nods.

He then asks Cooper's sister her name. Afraid to look at her shackled brother, she answers "Dalia."

Draden looks to Alvarez, "Please give them enough food and water to make their way to the closest town. Send 20 guard with them to ensure their safety."

Alvarez replies, "Sir, General, we need every fighting hand we have. Why would---"

Draden cuts him off and looks at him sternly, "We have a duty - to every soul on this planet – to save any and all who can be saved."

Alvarez scoffs tongue in cheek but obeys discordantly. As he reaches for Rebecca to escort her out, Draden raises his hand and requests a moment's pause for a final word.

"Rebecca," he begins. She looks up at Draden through tearful eyes, her heart sinks slowly – she knows what is about to happen to her husband, "we are not your enemy. Please be sure to remind Amalee of that. You will need each other now more than ever. The world needs you to understand that now more than ever."

Rebecca swallows sorrow-filled swallows and nods quickly. She cannot speak. Unable to form words behind unrelenting tears. She puts a trembling hand to quivering lip and nervously takes Amalee's hand in the other. Dalia also knows what's to come. Draden nods to Alvarez to continue their removal from camp.

Cooper breaks down in front of Draden, "Thank you General. Thank you, thank you. Oh bless you General. Thank you, thank you." He sobs clutching the snow and loose dirt beneath his hands.

Cooper is suddenly burdened by his own duplicity. He feels great regret for turning against Draden. Not just because he spared his family, but because he has just realized that Draden's commitment is to humanity, not just to victory. Cooper was given a choice between darkness and light, he chose poorly. He quietly and serenely accepts his fate; is taken a short distance from the tent by Nakano and Yver; his sentence is carried out swiftly and as painlessly as possible. Corporal James Cooper will never be heard from again.

Nakano returns with Yver. The trio exchange a silent understanding of what is transpired.

"What do we know?" asks Draden.

Nakano answers, "Darius' forces have split into three battalions. One hundred thousand in each battalion. They move more quickly now."

Yver adds, "We will be surrounded by three one hundred thousand blue-black brigades in less than a full day's march. Our only path is toward the ocean."

Haddad enters. "You called for me General."

Draden inquires, "Did you run into any trouble while foraging Commander?"

Haddad replies, "Yes Sir, General."

"Describe...please..." Requests Draden gesturing with two open hands.

"We couldn't see much General. It was getting dark. The snow and the forest was thick." He pauses as if his subconscious mind just grabbed his brain and unscrambled itself to his attention, "come to think of it, they were extremely well armored and equipped for a band of roadway brigands."

Draden confirms his suspicion, "They are already here." The room echoes with silence.

"What's the condition of our fighters?" asks Draden openly for anyone to answer.

Yver answers, "Many are still drunk General. Some have already passed out. Several thousand are still ill."

"Rouse them, muster them" urges Draden, "Strike Camp, we head north. With our number we can cross the channel there."

⸎

No sooner was the last tent struck than the blue-black flag of the global-imperial army appeared on the distances east, southeast and southwest of Draden's position.

"Rolling flare formation," shouts Draden.

On Draden's command, the Seventh Resistance assume Rolling Flare formation around Draden. Draden rides in the inner core at the very center of the flare. Haddad's archers insulate him from harm and form the first ring around him. Alvarez, Yver and their cavalry encircle Haddad's archers creating a third ring of protection. Nakano's infantry spear gather at the outer ring of the flare and form a wide elliptical phalanx. Their shields interlock and their spears overlap. In a shielded, rolling, military sphere, the entire Seventh Resistance moves in an orderly, disciplined, closely held, defensive formation. They commit straight north toward Denmark.

While marching, foot soldiers rotate constantly around the ellipse to ensure everyone can rest while fresh attacks are deflected. Archers launch their arrows into the oncoming force no matter whether they are near or far. Occasionally the phalanx and archer assault expose openings in the attacking enemy formation. Once exposed, cavalry and light infantry flare out onto the offensive exacting as much retribution as possible from each flare. Once exacted they return to the ellipse to close the openings in the first and second perimeter. It is the way the Seventh moves for the next 4 miles.

Attacks come from 3 different directions. They come at different times hoping to wear out each side of the flare formation. Global-imperial soldiers cannot penetrate the formidable shield wall. The Seventh counters ferociously. A full direct assault by the imperial army against Draden's troops results in horrendous casualties inflicted on their own number. They wage a battle of attrition awaiting their opportunity to come when Draden and his group tire under the ongoing force of attack. Their goal is Draden's full annihilation. They cannot win while the rolling flare is still fresh.

After 4 miles the entire phalanx is feeling the burn of their muscles and the bruises on their limbs. Some have suffered bone fractures on their arms and legs, yet they hold firm through the pain. Each warrior is desperate to not let their companions down. But series of sustained, heavy contact from repelling a charging army time and again has made clutching weapons an arduous task. The ill are getting weaker.

The next assault by the global-imperial army knocks shield and spear out of hands. Those who stumble are trampled by stampeding foot. Valiantly, the ones standing patch the breaches in formation with their weary bodies. The stalwart, intrepid wall of the Seventh reveals marks of deterioration. Cracks emerge in the flare formation. Sword and shield replace spear. The attackers erode Resistance lines. Soon horse meets horse and movement north stops. The battle is now waged standing. Three detachments of the global-imperial assault force converge upon the remaining forty thousand of the Resistance. General Draden is locked in hand to hand combat. Thousands are killed. The global-imperial army senses victory and is reinvigorated by the complete annihilation of the war movement's greatest general. Draden's elite fight on, but their numbers rapidly disintegrate. It is only a matter of time before there are none left to fight.

A horn sounds on the horizon. It starts to snow. The rumble of hooves and footsteps grow louder. Trumpets blare several more times. Snow clouds are kicked into the air and shift in the distance behind the advancing force. A striking figure emerges on the skyline at the head of thirty thousand horse, five thousand sword, five thousand spear and ten thousand arrow. His armor is silver and meets the pale blue spectrum. In the sun's reflection through the snow he appears as a blue flame glimmering in its light. The cavalry tightens its formation around the blue warrior – infantry fan out to the sides. He slowly draws his sword. The scratch of metal blade on scabbard rings in the ears and elevates the pulse. The blue general looks ahead and side to side – takes one final moment to assess the field – then beckons his army forward in a roar, "Attack!"

On his command they race forward directly on to Draden's position. Horses gallop neck and neck. Every living being's breath smokes in the cold afternoon air. Falling snow parts before them. Gradually breath gets faster and sharper as heart rates accelerate. The pale blue leader moves effortlessly with he and his horse mimicking centaurs of legend.

Draden looks upon the descending force. He contemplates his last days and inhales one final deep breath. He prepares to be struck from the earth and be reunited with his family.

The wedge that falls upon Draden's army suddenly separates around them leaving the Seventh unscathed. Global-imperial warriors are flung off their horse by powerful striking mace, sword and lance. Imperial archers are run down by charging cavalry. Foot-soldiers of the blue-black flag are impaled by streaking arrow.

Having not been struck and recognizing he has received nameless aid, Draden calls out to his remaining warriors feverishly to assist the anonymous, "Hammer formation! Ready!"

Enlivened by their turn in fortune, all remaining cavalry of the Seventh Resistance form a wedge. Alvarez is at the helm, Yver in second. Nakano's foot-soldier's muster behind and prepare to charge into the nearest foe. Nearly out of arrows, what remains of Haddad's archers draw swords and join Nakano. Haddad falls in with them – staff in one hand, scimitar blade in the other. Sa'eed growls at his side, Nabila swoops in close by. Draden spurs his horse into action and races to the front. "Attack!" He screams.

The entire remnants of the Seventh army collide violently with the holders of the blue-black flag. Wherever Draden's hammer falls, vengeance and destruction follow.

The pale blue warrior rides furiously upon his mount. From his saddle he draws a morningstar flail. The iron fangs of the spiked sphere fall at his side and glisten menacingly in the afternoon light. He glides over the plains toward an enemy officer. Spinning his chained mace swiftly in the wind it turns into a vicious whirling sledgehammer. With a yell, he slams a powerful, well-placed blow into the chests of many targets. The clang of iron spikes piercing armor and bone resonates loudly in the ears of the enemy. Confusion sets in upon them.

The pale blue rider takes many lives. Death by his hand is widespread. The enemy general turns. He singles out the blue-warrior for immediate elimination. A horde of global-imperialists charge at him. An arrow zings in front of the pale commander's fully armored head. Through the slits in his helmet he sees the projectile and reacts - tumbling off his horse. His steed protests in neigh and falls with him. They both spring up from the snow-covered earth instantly. Dismounted, the pale blue leader pulls twin swords from the saddle, one long and one short. He prepares to defend his ground. Friendly fighters scramble to his side. With the help of his horse, the bulk of the onrush is dispatched before much aid arrives. Draden looks on at the blue warrior with sustained impression. With every movement the blue soldier makes, Draden senses familiarity.

Having cleared his own way on the ground, the pale blue general whistles. His horse bends legs. With haste, he grabs a spear from a fallen adversary. The remount is effortless and unencumbered – spear is firmly in hand. The blue warrior and his horse rise connected once more. His green-brown eyes peer glaringly at the enemy general. With a series of sounds, he circles his steed quickly in place gaining momentum for the spear's throw – with a powerful release from his chest he launches it through the breastplate of the enemy general. The force of the throw knocks him back. He falls to the ground after having been lifted from it when the spear struck. Blood spills from the joints in his armor. The ground beneath him turns red. He grunts breathlessly. The victorious pale blue chief sits motionless on horseback assessing his strike – he grips the reins tightly in left hand. With a wrathful gaze, he wills the life out of his enemy and watches intently as life expires from him. The enemy general is vanquished. Retreat horns of the blue-black sound, tens of thousands lay dead.

⚬

The battle is ended. Still wary of their saviors, Draden and his commanders usher those nearby closer still. The soldiers of the pale blue make a path to Draden. The pale-blue chief dismounts his horse and walks watchfully through the space created toward Draden. Green-brown eyes look curiously upon him through the openings in his helmet. Nakano steps in front of Draden clutching her sais, Haddad, Yver and Alvarez move in next to him, weapons drawn. They are cautious and curious.

Draden allows the blue chief full access and gently motions Nakano aside. "I'll be alright." Draden confides in her.

The pale-blue general stands before Draden, 3 inches shorter. He is un-phased and untroubled by weapons scratching against his armor. In fact, he is so captivated by Draden he does not notice his proximity to death. He studies Draden a short while longer then opens, "They say you are the great Samuel Draden – General of the Seventh Resistance." He states though sounding as a question.

"I am. Who do I owe my gratitude to?" replies Draden.

The pale-blue deflects the question with a question, "Who are your companions?" speaking through plated helmet.

"Not until you answer the General's question first," Alvarez jumps in. Nakano gestures in agreement with Alvarez's question.

The pale-blue chuckles to himself, "You must be Lieutenant General Diego Alvarez, scourge of the imperialists from the Americas." He looks over to Nakano softly "And you," he continues, "are the daunting and fearless Lieutenant Commander Katsumi Nakano I presume. I heard you saved your General's life in Damascus."

Nakano does not respond. Draden laughs, "She does that a lot. Not just Damascus." The enigmatic general is amused with Draden's answer and smiles as though he knows that to be the truth.

"Then for that, Lieutenant Commander," the pale-blue says speaking to Nakano, "I am grateful." He pauses. "And the entire Resistance is grateful," motioning to everyone who is around and meaning the entire world. He looks back to Draden. Draden notices a hint of an expression behind the great metal helmet.

The pale-blue fixes his eyes directly on Draden's eyes. The mysterious man's eyes are the color of all the colors of the earth, with the sea readily perceptible throughout. Without blinking or moving his stare from Draden, he speaks to Nakano, "This man owes the world his service. He owes the world his survival. And it is he who owes the earth his leadership. Thank you Lieutenant Commander Nakano for seeing to it that he kept his promise to us." Tears well up in the pale-blue warriors eyes. Their color turns shades from green-brown to blue-green. At once Draden recognizes the words his son spoke to him years ago before their worlds were ripped apart. For the first time in nearly two decades, General Samuel Draden is overcome with emotion..."Nuriel!" he exclaims in disbelief, "My son..."

Nuriel removes his helmet revealing his father's eyes and his mother's hair. His face is entirely his own, "Yes father."

Without a thought, Draden throws his arms around his son. He cannot contain his emotions. Tears roll down his cheeks in a flood. Draden holds his son in his arms never meaning to let go. He sobs on his shoulder. Nuriel, with tears in his eyes, comforts and welcomes his father's embrace.

The impervious Nakano releases her emotion. A flood of feeling surges up from her heart and penetrates her soul. She is moved to tears. Fresh droplets slide down each of her porcelain, earth covered cheeks. Alvarez is moved. Yver is touched.

Haddad is ecstatic. With newly moistened eyes, he declares to himself in Arabic, *"Glory be to God, the exalted, the capable of bringing people together after a long separation! [Subhan'Allah al Alee al Qadeer al-lethee jama'ahum ba'ad foraq taweel]."*

Draden pulls away, his hands still grip his sons armor plated triceps. He looks at him proudly. "You're alive." Ensuring he is not dreaming or hallucinating. Nuriel nods. He pulls him back in and holds him tightly and exclaims again as if still convincing himself that the skies will not turn red and rip him away, "Nuriel...my precious boy...my son."

Draden sniffles, tears still warm upon his cheeks "And your mother? Where's your mother?"

Nuriel assures his father, "We have a lot to catch up on father. Come. I think I know where you are headed." He smiles.

⁂

Above the North Atlantic coast of Norway on the island of Torget rises the 846 foot granite peak of Mount Torghatten. Upon approach, the most prominent characteristic of the mountain is the 520 foot long, 66 foot wide and 115 foot high natural crater at its center. According to Scandinavian legend, the hole in the mountain was made by the troll knight Hestmannen while he was chasing a beautiful maiden Lekamoya. When the troll knight realized he will be unable to win her affections, he released an arrow to kill her. In her defense the troll-king of Somna threw his hat into the arrow's path to save her. That hat turned into the mountain with a hole in the middle.

Other legends link Torghatten to the Homeric myth of Polyphemus. Polyphemus is a man-eating giant who lives on the island of the Cyclops – an island the Greek General Odysseus had the misfortune of landing on while returning home from the Trojan War. Interpretations within the Scottish Rite of Freemasonry regard Polyphemus as a symbol for a civilization that harms itself by using ill-directed blind force.

Armies travel up a well-made path along the east side of the mountain. The passage climbs higher and higher until finally entering a chasm with sheer rock walls before ascending into the mouth of the mountain. Remnants of crashed aircraft speckle the surrounding landscape.

Taking in the sights of the unique and peculiar landmark, Draden recalls all the parables he read many decades ago that potentially identified Mount Tor as one of the final remaining strongholds that will stand against the tides of darkness. The descriptions in the scriptures of Mount Tor are vague. Some believe these writings were written with intentional ambiguity so that only those with purity of heart and innocence of intention will be able to decipher their true meaning. Mount Tor, as spoken of in legend could have been in any one of three different locations from three distinctly different regions of the world. It some instances of legend and scripture, what appears as one location can actually be several.

Despite the natural defenses of the island peak, inhabitants of the stronghold erected formidable walls around the entire island using the granite from surrounding land. The defenses blend stealthily into the rock face. A fortress was built into and underneath the crater and natural surface. Unlike traditional strongholds where attack and weak points are identifiable with a blue-print, the architects and masons of the stronghold on Mount Tor intentionally kept no such documents.

The only attack points are by sea or bridge across waters. And only if armies know that the stronghold exists. Many of the un-learned see Torghatten as a forgotten ruin. Sensational yet inconspicuous watch towers armed with forbidding weaponry guard those channels. Occasionally, barters and trades were made with pirates sailing the northern ocean to defend the banks of the mountain. The one thing pirates and freedom fighters have had in common over the ages is their hatred of being caged within a system with which they do not agree. Loose alliances are frequently made between pirates and the Resistance under this premise.

The price the pirates usually demand for their naval services is a retention of any and all spoils, treasure and manpower they deemed sufficient after a victorious defense against the global-imperial navy. A small plunder tax was agreed upon between the pirates and Nuriel's council. They agreed to a 5% share of gains, including the provision of some captured ships to the residents of Mount Tor. The plunder tax helps pay for maintenance and repairs of the stronghold as well as provide sea vessels for trade and transportation.

At the main entrance of the fortress is a massive banquet hall. It is not lavish nor ornamented in jewels or gold. It is plain, earthen and elegant. At the center rests a great granite table where all could dine if they pleased without regard to birth right or station. At each end of the table are large but simple chairs. Nuriel sits to the north and any can sit to the south. It is customary that the south seat remain reserved for whomever Nuriel appoints to sit in it. This is not a custom of Nuriel's choosing. Rather it is the strong suggestion of Nuriel's council that the south seat be reserved so.

At the end of the great hall are three separate and enormous rooms. Directly at the end of the banquet hall is the council chambers. It is a partitioned chamber that allows for decisions and discussions on law, economics, war and diplomacy. In all ways, the council chambers serves as the legislative body, the judiciary and the executive headquarters of the Torget community. One room joins the back of the council chambers. It is designated as the throne room with an impressive granite chair. Nuriel takes his seat upon the throne only when deciding on matters of justice and law for the accused. When trial is not in procession, he often returns here to pray and be left alone with his thoughts.

To the right of the council chambers is the chapel. It is two stories high. The first floor of the chapel opens to meet an elevated platform with a gigantic fireplace to the left. Here, minstrels play, actors perform and important announcements are made. Large stone steps at the right of the chapel rise east then ascend south. At the top of the stairs the floor is divided into three sections. Off to the sides of the second floor are enclosed rooms that act as Torghatten's library. Shelves are carved into the walls. The shelves are lined with scrolls that the stronghold's elders wrote from memory. These scrolls are some of the last remaining descriptions of history, fable, truth, legend and religious scriptures in the world. Almost every religious book and scripture was done away with and destroyed during the "cleansing of religious zealots," as decreed by Chancellor Darius when he assumed power and had long been practiced by those who came before him.

Archways without doors divide each of the three main sections. Originally Jews assembled in the west room, Christians congregated in the center room and Muslims worshipped in the east room. This is no longer the case. It is common to see members of each faith migrate between rooms on various days. Christians and Jews will join the Muslims for prayer and philosophical discussion on Fridays. Muslims and Christians gather among the Jews on Saturdays. Jews and Muslims attend mass and communions on Sundays. Lively and peaceful debates take place every weekend. Some go away from the conversations with a deeper understanding of their own religion while others are not swayed. Converts declare voluntary and un-coerced allegiance to a different religion from time to time. The most frequent question asked is, who is the Messiah and when will he or she show themselves? While minds differed about what form or shape the Messiah will take – all agreed the Nuriel was the most likely candidate to be that honor. Nuriel is not in agreement with that conclusion.

In so many ways he was too imperfect to be the Messiah maintains Nuriel. He was never ordained by a Godly power as such and suffers from the same humanity and afflictions that any other man does. He is not a healer, nor is he a prophet.

He cannot tell the future and God does not talk to him from His throne in the heavens. How could he be anything remotely resembling the Messiah he contemplates. He makes judgement errors. He does not have superhuman strength or genius intelligence. He stutters when nervous and has to slap his thigh repeatedly to regain control over his words after the stutters start. A presentment that developed over the years and has become more pronounced after many sustained impacts in battle. While otherwise healthy, he does not consider himself sufficiently divine to be the Messiah. In fact it is more accurate to say of Nuriel that he is simply a fighting clergyman who seeks only to preserve the fight until the real Messiah decides to arrive. Like his father, he has not declared allegiance to any one religion. He rather prefers to see the connecting thread between all religions and live by these interwoven tenets instead.

Spanning the left third of the back wall a large space is divided between the mezzanine and the kitchen. The mezzanine room serves as a landing between stories. The kitchen serves the main population of the fortress. Above the mezzanine, up slabs of granite stairs are the solar and sleeping chambers. The solar room is a great room that is used for casual gatherings and discussions. An oculus on the ceiling allows the suns warming rays to penetrate an otherwise chilly room. A fireplace rises from the left wall. Sofas and chairs are arranged for reading, conversing, or sharing friendly glasses of drink. At the right of the room is an archway that leads to a long corridor. The hallway opens into dozens of sleeping chambers. Nuriel resides in the largest room at the end of the hall overlooking 360 degrees of the ocean. From his room he can see for miles across the ocean in all directions and looks upon the 3 outside concentric walls that protect each wall behind it. Some of these walls are enhanced natural barriers while others were built and expertly blended into their surroundings. His guests sojourn next door and share an equally breathtaking view. A small kitchen is nearby.

At dinner, Nuriel excuses himself from the main banquet feast to dine privately with his father. Ignoring Nuriel's insistence to serve himself, attendants bring lamb, rice, fish soup, bread and carrots from the kitchen.

Nuriel looks at his father, "See what I have to put up with here. They treat me like I'm some kind of king who needs to be waited on hand and foot."

Draden replies sarcastically, "Yes, it looks like you have a lot to complain about." Laughing. He laughs partly at his answer, but mostly he laughs to express his overwhelming joy over seeing his son alive. He beams with pride as he looks, unbelievingly still, at his son.

"I thought you were dead." begins Draden.

"Almost was father."

"How did you escape?" asks Draden

Nuriel recalls, "Not long after you were hoisted away, mother and I were met by 70 of your riders who helped us fight our way out."

"Oh thank God," Draden praises. "Where's your mother?"

"When we escaped Virginia we agreed to separate. They would not let up trying to track us down. They had spies in practically every city. Owen, my second, and 30 others," he explains, "came with me. The rest looked after mother. We thought it best that we not know where each of us was being taken just in case we were ever captured." Tells Nuriel.

"Smart." affirms Draden. "It was also smart to not try to communicate with me." He pieces the rest together, "The global-imperial government thought you were dead. And that kept you safe."

"I hope you can forgive me for not trying to reach you sooner father." Requests Nuriel.

"Of course. I get it. It was the right thing to do. You're safe. That's all that matters." Answers Draden.

"You look well father," compliments Nuriel.

Draden laughs and bangs self-deprecatingly on the table, "Ha! thanks to you and your band of merry wanderers," he acknowledges. Then wonders, "How did you know where I was?"

Nuriel nods, "Well, the entire world heard about your assault on Damascus. The first invasion of the capital city in 30 years is big news in this world even without the media." Nuriel raises a finger in declaration, "And I will tell you, I would have absolutely paid to watch your invasion on pay per view." Both laugh.

"Your mother wouldn't allow it." Reminds Draden.

Nuriel continues, "Once word reached me, I dispatched, shall we say," he searches for the perfect word, "silent emissaries to keep me informed." He sighs, "When I heard things took a turn for the worst with Busellis and Cooper, I had no choice but to gather as many of my people as possible to come after you. I knew Darius wouldn't stop until he totally destroyed you. And," he pauses, "you knew that too." He considers, "At that point, I didn't care if I blew my cover and everyone knew that I was still alive. I had to try to save you."

"You put on quite a show my boy." Answers Draden. "Absolutely astounding. I am so proud of you and so proud of the man you have become."

"Thank you father."

"I never would have imagined in my entire life, that in my darkest hour, my son would be my salvation." He puts a large, gentle hand to the back of Nuriel's neck, pulls him forward and kisses his honey-blond head. "You still move like your mother," smiles Draden.

"She was quick on her feet." Remembers Nuriel.

"And you fight with your head and heart before your sword. I am most proud of you for that." Declares Draden.

"I am my father's son." Responds Nuriel.

"That you are my boy. That you are."

CHAPTER 4

False Prophets

*"And out came another horse, bright red. Its rider
was permitted to take peace from the earth, so that
people should slay one another, and he was given a
great sword."*

REVELATION 6:4

CHANCELLOR DARIUS STIRS restlessly back in his chambers.
He considers his triumphant campaign in India where he has
just returned from a six month war. The leader of the Indian
resistance lies now in chains in the dungeons of Damascus
and Darius' opposition there decimated. He is troubled as to
how the most notorious General of the resistance is still at
large and his son remains alive. Now nearing his 76th year,
the pronounced lines on his face cannot hide his frustration.
The years have deepened the red behind his eyelids so his eye
reflects more crimson in the light than they do deep brown.

Furiously he stampedes to the council chambers. The
scar across his face protrudes strongly where the veins in

his forehead bulge angrily. The ten governors of each sector are already there seated. They have been summoned by the Chancellor to address a growing problem. Draden's escape has encouraged new groups of resistance fighters to emerge across the globe. The re-emergence of Nuriel has spun the rumor that he is the resurrected Messiah sent back to earth to finish the fight against the global-imperial army. Darius feels his iron vice around the earth loosening.

He says calmly behind furious eye, "Someone tell me again how Nuriel Draden vanished from the earth 20 years ago and is now *resurrected* 20 years later?" He mocks directing the question to any of the ten governors seated in the room in terror.

Nobody answers. A moment later he loses patience and slams both fists into the table and screams, "Answer me!" he stands resting his aged yet sturdy frame upon wrist and clenched hands.

Baz Keating, the governor of Sector 0 fearfully recounts a version of events he heard from an elder 15 years ago. "I recently heard an elder say he was in Port Louis off the coast of Madagascar when word circulated that Nuriel Draden had arrived in port."

Governor Baz Keating is a native of Canada. Prior to obtaining his governor's seat in Damascus, he spent his entire life in the service of Chancellor Darius. His first opportunity to serve came as an officer in the Third Resistance under Darius' command. When Darius' ambitions become focused politically, Baz Keating was an outspoken supporter of the then general Darius. He was appointed to governor of

Sector 0 by Darius since the founding of the global-imperial nation. Every 6 years, Keating would win the re-election by an astounding margin. He regularly received 96% of the vote. Governor Keating is Darius' most loyal governor.

Satisfied that he is finally getting some answers Darius sits seriously and urges the governor to continue, "Yes Baz, please do go on."

The Governor continues, "when I asked the man when he had heard this, he said about 15 years ago." Getting acknowledgement to continue he goes on to say, "A man said to be Nuriel, son of Draden was travelling with 4 companions. He remembers one of them was called Owen. They were dismissed as pirates on temporary leave from the sea."

Darius rises to look at an immense map that covers the northern council chamber wall. He punches the wall after a moment's inspection. Port Louis is a tiny island port that sits approximately 300 miles outside the reach and borders of sector 5. Sector 5 begins on the African shores of the Mediterranean sea. It encircles the whole of the continent of Africa and Madagascar. Port Louis floats outside those borders. Darius returns and stands at the end of the table.

Calmly once more Darius beckons, "did you hear anything else Keating?"

The governor adds, "Yes, this elder told me that after three nights the pirates booked passage to India."

Darius rubs his gruff chin in contemplation, "Bring the elder here."

A frail man in his 90's is dragged into the council chambers. He is dressed in little more than a smock and cap. His sandals are simple and worn and his black eyes weakly make out the shapes of the people in the room. He is made to sit on a naked stone chair.

"What's your name?" begins Darius almost kindly.

"Kersely Begnaud," answers the fisherman.

"What did you do while you were in Port Louis?" follows Darius

"I was a fisherman your excellency." Replied Kersely.

"What do you know of the fugitive Nuriel Draden, Mr. Begnaud?"

"I only know what I hear now. I did not know he was a fugitive 15 years ago. I only remember any of it because there was a great commotion surrounding his arrival on our island." Recalls Kersely with an old and tired voice.

"How do you feel about him now?" asks Darius.

Unwittingly Kersely answers, "I think news of his res-urrection has inspired a lot of people highness." The back of Darius' hand cracks staunchly across the old man's face. Kersely's head is forcefully swiveled 90 degrees breaking open his lower lip.

Kersely is unsure what he said to deserve such a blow. His expression turns from obedient to fearful.

"He is not resurrected!" Barks Darius, "he is just a man. A criminal who has escaped!" he howls. "I...," yells pointing to himself, "I...," he glares with one red-brown eye, "I...am the one who brought order and peace to this world. I saved the nations from themselves, not some insignificant son of a rabble rouser."

Kersely answers with tearful eyes and bloody lip, "yes your majesty, yes, just a man. Forgive me excellency. Forgive me." He raises an open hand to Darius and gestures for forgiveness.

Darius massages the hand that struck the fisherman and softens his tone. "Take him away." Commands the chancellor.

Taking a seat, Darius warns, "You see ladies and gentlemen, this problem is starting to get out of control. People... common people, simpletons and idiots think a new God is risen on earth. Until we shatter this myth, it will continue to grow to scales we cannot possibly control."

⚜

Survivors of the battle of Hanover arrive to the council doors. "We have news," they call out behind the fully armed guards guarding the chamber.

"Let them come," order Darius. "What news do you have?

"He came from the west, then headed north. It is likely he came from Sector 7 and has headquarters in sector 2." The intelligence officer identifies.

Darius looks at the speaker confusedly, "Who?"

"Uh, forgive me sire, Nuriel Draden and his father. They are likely hiding somewhere in sector 2."

"Finally something I can work with," boasts Darius. He turns and orders his attendant, "Prepare my things." Darius motions the attendant out then speaks to Keating and Rachit

Mahajan, the governor of sector 9, "gather what you need, we're going back to India."

Mahajan asks cautiously, "Forgive me Sire, but, what are we going to do back in India? The uprising there is crushed."

"We will follow Nuriel's trail from 15 years ago all the way to Sector 2." He stares at Mahajan, almost annoyed that his decision is being questioned, "I intend to tear apart villages and towns to uncover and eliminate any perceived threat to our way of life along the way."

Mahajan replies carefully with his words, "Shall I send a detachment of soldiers to Sector 2 in the meantime your majesty?" wondering why Darius doesn't just attack Sector 2.

Darius pauses a moment and looks to the middle cuticle on his left hand tempering his reply, "I am not directly assaulting Sector 2, because there is no telling where support for Draden's armies will come from. We saw an entire legion of our warriors decimated by an unknown army that was somehow made to be invisible to our intelligence." He nods and continues nodding until Mahajan nods along with him, "the most prudent course of action is to ensure that when we finally corner Draden and his son, we will not repeat this same mistake." Still nodding, "It is best that we do not let ourselves be surprised again by an unknown military force...Yes?" he completes.

Mahajan nodding, "Absolutely highness. Brilliant highness. Of course. I will gather what I need."

⚬

Rachit Mahajan is a portly man in his early fifties. Preferring to dress in the traditional attire for Indian nobility he carries himself as a statesman. A full mustache runs the length of his upper lip and curves upwards toward his cheeks. The son of a wealthy banking and lending family in India, he and his family are riddled with scandals and schemes.

35 years ago, prior to Darius assuming absolute power, the Mahajan patriarch was indicted for and found guilty of running the world's largest ponzi scheme in history. During the investigation into the Mahajan family businesses more horrific crimes against humanity were uncovered. Among them was the abduction of young children and adolescents for the purposes of human trafficking, prostitution and forced labor. The majority of children were abducted from families who racked up debts they could not repay. When questions arose about transacting human beings for forced labor, the answer was given that the children's wages went to paying down the owed debt. The interest rates charged were too high to ever pay down a significant amount of principal in a parent's lifetime. Once abducted, a family lost their child for life.

Rachit was the Chief Operating Officer of his family's abduction and trafficking enterprise. Taxes for their trade were subsidized by the local government. Ever an ambitious man, Rachit spun off a subsidiary company that boasted the largest opium trade in east Asia. In classic mercantilist-protectionist fashion, this subsidiary also enjoyed government subsidies and reduced tariffs across borders for its opium trade. The government of India claimed no knowledge of the inventory Rachit and his family were exporting.

Rachit Mahajan and his father were arrested and their family assets were frozen. They were both convicted and directed to serve consecutive life sentences in prison. When Darius assumed power he reviewed the names of all prisoners serving life sentences for so-called non-violent crimes. The crimes of the Mahajan family were classified as white collar and non-violent. Darius was aware of the immense influence this family wielded in the criminal underground and saw their usefulness immediately. He granted both Rachit Mahajan and his father full pardons because they were non-violent criminals and gave Rachit a seat in parliament in order to bring India under quick control. Shortly after being pardoned and operating under the cloak of governmental immunity with a seat as governor, Rachit made short work of financial and opposition rivals. The once mighty and developing state of India was weakened by the swift destruction of opponents. It quickly plunged into a state of poverty, hunger and famine. It was an easy target for submission.

Rachit gathers items in his chambers preparing for his trip to New Delhi. He addresses his servant, a 16 year old female. She is a product of the Mahajan forced labor enterprise. "He talks to me like I'm a child sometimes." He says to her, referring to Darius.

The young girl hears what is being said, stops what she is doing, turns toward him and keeps her eyes down letting him speak. She obediently clasps her delicate hands in front of her - one hand over the other - she listens.

"I gave him India," continues Mahajan, "I can take it away. Doesn't he realize that?"

The young girl remains nervously silent. Eyes still down fearing a blow from her keeper's belt or whip that would ease his discomfort.

Mahajan walks over to the trembling girl and grabs her by the arms, "You know me. You see that I am powerful. You know that if I snap my fingers, India goes away from the Chancellor."

She nods her head fearfully agreeing with whatever he says.

Mahajan relishes the sight of this timid creature cowering in his presence. "Oh my scared little angel, don't be scared. I am not going to hurt you. You please me. You please me a great deal. That's why I keep you. You know you please me don't you?"

She nods, tears begin to well-up in her eyes, she recognizes his advances just before he satisfies himself with her. Weakly she responds, "Yes Sir. Thank you."

Mahajan kisses her forehead - her cheek - her mouth – then slowly undoes the top buttons of her simple and plain dress. He takes his time. He delights in her timid sobs and the unease she must feel of what may come next.

With one finger he slides the thin strap of her gown off of her right shoulder then off of her left. The dress falls to the ground. She stands before him quivering, naked - awaiting his next command.

The Last Days of Draden

Mahajan, Darius and Keating arrive in New Delhi.

Darius enjoys coming to India. India is rich in mysticism, lore, magic, superstition, legend and tradition. Mysteries of the universe have been grappled with here for centuries and from the esoteric underground was dug up to the surface dozens of theories and practices in ritual magic. The mysticism in India takes him back to the life he was raised in. A life replete with conjuring, incantation, wizardry and alchemy. Even the air, heavy laden with the smell of incense and jasmine flowers reaches the core of his roots and ancestral memories. The energy in the air uplifts his soul. His core psyche feeds off the residual particles in the air left from thousands of years of sorcery, black arts and transformation.

Smoke still rises from towns recently pillaged by the global-imperial armies. The band of rulers walk the streets with their guards. Displaced, homeless and diseased villagers shrink and retreat from their path. Others scatter fearing abduction or assault. The larger, healthier of the towns people do not cower away in horror. They look on the parade with expressions of sorrow, despair and anger. Those that stare too long are met with deathly glares from the guards. Onlookers that did not easily avert their gaze are placated with a solid clubbing to the ground. Darius does not flinch at the violence preferring not to trouble himself with the trifles of peasants. His long dark blue-black cape shimmers with crimson accents and drags behind him. Marching boots leave puddles in the mud.

Darius approaches a structure that was erected from large marble slabs individually arranged in a large circle. In the middle of the circle is the largest stone. A massive slab in the middle of the ring rises 20 feet into the sky and spans an equally imposing radius on the earth. Just beyond this shrine is a tower that was seized and re-fitted for ritualistic magical operations. Darius instructs his followers to remain outside the sphere while he ascends into the tower ahead.

After rising 4 flights of stairs Darius enters a wide chamber lit dimly with torches around the walls. Just ahead is an iron throne. On the floor below are circles, shapes, etchings and markings in Sumerian, Hebrew, Arabic, Aramaic, alphabet of the Magi, celestial writings and invocations in the language of *Passing the River*. Darius walks to the center of the center circle and unclips his cape from around his shoulders. He holds it out in anticipation of it being collected by another. From the dark corners of the walls emerge 30 adepts and disciples. 20 are female, 10 are male. Each group of three represents leaders of covens from each of the ten sectors of the world. All the heads of every coven have been hand selected and sired by Darius himself. Some of his disciples here sprang from his own loins. His offspring from encounters with their mothers in ritual magic, tantric invocations or just because he willed himself upon whomever he wanted whenever he pleased. One ahead of the rest takes his cloak and lays it on the throne before returning to the circle. She returns to fill the open gap in the circle and stands directly before him. All are dressed in garments that barely cover sensual parts of their bodies.

Darius extends his arms and begins an incantation, "All you creatures that dwell here now in the unseen, present yourselves in a manner that pleases me. Do not resist and do not disobey." The room gets cold and shadows scale the walls. Low murmurs and whispers come from the shadows - Inaudible to all but Darius.

Darius stands without fear. Unflinching, he continues, "Welcome. I command thee to guard this tower from all ears not meant to hear what it is we are about to discuss. Do not whisper our secrets into the hearts of any others but to those in this room right now. Do you understand me and will you comply?" Low, inaudible whispers and murmurs.

"Should you fail me, I will assign a most grievous punishment for you. Do I make myself clear?" murmurs and whispers.

"Good. Go now and do as I have commanded." Completes Darius. The shadows scatter from within the walls to circling the tower from without like a dark fog not visible to any but those who took part in the circle.

Casually, Darius makes his way to the throne. Assembled here is the imperial council of mystics. Sorcerers, sorceresses, adepts, disciples, witches and warlocks who preside over all ritual practitioners in the world. Their primary role is to prevent the emergence of a counter force utilizing practices commonly known as *antithetical magic*. They hunt any ritualists who do not conform to their ideals and deal to them gruesome retribution for non-conformity. The council served Darius when he subdued the world under his reign as far back as the war between the hemispheres. When one would die, another was recruited promptly in their place. Darius personally trains and mentors each new adept. When the antithetical forces strike a blow, Darius acts swiftly before the circle is found, disrupted and dismantled. Darius believes that metaphysics is the truest power above all things earthly. The world between realms is mightier than military might. He has often said he would trample adversaries through incantations before he ever raised a sword. The Chancellor's legions include forces that can never be accounted for and those that are specifically isolated as to be beyond human dominion.

Speaking to the council, "I have summoned you all here to address a very troubling matter concerning Samuel Draden and his son." The circle falls silent paying attention to him as would followers pay a revered cult leader.

The woman that stood before Darius in the circle speaks, "Sire, the threat of Nuriel Draden and his father is real. Samuel Draden will raise another great army and attack the walls of Damascus once more."

Darius replies, "Yes, I have seen it too Maera. I have also seen that he dies by my hand. This future remains constant in my visions."

"Indeed Sire. And what of Nuriel?" Presents Maera.

"I cannot see him. The moment I get a glimpse of him a blinding flash disrupts my visions. I know Damascus does not fall while under my rule." Says Darius.

"It does not Sire. I know this to be certain." Assures Maera.

"It puzzles me. Very puzzling. I am puzzled," toils Darius. "This is why I summoned you all here. Perhaps in my aged years, my sight does not extend as far as it once did. Have you made the necessary preparations Maera?"

"Of course Sire." Maera raises her right hand and rotates her right finger prompting obedient compliance from the crowd.

The coven places the instruments of ritual in their designated and prescribed locations. A podium and ingredients for invocation are placed at the center circle where Darius will stand. Atop the podium is a book of incantations and invocations. Incense and vials of freshly drained blood from animals and humans are placed on the floor next to the podium. Inscribed knives, staffs and robes are handed out and attired. Symbols of the four corners of the earth decorate the floor north, east, south and west. Carvings of the five elements that are necessary for their purposes are displayed in plain sight, earth, wind, water, fire and human soul at the center. Names of the spirits and demons to be summoned are carefully written in the appropriate language or symbol in the correct place. Jewels of gold, silver and precious metals are adorned to please the spirits that will be called. The circle is prepared. Darius takes his position in the center of the center circle. The 30 disciples surround him dressed in nothing but the required items for summoning and protection. Much of their skin is bare however.

Darius performs the necessary invocations. He spills and combines the required ingredients together for such an operation and calls forth the demon who will assist him in his earthly vision. The life force of the 30 disciples will be focused on containing the spirits under their command.

"I summon thee to come forth dark duke of sight, complete for me the visions that have been left incomplete." Calls Darius.

The disciples squeeze their hands together uniting their life forces in defense should the spirit choose to retaliate against them.

A large and wild creature leaches into the tower from the walls directly before Darius and appears behind the disciples standing in front of him. The members of the coven ensure that every inch of their bodies are kept inside the circle. Any who step or hover for a moment outside the protective ring risk death. The ushered spirit stands as a faceless burning man enveloped in fire. When he speaks the smell of sulfur penetrates the nostrils.

"Of whom do you speak?" asks the creature.

"Nuriel Draden." Testifies Darius.

The creature laughs, then replies in a low growl, "You cannot see the comings of a man who's destiny is hidden."

"He comes for me, does he not?" asks Darius.

"He comes for no one." Answers the spirit.

"Do not lie to me spirit." Commands Darius becoming angry with the riddles. "Stop speaking to me in riddles."

The fiery demon is enraged by the charge and bursts into a fireball that erupts throughout the chamber. The circle protects those inside. "I do not lie mortal." Rumbles the demon erupting even larger.

"Calm yourself before I entrap thee in this vessel and torment thine soul for eternity." Orders Darius.

The fiery fiend's flames defiantly and reluctantly return to their origin. Darius senses his circle weakening. It took a tremendous amount of life force to defend its borders from the anger of the apparition. He is running out of time. The spirit senses this as well and is eager for one of them to collapse the circle.

"One more question demon." Indicates Darius

"One more question mortal. For it is best you release me before they break." Referring to the coven. "None will survive."

"Is Nuriel Draden the man that the prophecies predict?"

"No." hisses the demon.

The power of the circle is at a critical low. Darius must release the demon now back to where he came from.

"Thank you spirit. You may now return to the habitation that has been destined for you. I release you from this world back to yours. You may depart."

In a fiery vacuum, the demon is dismissed from this telluric realm. The members of the circle fall exhausted to the floor. Breathless and panting. The smell of sulfur lingers in the room making it more difficult to breathe.

Satisfied, Darius returns to his throne and waits for the group's strength to return. He sits pensively.

———※———

Maera approaches the throne and fixes her thoughts on Darius. She takes his right hand in hers and with gentle adulation pulls him toward her breast – speaking softly "Sire, the demon brought good tidings. Nuriel is not the one the prophecies speak of."

Darius returns, "Yes. That is what he said." Still cautious in his conclusion.

"What do you command Sire?" asks Maera.

"Let's not make it easy for them to return to Damascus." Prompts Darius. "What can we do to disrupt their little band of merry warriors?"

Maera provides, "I believe we can tear them apart before they even set foot in Sector 1. There is one among them who is weak and can be easily led off."

"Who is that?" asks Darius.

"I will save the name for the spirits. You know I can only utter it once for the operation to be successful. Listen to the shadows and you will hear it." Maera looks outside a window and recognizes something she hadn't considered until this very moment, "The moon favors us Sire. It sits in Scorpio tonight." delights Maera.

Darius simpers, "I have always enjoyed your handiwork my darling." He sits on his throne rests an elbow on the metal, rubs his fingernails together and observes.

Maera sits in the center circle and draws a figure on the ground. Her markings and etchings are written in freshly gotten dove's blood. She pours melted copper over iron in a container meant for mixing. As the metals bind to one another she adds cedar and myrtle. A fragrant blend that replaces the smell of stale sulfur which still leaves traces in the chamber.

She begins repeating a steady chant almost as if in a trance. "Ancient spirits, creatures of the realms, I call upon thee to rend asunder those who are them..." with the dove's blood she writes names of Draden's party on the ground. "Do my bidding, upon high and low, across the surface of the earth, above the clouds and all below." She rocks back and forth her eyes are closed, her concentration increased, "disrupt their harmony their unity their bond, destroy them all with the wave of this wand."

Portions of the dark fog that surrounded the tower tear away and disperse west.

CHAPTER 5

Lamentation

Mansour Haddad stirs in his bed and awakens in a sweat. He had the strangest dream he has had in a long while. Immediately he sits at the writing table in his room and scribbles out all that he can remember. He must capture every aspect of the dream, colors, smells, words, and people. Even how he felt when he awoke can change the very meaning of the same dream. He finishes writing and hurries to Draden's room. Nakano hurries close by sensing something is the matter. He leaves his chambers clasping his papers in hand with one shoe on one foot and barefoot on the other. He fights to keep his spectacles evenly on his face but settles with one lens higher than the other lopsided on his nose. He walks doggedly on the cold stone.

"General, general, wake up." Haddad says, shaking Draden awake.

Nakano stands at the other side of Draden's bed.

"Wha...what is it Haddad?" he asks with one eye open struggling to open the other.

"You must be fully awake for this general," he says then annunciates more clearly and simply, while touching the empty air in front of him with his pointer finger as if he was touching the words like they were just hanging there invisibly suspended in space, "fully, awake."

"Okay, okay. Grab Nuriel, bring him here. I want him to be a part of this too if it is urgent." Draden requests.

Nakano returns with a surprisingly fresh and alert Nuriel.

"It is 4:30 in the morning Commander," states Nuriel, "what is so urgent?"

"Yes, exactly...exactly," says Haddad. "The angels are closest to us during 4 and 6 in the morning. A warning from them at this hour cannot be ignored."

Nuriel smiles remembering that his father had read the same thing about the angels to him from somewhere when he was still a small boy. Haddad repositions himself at the foot of Draden's bed to be sure to include everyone in the conversation.

"What is it old friend?" asks Draden.

Haddad begins, "I had a dream." He stands silently for a few seconds scanning his eyes about the room waiting to be mocked, anticipating jokes and remarks about making all the commotion over a dream. None come. Every person present has had meaningful premonitions that came from what seemed a harmless dream.

"Go on..." says Draden.

"It was all of us. You," pointing to Draden, "me," pointing to himself, "Nakano, Yver, Nuriel and Alvarez. Points to the others in the room. We were abandoned by our army. They just disappeared out of my mind. Poof!" He makes the gesture of a thought cloud leaving his head. "Then we were surrounded by a pack of hyenas…" he shudders remembering their image.

He goes on, "their hungry eyes were focused on us all, I could smell their rotten breath. They would bark and with every snap would spray us with sprinkles of blood."

The group pictures themselves in the dream with Haddad. They are slightly disturbed about the image of hyenas spraying blood from their mouths.

"Their snarl revealed razor teeth that were eager to tear apart our flesh." He steps forward representing the lunge of a dog, "they jumped at us from all directions. We would hit them and cut them and they would jump back. But they would heal. We did no damage. They lunged again and again." Exclaims Haddad.

They listen more intently, "then, after maybe 100 lunges, Alvarez jumps out in front of you," pointing to Draden, "then hacks at the hyena leader, then cuts him to pieces, then leads the rest away." He demonstrates the sword strikes and slashes while speaking.

"We sent a search party," he continues. "We went to look for him. We must have covered 50 miles but we could not find him. Every now and again we would come across dead hyenas, struck down by Alvarez's sword but he did not answer to our calls nor did we ever find him."

The party of four sit quietly for a few seconds in contemplation.

"How did you feel when you woke up?" asks Nuriel.

"Betrayed." Replies Haddad.

"By Alvarez?" asks Draden.

"I don't know," answers Haddad, "He did not do anything in the dream that would indicate he was going to betray you, or us. He saved us."

"But you think one of us six?" inquires Nakano, "one of us will betray?"

"I did not say that." Replies Haddad. "I felt betrayed, but I cannot say that absolutely one of us will betray the rest of us. It is something very troubling still."

Draden scratches his head. "Whew." He breathes out, "okay. It's probably a good time for me to get out of bed now." Jokes Draden in his usual way of dealing with surprises.

In the breakfast hall, Alvarez, Nakano, Yver, Draden, Haddad and Nuriel all sit in close station to one another. Nothing appears out of place. Nakano directs a watchful eye on Alvarez while remaining discreet. The conversation flows normally and non-threateningly.

"Thank you for your kindness and hospitality Nuriel," begins Alvarez.

"Thank you." Responds Nuriel, "You are my father's companions. You fight alongside him and keep him safe. I wish I could do more for each of you."

"Here, here!" drums the party at the table.

"Your father has said so many wonderful things about you Nuriel. He is so proud of you." Shares Yver.

"He taught me everything I know and made me all who I am today." Answers Nuriel humbly.

"Well, your mother would disagree with that." Draden quips.

Laughing - Nuriel answers, "Yes, she did say you were a bit clumsy and that if I wanted to stay alive on the battlefield I had to master *her* gracefulness instead of yours."

"How did you escape?" asks Alvarez.

Nuriel points to Owen across the table and says loudly enough so Owen can hear, "my man Owen there saw to it that I remained alive."

Owen overhears the compliment and raises a turkey leg in a toast to Nuriel. Takes a bite out of the turkey and drinks the rare commodity of coffee resting warmly in his glass.

Alvarez returns to the question, "but how did you stay hidden all these years?"

Nuriel recounts, "We fled along the east coastline of sector 0 then followed the swamps of Georgia, Alabama, Mississippi, Texas then into Mexico." He shrugs as if everyone at the table knew that this route was the only obvious route to survive. "Mexico had been so decimated by the wars that we didn't expect much trouble. What we found was that there wasn't much left alive there at all. It is a no man's land. We moved through the desert and eventually crossed into the southern jungles from Guatemala."

Alvarez listens, not maliciously, but curiously. Nonetheless Nakano starts to get suspicious over the line of questioning. Nuriel does not see any harm in continuing a series of events that happened 20 years ago goes on sharing how he escaped.

"We had a lot of help from the villagers who were dismayed by the state of the world. Some took us through underground passages, while some escorted us through the rainforests, across Brazil and into Uruguay. At Montavideo port in Uruguay, we found transport away from sector 6 aboard a pirate ship bound to a search and destroy campaign in the Indian Ocean. Part of the arrangement for us to come along was to serve under the captain of the ship and hunt global-imperial naval vessels and supplies. We didn't have any money or anything else to trade, so we agreed. There were 9 of us left and the Captain was short on men."

Yver is surprised, "You were a pirate? I can hardly picture that." He chuckles.

"Indeed I was. But a good pirate, hunting bad ships." Responds Nuriel. "Captain Frederick Nesbit was his name. A super fellow really. I wouldn't think he was a pirate either."

"Why do you say that?" asks Alvarez.

"Well," starts Nuriel, "He graduated West Point Military Academy with top honors and was an actual captain in the US Navy during the wars between East and West."

"No kidding," says Yver. His admiration for West Point Academy is clear.

"Yah, he considered being a fighter pilot he told me, but thought that was too easy of a job, so he opted for Surface Warfare command instead. When the true designs of Darius' government were unmasked, he could not continue to fight for globalist supremacy. Having lost patience with the politicians, he defected to piracy." Motioned Nuriel.

"Good man," boasted Alvarez.

"One thing that really stood out to me and that he was the most proud of was his involvement with the Illustrious Order of the Red Cross, a secret order of Freemasonry. He was so outspoken about it that we regularly feared for his assassination. But, he didn't care. He proudly proclaimed that he was a mason and if anyone had a problem with that, Providence would settle the dispute." Puzzles Nuriel.

Yver exclaims without thought, "Yes, the masons had all but gone underground when Darius put a target on their backs. They are..." he corrects himself, "..er, *were* a huge obstruction to his ambitions."

Draden catches the error, "Yver?" he questions, "Are you a freemason?"

Yver sits silently deciding whether to answer. "I guess, there is no safer place to come out about it then here, with all of you." He nods, "I am."

Alvarez jokes, "Ah, our very own Ezra Yver has decided to come out of the closet as a freemason. No kidding. Had I known, I would have watched my back a little more closely around you." He nudges jokingly.

Nakano asks Yver, "Why was the elimination of the freemasons so important to Darius?"

Yver thinks about his answer. Before replying he swallows the egg he was chewing, "We are primarily a humanitarian organization that toils in charitable works and human advancement materially and spiritually. We have to believe in God in order to be accepted as freemasons. Darius wasn't happy about God being ever-present in our lives, nor was he happy that we would keep people from relying on his handouts. We regularly served the poor giving them stuff and keeping them housed and fed. We were the first movement to organize a military answer to him when his plans to build his global empire were confirmed."

He looks around the table to gauge the reactions of those listening. He adds, "You see, in addition to charity, another one of our main tenets is freedom to forge our own destinies. Freedom from corruption, freedom from oppression and certainly freedom from tyranny. Thousands of years ago, we were the first group of people who were able to move around the world freely because we were building stuff. By crossing in and out of various sovereignties we were among the earliest travelers to bring culture and tradition from other civilizations across borders. Our pursuit of multi-culturalism and independence threatened Darius' plan for one brain-washed and conforming culture and one tradition. In short, we stood for everything he was against and that he was trying to reform away from. So now we hide our identities from even our closest friends."

"Makes sense." Says Nakano. She pops a spicy radish into her mouth and crunches on it until it dissolves.

"Absolutely," acknowledges Nuriel. He returns the conversation to Nesbit and reinforces Yver's point, "When he took us in, he made sure we knew where he stood against Darius. And now he commands over 200 ships. They fly pirate flags, but make no mistake, they are an organized anti-imperial naval force."

"I would have loved to meet him," responds Yver.

Nuriel smiles, "Good. You will have your chance."

Yver's eyes widen.

"Yes," answers Nuriel, "in fact he is due to arrive tomorrow with plans on how we can return to Damascus by sea. We will need to use the sea this time. It is likely Darius has doubled or tripled his reinforcements from here to Jerusalem by now."

Draden beams proudly at his son. Owen smiles at Draden acknowledging his pride.

⚓

Admiral Frederick Nesbit arrives at port early the next morning. His escort is comprised of 50 battle ready warships equipped with grappling hooks, ramming heads, fire bombs, flame throwers, and ballistae. Each ship was bearded with iron bands across the bows for protection and to inflict maximum damage when ramming. Each massive vessel carries 200 fully armored and weaponized warriors.

Nuriel meets him at the dock. When the Admiral disembarks, Nuriel embraces him warmly and shows him to the council chambers. Draden is in the room with his commanders, Owen and the others await in eager anticipation of the plan to return to Damascus. Admiral Nesbit enters the room augustly but with an air of complete humility. He scans the room looking for Draden.

The 6 foot tall, 74 year-old Nesbit walks energetically over to Draden - as energetic as a man half his age. He stretches a hand forward and in a firm, military handshake takes Draden's hand and says genially, "General Samuel Draden, you just can't die can you. You stubborn son of gun. So good to meet you. I've heard a great deal about you."

Draden smiles and returns the handshake. Nesbit extends his other hand toward Draden and grabs his upper arm, squeezes a little more tightly, "My congratulations to you, you've done a tremendous job with your son over there." Nesbit says tilting his head toward Nuriel.

"Thank you Admiral," answers Draden, "It is a privilege and an honor to be standing here with you. I had nothing to do with my son, he decided to be that way all on his own." The two supreme commanders guffaw and reminisce briefly about battles and victories come and gone. Each is more gracious to the other in their praise.

Draden then continues genuinely, "And thank you for looking after my son for 5 years Admiral. He could not have had a better captain than you."

"Nonsense general. Nuriel was the finest first mate I ever had. He didn't need much looking after." Replies the affable Admiral.

"Thank you for saying that," answers Draden.

Commander Ezra Yver introduces himself, "Admiral, its so wonderful to meet you." He extends his hand and greets Nesbit in the surreptitious way Master Masons greet one another to identify their affiliations. Nesbit recognizes and gives Yver an extra nod of approval.

Alvarez comes forward to shake the admirals hand, "Welcome Admiral, it is a pleasure and an honor to meet you." Nesbit returns his greeting. Behind his cordiality he is very formal with Alvarez and not impressed. He does not return the smile but keeps control over his demeanor so his disappointment is not so evident.

Nakano makes no attempt to get up and greet Nesbit. She continues to sit casually on an end table, her back rests against the wall, right leg bent, right knee up, left leg outstretched. The sole of her outstretched boot faces the door.

Her right arm rests atop her bent knee. She nods nonchalantly to the Admiral when he enters having little interest in persons of authority except for Draden. Nesbit nods back and smiles appreciatively. He respects her and recognizes the vital role she continues to fill in this struggle. Nesbit is not insulted. She doesn't have anything to prove to him. Still, Draden gestures to her with a tilt of his head. She rolls her eyes and reluctantly hops off the table.

Haddad cordially presses a closed fist to his chest and bows his head slightly. In keeping with Muslim tradition, bowing low is reserved only for God not another human. Still, Haddad represents a heart-felt welcome to the admiral, "Al-salamu Alaikum," says Haddad. Nesbit responds respectfully, "Wa Alaikum Al-Salam." Nesbits return greeting instantly receives a cheerful glow from Haddad. Draden and Nuriel exchange glances with one another on Haddad's child-like appreciation of such a simple give-and-take.

Nesbit turns to Owen, "There he is! The man who looks after my boy Nuriel." The hearty Admiral hurries toward Owen and lifts the 6 foot, 210 pound soldier off the ground in a powerful bear hug. Afterward, Nesbit jokingly grabs his back, "OH! You've put on some weight there since we sailed together young man." Owen throws his hands in the air as if gesturing to an uncle making the same remark and laughs.

The mood turns serious and focused. Owen pulls maps from off the wall and spreads them across the table. "Whew, that's a big world," remarks Nesbit.

He studies the maps intently to ensure that they are the most up to date maps. Maps that take into account the most recent receding shorelines and dried up waterways. He confirms the maps will work and serve their purposes. One of the Admiral's assistants places a box on the table. Nesbit spills the contents of the box on top of the maps. Out of the container pour 200 miniature models of all his ships. Each piece is an accurate replica of the actual ship sailing the ocean. Nesbit begins sorting them out on the maps. Meanwhile, Draden watches the motions of the admiral and imagines where his ground troops must be positioned and which route they must take in order to align with the picture Nesbit is creating. Once all the ships are in place, the discussions of troop movement, supply logistics and timing get underway.

After several hours of planning, the final details are confirmed. "A large portion of our troops can travel exclusively by land through Sector 7 using Moscow as an outpost, maybe even crossing over into sector 4 if we need to establish surprise. We have all that eastern land mass of Russia in sector 4. With all that space, it would be difficult to pin us down anywhere here." Suggests Draden pointing to the map on Sector 4 which encircles central and western Russia. Moscow is in the easternmost point of Sector 7 approximately 300 miles west of the border to Sector 4.

After more contemplation and study Draden continues, "Then we could come down into Sector 1 through the north side of Damascus. The opposite route we took last time. Your ships can unload our soldiers into Kuwait, Cairo and Southern Turkey to meet us directly at the capital city." Suggests Draden.

"Yes," adds Nesbit, "We create a large, geographic blockade of every major entry way into Sector 1. Our ships will sink any relief attempting to get in and the troops we leave on board the ships can disrupt reinforcements coming from Sectors 9, 4, 7, and 5."

Draden thinks through a moment. He calculates several different scenarios in his head in a fraction of a minute, "But, in order for this whole thing to be successful, you're talking about a ground force of at least two million and at least another one million by sea. How are we to come up with three million warriors ready to go?"

Nesbit looks around the room as though he has a secret to share then speaks plainly, "General," he starts, "You were the first person to successfully lead an army, *undetected*, into Damascus in over 30 years. You were outnumbered and out-gunned, and you still almost sacked the capital city. You would have taken it had Busellis held out for just a little while longer."

Draden breathes in remembering his friend Colonel Busellis, "He was a good man, and a loyal soldier. May he rest in peace."

After a few seconds pause in memory of the fallen colonel, Nesbit heartens, "You have awakened a movement Sam. Millions of people are just waiting for the opportunity for you to take them back to the capital. They believe in you. They believe that Nuriel's return is a miracle. Millions of silent dissenters want to be a part of this movement with you now. They want to be a part of history. The history that ushers balance back into this world." He is inspired, "And we will Sam. Only this time, we finish the job. We will be our own reinforcements."

Draden crosses his arms thoughtfully, "You really think so many people are just silently waiting for the chance to take up arms against the imperialists?"

Nesbit nods reassuringly and with certainty, "I don't think it Samuel, I'm sure of it. Even in my own order, tens of thousands have already pledged loyalty to you, to the Seventh Resistance and to mankind."

Draden nods his head and accepts his role. "Who would have thought we could essentially seize an entire sector and cut it off from the global-empire with a few warships and an assorted collection of pirates, mercenaries and freedom fighters." Draden rubs his chin and chuckles to himself. "This could work. This could quite possibly be the most decisive confrontation of the century. A free world once again. How about that!"

Alvarez enthusiastically slams an open-hand into the table, "Its brilliant. Flawless. What are we waiting for, let's get moving." Some of Nesbit's replicas fling off the maps and onto the floor by the force of Alvarez's slap. He hurries to pick them up and replaces them on the map amongst disapproving looks from the Admiral and his aide. Nesbit's aide straightens up the models where they were pre-Alvarez.

Yver speaks to dispel the awkwardness, "Alvarez is always ready to charge in. That's why we love him." Nesbit does not smile but the scowl on his face lessens.

"Excuse me," says Alvarez abashedly noticing Nesbits disapproval, "I seemed to have gotten ahead of myself." Alvarez escorts himself out of the room to the kitchen where he helps himself to a drink.

Back in the council chambers Draden tries to excuse Alvarez's disruption, "Forgive him admiral. Alvarez is a bit of a hot-head and is extremely passionate about what we're out there trying to accomplish. He is also a very good soldier and the men look up to him."

Nesbit shakes his head, "Hot-head indeed. I heard about what happened at Damascus. There in the walls, in the breach. I heard how he almost got his entire division slaughtered because he disobeyed your direct orders to pull back. I understand that if not for Commander Yver there, your second would have been just another corpse they dug up out of the rubble. I mourn for the families of the sixteen brave men and women who died senselessly trying to bring him back to his senses. That boy is a prima donna in a metal suit. He's a liability." He exclaims pointing out the door in the direction of Alvarez's departure.

Yver looks down, embarrassed about Alvarez's diminished reputation.

Draden ponders how to respond for a moment, "He is a good soldier. What happened at Damascus was unfortunate. He felt awfully about it afterward and came to see me. He begged me to forgive him. I did. He deserves a second chance."

Nesbit nods, "And I would expect nothing less from the Resistance's greatest war general."

Draden nods modestly, "Thank you. Please give him a chance to prove it to you."

Nesbit places a friendly hand on Draden's shoulder, "You're a good man Samuel." And takes his leave to his quarters.

Draden turns to Nuriel and the rest, "We leave tomorrow. We have a lot of ground to cover and many war clans to unite."

⚓

Draden and Nuriel march with shared command over four hundred thousand soldiers. Only thirty thousand of the troop marching are the original combatants that assaulted Damascus with Draden last October. The remaining soldiers have only ever fought under Nuriel's leadership.

The inhabitants of Mount Torghatten are professional raiders and expert warriors on short-term campaigns. Once a season, fifty thousand to a hundred thousand warriors would participate in raids that covered stretches of coast-line along Sector 2. They appear unexpectedly from the sea, hit their targets then return to their boats and safety of their homes before the global-imperialists have time to organize and launch any counter attack. At times, though rarely occurring, when warriors were emboldened and supply and their transportation lines were unmolested by the global-imperial navy, they would venture to raid as far as South Africa in the southern most coastline of Sector 5. The campaign to Damascus by ground will be the longest stretch of land ever crossed by the soldiers of Mount Tor. It will be the most exhausting, demanding and disciplined march ever before undertaken by many of the men and women from the invisible island.

It is agreed that all the commanders answer to Draden and Nuriel equally. Nuriel defers absolute authority to his father. Alvarez retains his rank as Lieutenant General, though he also now reports to Nuriel. Consequently, as a result of Nuriel's deferment to his father, Alvarez is third in command.

Alvarez begrudgingly accepts his role as third in command. But that is not what tears at him the most. In the depths of his heart he understands that he has lost his place as second to Draden forever. Nuriel now fills that role. So long as Nuriel rides with them, and whether or not Alvarez serves under Draden on the battlefield, he will never again be able to consider the possibility that Draden will look to him as a son, or at the very least as his "second". He has sought Draden's fatherly affections since he lost his father nearly 11 years ago. Draden had always treated him kindly and with respect. He saw his talent and put the young lieutenant general's pride and passion to work in a manner that furthered his own growth and that contributed positively to the Resistance. Alvarez revered Draden as a son does a noble and benevolent father. He only ever wanted to make him proud. Alvarez starts to feel his heart sink and begins to get confused about his place and role in the entire Resistance. He is trying to be a loyal and dutiful soldier to his general, but a piece of his purpose has been torn out of his chest. He feels lost and unimportant. A struggle he now carries with him on the 3,500 mile road to Damascus.

Nuriel senses tension between himself and Alvarez. He rides over. "Lieutenant General, you are a vital and important part of this movement. You are not lesser than I. I hope you understand that."

Alvarez is ashamed to have been called out on his envious ambitions yet angered that Nuriel feels the need to share it with him. The embittered Lieutenant General battles with his jealousy and fights to subdue his anger, tempering his reply.

After several seconds Alvarez turns his head to answer Nuriel, "Your father adores you. You are a gifted warrior. The men and women marching with us now are your people. They love you, they love your father. They mock me for what happened in Damascus. How dare you tell me that we are at the same level in this conflict. How stupid must you think I am to actually believe that I would believe what you just said?"

Nuriel bites his lower lip maintaining his composure, "You are the most famous tactician who ever took part in the wars of the Americas. People still sing songs about you all along both coasts. Surely you haven't lost sight of how essential your participation on the field with me and my father is to the well-fare, safety and victory of every man, woman and child who marches with us?"

Appreciating the response, yet still bitter Alvarez answers, "That's just it *General*," he emphasizes impetuously, almost scornfully "all I will ever be now is a tactician. I will never be known as a field general like you and your father. I am the man that followed the direction of the greatest war general and his son in the greatest uprising in history. I was the loyal puppy who basked in the light of your father and now who basks in your shadow too. It's humiliating."

"This is not the conversation I was hoping to have with you Lieutenant General. I will have you know my father respects you and your abilities tremendously. Never would he think that *anyone* walks in his shadow. He has never once said a bad word about you and defends you to all who question your leadership." Says Nuriel. Seeing an opportunity to offer encouragement adds, "You chose the actions you chose in Damascus Lieutenant General. Nobody can change that. You cannot blame anyone else for those choices but yourself. But one thing my father believes uncompromisingly is that no matter the mistakes we chose to make in the past, what we choose to do now defines who we are and how we are remembered." Nuriel nudges his horse gently with a few clicks of his tongue and returns to his original position next to his father.

"What was that all about?" asks Draden.

"Alvarez is not very happy with the current state of affairs between us." Replies Nuriel.

Draden nods empathetically, "He is a passionate man. He only knows how to do things one way. All out. It is his strong suit, and it is also his Achilles heel. He is a good soldier and a gifted tactician. Nobody can take that away from him. You've said what you could say. Give him his space for a while. He'll come around." Answers Draden assuredly. Though in his own mind it is more of a hope that Alvarez will come around rather than a certainty.

Nuriel nods, only half-way believing the same.

Alvarez rides silently and in formation. Presently, he detests the Dradens' and this war effort. Riding along solemnly, he runs the conversation he had with Nuriel over and over again in his head. Each time, the anger dissipates a little. He realizes, he is not angry with either one of them. He is ashamed of himself. He lost his cool and made dangerous decisions. Nuriel was right, he cannot change that. Nuriel was also right in that what we choose to do now defines who we are and how we are remembered. He sits with that for a month.

⚜

Since his conversation with Nuriel, Alvarez kept mostly to himself, fulfilling the requirements and duties of his station in a disciplined, soldierly and organized manner. He is not defiant, nor is he openly scornful. The subject of jealously and legacy is never spoken of again - out loud. The battle of his role and position in the Seventh Resistance wages on - silently - within himself.

⚜

St. Petersburg Russia in Sector 7 is one week's march ahead. The city was flattened during the wars of the hemispheres. Darius restored the city completely a few years after he assumed power but very little is known as to why Darius chose to restore St. Petersburg and ignore other more militarily significant cities. St. Petersburg does have a rich cultural and trading history. Once it was revered for its architecture, art and fashion for centuries and twice it stood as the capital of the whole of Russia but otherwise has very little strategic value. Darius is not known to be a lover of art or architecture and no advantage could be gotten from fully revitalizing the town. Many whispered to one another around dining tables

133

that restoration was a waste of time and resources. The speculations behind his motivations continued.

Maera Lynx is a woman of average height. She has a slender frame and a full red mane that waves wildly down her neck, just past her shoulders. The redness of her hair is accentuated by the deep emerald color in her eyes. She is middle aged at 45 though youthful in appearance. Often she is mistaken for a girl of 25 years.

Her mother was a prostitute and opium addict. When Maera was 4, her mother left her at the steps of a foster home not far from the run-down, ruined and dilapidated structure that served as the St. Petersburg town hall. Before Darius restored the city it was overrun by squalor, disease, crime and sex. Pirates, brigands, ne'er do wells, thieves and cutthroats found solace behind the shabby, crumbling walls of the city. Occasionally, while traveling through Sector 7, the bored and underwhelmed politician would savor the services offered by the town. With the angled, traditional Russian features of her face, natural slenderness, green eyes and red hair, Maera was a very popular woman of the times. Her skin was soft, porcelain and unblemished with scars, marks, lesions, redness and cracks. Her appearance was different from that of the common, field worker, servant type that occupied much of the new world today. Many of the sex-workers these days aged quickly from delicate and supple flowers into weather-beaten, scornful, embittered and sickly human beings. They are no longer desired and can no longer ply their trade as they once did. Many enter their middle years as a housemaid if they maintained sobriety, if not, an addict, or beggar. Maera did not suffer from this inevitability. She serviced her first politician when she was just 9 years old. She quickly discovered that she could charge higher rates and be paid more handsomely than most of the other prostitutes simply for being born as she was. She grew her practice very rapidly. Eventually, she owned the most popular brothel in Sector 7 offering a diverse group of 210 girls and 150 boys to wayfarers and regular clients. Gaining region-wide success, Maera no longer personally serviced numerous clients. She had scores of men and women working for her but found it good business for herself and the prestige of her organization to maintain an exclusive arrangement with only a few of the highest paying, most influential patrons of the global-empire. Many of her labor force came to work for her voluntarily, but whenever she had a shortage, Rachit Mahajan, the governor of Sector 9 supplied the human product from his family business at a substantial discount to her from his regular prices.

Chancellor Darius heard of the mesmerizing enchantress of sector 7 that catered to the imperialists elite. Succumbing to his intrigue he paid her a personal visit. For eight consecutive weeks Maera cleared her schedule while Darius visited with her. No other patrons were allowed to see her. She devoted every second to the words, wishes and desires of the Chancellor. Ultimately Darius convinced Maera to stop servicing anybody else but him. Rather than simply ordering her to service him exclusively, he felt differently about Maera. His feelings for her needed to be validated. The only way they could be genuinely validated was if Maera chose to serve him freely. Not long after, stories began to circulate that Maera was actually the one who got Darius to serve her freely rather than she serving him. She was a very skilled seductress.

To show his appreciation to Maera for her devotion, loyalty, and commitment to him, Darius ordered the entire city of St. Petersburg restored to how it looked during its richest, most golden era. He gave Maera the home she always longed for. Under Darius' tutelage in the dark arts, mysticism, occultism and summoning, Maera became an expert enchantress and sorceress. Skills she would come to use regularly and with impunity against her enemies. Maera was the most feared and respected woman of the global-empire. She was also the least identifiable woman across the hemispheres as she had mastered metamorphosis through Darius' teachings. Through specific incantations and the right application of disguise, Maera could vanish as one person and within the hour, re-appear as another.

⚬

Lieutentant General Alvarez is on a stroll alone while the rest of the camp settles in for the night. In his mind, he cannot reconcile how his current position came to be. He knows that he chose certain actions that set into motion a series of consequences and results, but he could not wrap his head around how he went from the greatest tactician in an entire continent during his early years to an un-respected, humiliated has-been in what is supposed to be his peak performing years. Or so he would tell himself. His self-confidence is shattered and his heart is broken. Indeed, his heart has been broken by a man who he looked up to. But how could he feel this way about a noble and compassionate man? Even though Draden only ever showed him love and appreciation, never taunting him with harsh word or contempt, he hated him. He could not understand this either. His hate is mixed with guilt. How could he feel so much admiration for someone yet so much resentment for him at the same time? A man who only sought to bring the best out of him? Was I evil, he thought? Am I forsaken? Have I done something that God feels I must now pay for?

He sits on a moss covered rock, chin rests atop a closed fist interchanging with an open palm that he would run from his forehead to his chin, press his temples and his eyes, over his nose and closing a hand on his chin returning once more to resting his chin on his fist. He feels his chest swell with hurt and sorrow, he is ready for his tears to fall on the patchy earth beneath his face. His eyes water and his lips quiver, but to let a tear fall would be to accept that his star has fallen and that he is doomed to stay third. He challenges gravity, he challenges his emotions with every beat of his heart and every muscle in his countenance. He cannot contain his pain. First, one solitary drop falls to the ground, then, two, then several trail down his face and moisten the ground below. His face is now firmly placed in both hands. He laments and shuffles to placing an arm atop a bent leg resting his forehead on his forearm. He sniffles trying to regain control of his heart and his mind.

In the night breeze, distant footsteps pace closer to Alvarez. He hears them but leaves them be. He is too caught up in his own thoughts. Only the gentle hand that rests on his shoulder compels his attention. He looks up into mesmerizing emerald green eyes. She smiles the purest smile and softly asks the grieving Lieutenant General, "May I join you?"

Alvarez considers her request, not sure whether he is interested in entertaining visitors or not. Having willingly isolated himself for over a month he has convinced himself that he is not worthy of any company. Yet something comes over him. Something he cannot explain. At this very moment he no longer wishes to remain alone. "Of course." He answers and moves to his right to make room for the slender beauty that entered his life at his most vulnerable.

"I've noticed you haven't been yourself lately Lieutenant general, and was hoping you could use some company if you ever wanted to talk or share what has been on your mind for the past weeks?" says the seductress.

"I...," studying her, "I'm sorry miss, I don't recognize you from camp. Forgive me." Returns Alvarez with a hint of chivalry.

Maera chuckles innocently to herself, "No of course not, I'm with Nuriel's people. It's been rather chaotic around here. I am not surprised you never noticed me. You have so much on your mind. And you're always so busy." Extending her hand she introduces herself, "I'm Susie."

Accepting her explanation Alvarez smiles back. Wiping his moist cheeks with his sleeve on the back of his hand he answers, "Yes, there are a lot of new faces around here. And yes, I have had a lot on my mind lately."

"You feel like talking about it?" asks the enchantress.

"Not really. We are a product of the choices we make I suppose. That's kind of where I'm at right now. Maybe some of us are meant to remain in minimal roles in order to do our part in creating the larger picture." Alvarez notes aloud attempting to convince himself from within.

Maera laughs, "Surely you don't mean you? You are the greatest field commander in the history of the Resistance. Your destiny in the bigger picture is huge."

Alvarez snickers, "From what I hear, I'm only the greatest from the Americas. Not the Resistance. Maybe my destiny *is* actually minimal?"

"Nonsense and rubbish," answers Maera. "People are talking. They are saying that Draden and Nuriel don't stand a chance against the global-imperial armies and certainly not the Chancellor without you. Some have even said they would rather have you as their general. Draden and Nuriel are over reaching they say. I've heard that."

Alvarez answers disbelievingly, "that's crazy. How could anyone say those things. General Draden is a legend. Nuriel Draden is a skilled warrior. They both love their people unconditionally and would give their lives willingly in exchange for any of them. And the men and women of the Seventh would do the same for them on any given day."

Maera manipulates, "Sure. They would. For everyone else. But not for you."

Alvarez stands up angrily and suspiciously, "What? Who are you? Get the hell out of my sight. I've never heard anything so ridiculous. I should have your tongue cut out for treason." He walks angrily away.

Maera chases him pleadingly and grabs his harm, "No. wait. Stop please. I didn't mean to anger you. Please stop. Sit with me. I'm sorry. Hear me out."

Alvarez takes a deep breath in, eyes her glaringly, asks still angry "Who are you? How did you say you got here?"

Still holding Alvarez's arm, Maera plays her character expertly, "I told you, my name is Susie Blankenship, I am from Tor. I've wanted to sit with you for so long, but you seemed so unapproachable. Not your usual self. The gallant and admired Lieutenant General that I heard so many stories about hasn't been present on this march with us. He's been somewhere else. He's been in the stories and in so many songs. But he's not here. I didn't mean to upset you. I was only…" she bids forth her best tears while keeping an air of dignified sorrow, "I was only…"

Alvarez softens at the dismay of the beautiful damsel. He asks, still detached but thawing, "You were only what?"

She keeps her head down and summons a tear, looks up, calls forth a second tear to balance the ruse, "I only want to get closer to you. Be alone with you." Her act now in full swing she adds, "Please, don't walk away. I've waited so long to get close to you." She looks dead in his eyes, "please, please just sit with me a little while longer. I won't mention Draden or

Nuriel again. I promise. It was foolish of me. Please just stay. Don't walk away."

Alvarez accepts her explanation once more and looks for a place to sit. Maera pulls a hidden knife from between her full breasts. Alvarez jumps and grabs for his sword. Maera laughs playfully though keeping in character, sniffles still through grateful tears. "No. Silly. Not for that. For this." She bends slowly at the waist and offers the base of her dress as a make-shift picnic blanket by cutting away the fabric. Her gratitude is real. For surely had Alvarez reported her to Draden, she would face the possibility of banishment or execution for inciting treason. A few short cuts and Maera's dress is separated away from the bottom exposing perfectly sculpted calves. Clear, porcelain, soft, and hairless skin tempts the onlooker's eye, slowly, all the way up to the middle of her thighs. For a brief moment Alvarez's instincts commanded where his eyes gazed. He scans her legs and takes in her youthful and supple shape. Her entire being exudes sexuality, sensuality and a longing for raw, carnal intimacy. The way she moves, the way she speaks, how her eyes meet his. All of it. Every gesture beckons him to her, desperately pleading with him to be inside of her. By the time he catches himself, Maera has already placed the fabric on the ground, is sitting, and waits for Alvarez to join her. She rubs her hand slowly, back and forth on the material. With a movement of her eyes she says with a distinct primal urgency, "please stay with me," Alvarez acquiesces almost involuntarily.

CHAPTER 6

Judges

"Maera's mark ought to be fully entangled in her web by now." Brags Darius from his command post in Astana, northern part of Kazakhstan, in Sector 4.

"I would imagine so," replies Keating, "She is unmatched in the ways of cunning and temptation."

With a grin that conveys secret knowledge Darius reflects on the lessons he has taught and imparted to her over the years.

The heavy wooden doors of the room slowly swing open. The governor of Sector 4 enters with an entourage of armed and burly guardsmen. Each of them stands more herculean then the next. The largest of whom closes the doors behind him and stands in front of it preventing any entry. He folds his great big arms across his barreled chest and stands firmly planted, the size of a tree.

Vasili Karakovnic approaches Darius warmly with arms outstretched. "Don Darius" he jokes in a heavy Russian accent. Even though he is joking Karakovnic is fully aware of Darius' superior position and yields knowingly to the existing order of things. Darius gets up from his chair and allows a much taller Vasili to pay him his proper respects. Karakovnic puts two hands to either one of Darius' soldiers and kisses each side of his face properly wetting his cheeks.

Vasili Karakovnic is a strong, strapping man. He is tall and toned but not as muscular or beefy as his guardsmen. Especially well-dressed, Karakovnic amassed a fine collection of modern men's suits over the years. Italian suits were his favorite. He would either take them from the homes of his victims or find them among the wreckage. If he liked what he found he would instruct his seamstress to salvage them. She usually succeeding in restoring them to their original condition. He made sure that those in his closest circles were always dressed in the finest garments. His biggest challenge was finding suits large enough to fit his guardsmen. But, he typically managed to dress them to the hilt.

The last time somebody asked him how tall he was, he told him he was 6 foot 3. When he was questioned and doubted about the accuracy of his height he answered him promptly by a jolt with the bottom of his dagger across the temple. While the questioner was unconscious, Sergei, the largest of the guardsmen hoisted him over his shoulder, took him outside and kicked him awake. Then he kicked him again and again until the poor suppliant curled up in a whimper begging to be left alone to nurse his broken bones. In reality Karakovnic is 6 foot 1. When not pressing to express often disingenuous emotions, his face remains expressionless. One of his favorite pass-times is to lock his eyes on an unsuspecting passerby and stare at them with piercing, cold blue eyes to the point until panic overtook them. Once he reached a satisfactory level of tension he would break his stare, bang on the table laughing as if to say he was only kidding around then would send over a drink as a peace offering.

His face is sharp and chiseled like a roman sculpture. Well-known for disguising what he was truly thinking even when he was entertaining the most gruesome and horrific thoughts; he could smile to someone convincingly in one word then cut his throat in the next. His lips are barely present. Rather, his mouth is more like a slit just three inches above his chin. A young man of barely 30 years old, Karakovnic grew up in Russia 20 years after the war of the hemispheres started.

His father, Alexei Karakovnic, was a former intelligence officer under the previous Russian regime. Alexei held an intense hatred for anything western. He made a name for himself sabotaging and disrupting many major western operations designed to overcome and topple the east. A deadly assassin and powerful spymaster, Alexei earned great respect from Darius himself though originally they fought on opposing sides. By the same token, Vasili's father admired Darius' reputation as a ferocious, fearless and brutal combatant. In fact, he would copy Darius' tradition of capturing the opposing commander, securing him by the four limbs on immovable wooden posts and slicing him in half from head clear through to the torso. He didn't bother using the halves as target practice like Darius would do in his camp. Rather he felt the severed corpora were best used to feed the hyenas that he kept as pets. The tradition of keeping hyenas is a tradition that his son would carry along with him.

After Russia fell to Darius' forces, Vasili disappeared into the landscape penniless, hungry and desperate for a means to survive. He returned some years later at the head of the region's most powerful, notorious and violent crime organization. No trade was beneath them. Initially, Vasili used the skills he learned from his father and cashed in with murder for hire. Regularly he would collect his pay then kill his benefactor after he secured as much of their assets and property as he could. Using his new found wealth he extended his reach into other markets. Drugs, prostitution, murder, extortion, gambling, loan-sharking, sabotage, kidnapping, torture, arms and armor, raising armies, militias, horses, food, grain, and water were all things that were available to a paying customer through Karakovnic's organization. Literally, anyone and anything could be bought and sold for the right price. With the same reasoning Darius used for installing Mahajan into governorship, he delivered Sector 4 to Vasili. Karakovnic Enterprise's would be free to continue operating unchecked and unmolested in exchange for loyalty, obedience and keeping order in Sector 4. Eventually Karakovnic branched out into some legitimate enterprises but they were all funded by and funneled through to his criminal ventures. His father's hatred of the west remained with him.

"Thank you Vasili, it's good to see you." Says Darius. Governor Keating moves a chair closer to Karakovnic. With an open palmed hand gesture Darius offers him a seat.

"To what do I owe the pleasure of this meeting Chancellor?" asks Vasili.

"I need you to round up and raise an army of the craziest lunatics to ever set foot in Sector 4. They will be instructed to march on Draden's forces in Sector 7. I don't want to use our main military forces just yet until I know what we are marching into. I understand Draden and his son are a week's march from St. Petersburg. What I don't understand is their number and grand plan. It doesn't make any sense to me. They're too few. They need at least three million soldiers to even have a chance to take Damascus. They only have four hundred thousand. They are up to something. I need to know what. I have someone on the inside slowly dismantling their campaign and gathering information. If you act fast your militia shouldn't face too much trouble and may even survive the confrontation." Answers Darius.

Vasili's invisible lips part and replace an expressionless countenance with a broad and understanding smile, "Maera! She is quite the woman uh? Of course, she is one of us, made in Russia."

Darius beams back proudly. "So, can you deliver?"

Keeping a confident grin Karakovnic replies, "Does a pigs mother have tits? Of course I will. I need few days but I know where to start. How many you need?"

"To move as quickly as I would like? Three hundred thousand - to take Draden at St. Petersburg within the week. Will that be a problem?" inquires Darius with an expectant expression.

"No problem at all boss." Promises Vasili.

"Excellent. Your payment is just downstairs with my... *treasurer*," Darius says sarcastically but truthfully, "I believe you'll find your compensation more than adequate."

"It always is boss. Kiss Maera for me when you see her. Tell her Vasili sends his love." Saying as a brother would about his sister. Darius nods. Keating walks down to the *treasury* with Karakovnic to oversee and authorize payment.

Maera and Alvarez have been inseparable for the past three days. She has stayed with him in his tent every night, sometimes well into the mornings. Alvarez no longer moved with his usual flare and pizzazz. Now instead, when the bugles sound the start of the march, he walks nonchalantly to his horse and takes his time.

He remains disinterested and disheveled as he leaves his tent - tucks his shirt into his pants while approaching his mount. Duty-bound and torn he serves as ordered then retreats to be alone with Maera in an attemp to reconcile his loss of authority with his role in the Resistance.

"Father?" starts Nuriel, riding alongside Draden.

"Yes?" he answers.

"I have asked around and nobody knows who Alvarez's companion is. I know who she claims to be and where she insists she's from, but I have been unable to verify anything she says. I know we want Alvarez to be happy, but I suspect something more sinister is happening here." Nuriel points out.

"A spy?" asks Draden.

"Maybe. But its also more than that. She feels like a wedge. A wall between us." Speculates Nuriel.

"I get that too," confirms Draden.

"What does Nakano say?" Nuriel asks.

"She is keeping an eye on her. They haven't done any-thing but sleep together and disappear into the wood to be alone. On occasion, they meet with a handful of Alvarez's men by a fire, exchange stories and then disappear by themselves again. Nakano is hearing some discontent from the army. They aren't used to travelling so far for so long." Relays Draden.

"Mutiny?" asks Nuriel.

"Perhaps." Replies Draden, "maybe desertion."

⚜

Draden, Nuriel, Nakano, Yver and Haddad settle in at the end of the days march. Alvarez and Maera leave to be alone in the wood.

"Nakano?" beckons Draden. Nakano obliges in his call and comes. "Yver?" he adds. Commander Yver stops what he is doing and goes to Draden's tent presently.

"Yes godfather?" asks Nakano. Yver asks the same question with a tilt of his head.

"I know I asked you two to keep an eye on Alvarez and Susie, but I have a slightly more pressing matter I need you to focus your attention on instead." Stipulates Draden.

"No! I will not leave you alone with that woman and Alvarez. No! I do not trust either of them alone and I especially don't trust them together. And you? Alone? With them? No! No!" says Nakano defiantly. Yver stands next to her in agreement with tongue in cheek. He nods.

"Nuriel is with me. He won't let anything happen to me. And Haddad, he senses these things." Says Draden.

"And…" Yver points out, "…lest you forget, he had a dream where Alvarez left us for a pack of hyenas. I don't trust them. I don't trust this. I don't trust what Nakano and I think is about to happen."

"Okay, listen I appreciate your concern, but I need you both to make contact with the people Nesbit arranged for us to meet near St. Petersburg. They are expecting an emissary from us tonight. We can't miss this communication." Draden reminds Yver, "they are expecting you, their brother Master Mason to give them the go ahead to form up and move on Damascus."

"Alvarez knows this too. He knows all our plans. It's too risky now." Yver says starting to get slightly nervous about leaving Draden to a pack of hyenas.

"Agreed." announces Nakano.

Draden sighs. He rubs his face and chin with open hand and thinks what to say next. "You'll be gone six hours max. Nuriel, Haddad, Sa'eed and Nabila will look after me. Besides, you two seem to forget…I can defend myself too. You don't need to treat me like a feeble old man."

"You *are* an old man godfather!" Nakano fires back angered at being ordered to abandon him, "you're not as fluid as you used to be," she proclaims with equal discontent.

Try as he would Draden could not hold back his laughter at Nakano's fiery answer. Yver bites his lip fighting back a chuckle. He could never speak to the general the same way Nakano does and respects their father-daughter type relationship. Smartly he stays out of it. Draden re-centers the conversation to what is important. "I am not as young as I used to be, but this mission that I am asking of you two here and now is more important than me."

Nakano pulls twin daggers out of her belt and pictures herself hurling them at – and fatally wounding Alvarez and Susie before she goes - just to make sure they can't hurt her godfather while she is away. When she realizes Draden does not want that she sneers, takes a quick breath in and angrily forces the weapons back into their sheaths. She looks at Yver as if to say, dammit man let's go, and storms out. Yver nods to Draden in a casual salute and proceeds with Nakano on his mission.

Draden breathes a sigh of frustration. Rather than dwell on the worst portrait painted by Yver and Nakano, Draden prefers to mingle with his people. He moves freely and casually among them. He favors this way of gauging morale, confidence, determination, fatigue, etc. over second hand reports and other people's opinions. All the while, under strict command by Nakano, Haddad and Nuriel keep the general within their line of sight at all times.

Nabila suddenly screeches loudly from the sky. Sa'eed starts to growl uneasily. Haddad and Nuriel are alarmed and rush in closer, closing the space between them and Draden. The sudden commotion raises heads and eyebrows. Nuriel and Haddad avoid drawing their weapons in attempts to defuse further anxiety. Tensions quietly mount. Haddad places five fingers to his right temple and reaches out to Nabila.

"What is it?" asks Draden.

Haddad finishes listening to the graceful eagle soaring high above with watchful eyes and protective wings. His hand drops sorrowfully from his temples to his side; with grave regret he confirms that his dream has come true. Alvarez and Maera ride southward toward Moscow with one hundred thousand troop deserting.

"Desertion." acknowledges Draden with a heavy heart and deep disappointment.

Haddad corrects him, "Betrayal."

Nuriel and Haddad stand guardedly together within a couple feet from Draden, cautiously awaiting and considering what next may come.

"Shall we send a company after them father?" Asks Nuriel.

After a few seconds contemplation, Draden considers all possible outcomes of such a proposal. "No. We need every man and woman we have. We are exposed from all sides here. Rally the troop, tell them to maintain defensive guard until Nakano and Yver return."

Just as Nuriel takes his first step to pass on the order, Sa'eed darts away from Haddad and sprints eastward, angrily barking and growling while dashing ahead full speed. Startled and concerned, Haddad, Nuriel and Draden follow. Nabila redirects her flight path 180 degrees to stay above her master, keeping watch over him. A quarter mile sprint from all parties reveals more distressing news. Thousands of Nuriel's soldiers have made a fast break away from the camp. They have deserted too. Not used to the rigors of long march, scarcity of supply and scorching solar heat under full armor, fifty thousand more fighters flee northwest away from the campaign longing for the safety and plenty of the forgotten walls of Mount Torghatten.

"Traitorous wretch," proclaims Haddad speaking of Alvarez.

"How now Haddad. He is misguided. Those fifty thousand are not with him. They simply have had enough. We need to focus our attention and energies on the forces we have left. We are still dangerously exposed out here. Nuriel, please carry out my order and inform our men and women to maintain defensive guard for the time being." Draden instructs as he reasserts calm order over erupting chaos. Nuriel steps away to do as he is instructed.

The remaining two hundred fifty thousand warriors fortify the camp and are arranged in defensive guard. Scheduled, rigorous and vigilant watches rotate every third hour. Scouts have assumed inconspicuous positions at all corners of the camp a mile and a half away in tree-tops, dug into ground holes and pressed up against the brush wherever the brush is dense enough to provide adequate cover and camouflage. They are not demoralized, they are not discouraged. They remain stalwart in mind and high in spirit. None of the remaining force have any thought of desertion whatsoever. Their main concern is whatever Alvarez intends to do next?

Certainly Alvarez and Maera would have liked to break away from Draden with more than one hundred thousand. They did try. Many of those who were invited along with them were among the separate fifty thousand who fled to return to Tor. They feared that the hint of treachery at the highest levels was enough to bring the entire war effort crashing down on them. Pre-emptively they dropped their weapons and armor and sped away from camp fleeing impending destruction. Defeat is an inevitability they concluded. Some of the remaining two hundred and fifty thousand had heard whispers and gossip but dismissed these distractions promptly as petty and passing. Never a one of them imagined Alvarez, their trusted and loyal lieutenant general, could concoct such a plan to move against his friend and mentor; the greatest Resistance general of all-time. Especially never on such a campaign to take back the capital of the new world. A day of contemplation however returned the consensus that Alvarez is not acting out of his own volition. Susie is the culprit. She is the villain that has seized control of Alvarez's mind. For the soldiers, the complete belief of this concession allows them to minimize their resentment, hatred and disgust toward him. It was comforting to believe that if it wasn't he who thought up such a sinister plan, he could be saved and reconverted back to their brother, their commander.

Believing in him this way opens the possibility that he is not so deserving of their disdain. The alternative possibility is to one day meet him on the battlefield and strike him down fatally for desertion or worse, for treason. But how could they? How could those who fought alongside him, trusted him and stood ready to lay their lives down for him on his command deal such a blow to him? Yes he deserted them but he hasn't physically harmed anyone yet. He surely isn't a full and complete traitor at this point...is he? Has Alvarez just needed a break from his humiliation? Or, have the fires of contempt, rage and pride been stoked to irreversible levels? Has the wicked work of the red-headed vixen that crept insidiously into his mind permanently consumed him? And for what purpose? To what end?

⚜

"Give me the order godfather. Let me go find them and let me go kill them! That traitor *and* his bitch!" demanded Nakano.

Draden shakes his head in slow side to side motion. Elbow on his chair supporting his arm, his mouth rests on the two first fingers of his left hand. Without speaking, he denies her request. Nakano throws her hands in the air. She is considerably frustrated and is unable to understand how Draden could be so calm and why he is not ordering Alvarez's immediate retrieval and execution.

"This man has no honor godfather. He does not deserve to breathe the same air as us. He does not deserve to live. Not a single moment more on this planet. He must die!" Blasts Nakano.

For the first time in several moments Draden speaks, almost yelling but not quite, "Nakano, calm yourself!" he waits for her to calm down until she is finally receptive to listening. "Alvarez will have his day. But right now we have more pressing concerns. Our scouts reported an incoming attack force from the east. They are not flying imperial colors. But they are bent on our destruction nonetheless. They estimate three hundred thousand."

"Outnumbered again. By who?" asks Yver.

Draden answers, "They're carrying the Sector 4 standard. No doubt they are doing the Chancellor's bidding anyway." He thinks through why. "He must not want to endanger his main army and is not sure what we are up to. Feeling out our plans."

Nuriel moves off of the wooden post he was leaning on and uncrosses his arms. Anticipating what his father is about to ask next he moves in closer to the circle of commanders and puts forth a plan to deal with the threat. "Cyclone." He says.

Their interest piqued, Haddad, Nakano and Yver give Nuriel their attention. Draden remembers teaching him the strategy of Cyclone when he was a boy. "That could work." Agrees Draden from his chair. The three commanders look to Nuriel for an explanation.

"What makes a cyclone so powerful?" he asks everyone. The three commanders don't know the answer and look to Nuriel to elaborate.

He takes a writing instrument to the parchment map on Draden's strategy table. "A cyclone has *three separate parts* that on their own cause severe damage and destruction but together cause absolute devastation and havoc on areas much larger than itself…severe wind, heavy rainfall and storm surge." Nuriel finishes drawing his initial diagram on the map and looks up to see if he has lost anybody in his opening. He is met with puzzled looks on how this applies to a human army on the field of battle.

Nuriel points to Nakano and asks her to come over to the table to his right side, "you…," he explains, "…and your infantry are severe wind." Nakano is intrigued. The association of a martial artist with nature's elements is a comparison she readily understands. He continues, "You meet them head on. Frontal assault. Engage them quickly, inflict maximum damage then disengage just as fast. Keep them moving and make them focus their attention on you. From our intelligence, your people should handle multiples of them fairly easily. They are a larger force but they are undisciplined and fragmented." Nakano understands the strategy.

Nuriel looks to Haddad and motions him to come over excitedly, almost reminiscent of a young boy showing off a new invention to an old friend, "You," he says to Haddad, "are heavy rainfall." Haddad looks at him wondering what that means in the context of battle. "Arrange your archers here," Nuriel says pointing to a spot on the map that is far enough away from Nakano's forces and concealed behind cover of tree. He continues, "after Nakano has disengaged three times and is far enough away, fire off your foray from behind the mercenaries.

Let loose several salvos, at least five. Black out the sun with every release."

Nuriel speaks to Nakano once again, "in their confusion, loop out of sight onto the other side of the hills over here." He points to the spot on the map with firm finger.

Back to Haddad, "you keep pounding them with volleys. Give her cover while she moves away."

Yver anticipates his role will be described next and comes over to the table where Nuriel and the rest are standing, "Let me guess," Yver says, "I am storm surge." Nuriel smiles and gleefully says you got it. Yver moves in to get a better look of the map, "Now, what does that mean?" he asks.

"After the fifth salvo," Nuriel explains, "you ride them through with your cavalry from the east. I will join you from the opposite end of the field from the west. We will meet in the middle. Once we have them pressed in between our horses Nakano and her infantry blow back in from the south. Now Haddad, this is important, listen carefully..." Haddad nods and is ready to hear what the young general says next.

"Once everyone is engaged, you become the sniper. Give us cover from your location and make sure nobody gets a clear shot at us from our blindspots." Instructs Nuriel. Haddad nods in understanding.

"And there we have it, Cyclone." Presents Nuriel dropping his writing instrument on the table. "Like the elements of the storm we come from different directions, gain momentum then combine at just the right point to inflict maximum, sustained damage. Any questions?"

Everyone in the room has a clear picture of what's expected. Draden never left his chair while Nuriel was talking. He watched, listened and observed proudly while his son marked up the map and illustrated the advantage.

－✦－

Three hundred thousand mercenaries from Sector 4 line the landscape just ahead of Nakano's ground forces. Several hundred feet away to the north, Haddad and his archers lie in wait, concealed in the bush. They breathe quietly and patiently – each staying more still then the next – waiting for just the right moment to spring their trap. A distance away to the west Nuriel's division stirs quietly in anxious anticipation of their call to action. The riders sit eagerly atop them swaying side to side as the horses grapple with the terrain beneath their hooves. Yver's cavalry is camouflaged by the foliage to the northeast about 200 yards away from the rear flank of the enemy. They rustle gently against the leaves on the trees and under their feet. Yver will count five salvos then order the attack from behind. He overhears the enemy commander laugh mockingly and say to his mercenaries, "Hah, that witch did it! Her spell actually worked. I wouldn't have believed it if I didn't see it with my own eyes. The great General Draden has been abandoned by half his force. He's been bested at the hands of one tiny red-headed sorceress bitch."

Yver listens in disbelief. He thinks to himself, "...this, this was all Darius' doing. Can it be? Is Alvarez actually innocent of the crimes we've pinned against him? Has he actually succumbed to the enchantments of a sorceress? Do such things actually exist? Do those things, spells, enchantments and castings really actually work?" Shaking away thoughts and questions overtaking his mind Yver looks around and confirms that others nearby him just heard the same things and just had the same conversations within themselves. With a hand gesture and a steady look he manages to redirect their focus back to the task at hand.

Yver hears the enemy commander's voice boom through the air once again, "Are you ready for a quick victory boys and girls?" Yells the militia captain with inflated confidence. His army is comprised of the most vicious, cruel and ruthless cut-throats to ever walk Sector 4. Eager and bloodthirsty they scream their battle cry feverishly into the skies of Sector 7. They are fresh. They are ready. And more chillingly, they are consumed with the most vile bloodlust imaginable. Believing the rest of Draden's army has abandoned him and has made a run for the hills in the wake of their arrival, he directs his forces fully on Lieutenant Commander Nakano and her eighty thousand foot soldiers who stand bravely in place prepared to execute any feat at her command.

"Attack!" rages the enemy commander cutting his sword through the air completing his cut with the point of his blade facing Nakano.

At the first sign of the attack Nakano responds with her own umbrage pulling her twin katanas out from the sheathes on her back.

"Attack!" She blasts then immediately springs into full sprint head-on into the fray. Her brigade follows with matching tenacity. Just as scripted, the clash is severe, bloody, quick and devastating on the advancing army. Nakano signals disengagement and rushes away from the enemy. Brimming with confidence, the Sector 4 commander believes Nakano is retreating and orders a full press against her.

In line with the plan, Nakano orders re-engagement but commands her warriors to linger a little while longer in combat this time before they disengage. She has unfinished business with the enemy commander.

As ordered the armies are engaged once more in bruising, crushing, ferocious combat. The weight of advantage is with Nakano and her warriors. Each of her infantry men and women single handedly dispatch two or three mercenaries at a time. It is as Nuriel said, they are larger in number, but smaller in skill, organization and discipline.

Nakano moves swiftly between the combatants. She ducks beneath a blow before it severs her head. From underneath the swinging enemy blade - clutches her katana with both hands - explodes upward with lightning speed - cuts into exposed armpit - slices the arm clean off bottom to top. She catches the severed arm in mid-air – her victim's blade is still tightly gripped in nerveless hand. With a breakneck pivot from her hips jams the sword into the eye of another pushing it cleanly through skull. She is attacked from behind. Nakano kicks up a heavy rock from the earth – with the top of her boot drives it squarely into her assailant's mouth smashing teeth. Her attacker is bloodied, dazed and disoriented. Nakano spins to sweep her while still vulnerable. With the sharpest edges of her blade - in a grisly slash to the knees - cuts the legs out from under her. When her spin subsides, Nakano jumps into the air off one leg in a backwards summersault behind another assailing her from back. She glides through the air in one full rotation and lands in splits beneath him - thrusts her sword upward through pelvis - cuts his intestines loose. Another blade comes at her from above. Before it cuts, she throws herself flat on her back - crosses defensive swords over supporting soles - deflects the blow. She rotates her hips quickly. With a swift kick to the ankles from the ground - knocks the legs out from underneath the other - rolls rapidly over the earth and impales the fallen assailant with his own sword through the neck.

Satisfied she has done enough in this engagement Nakano orders another feigned retreat. She repeats the cycle one more time as planned. Just after the final disengagement the clean whistle of arrows penetrates the atmosphere from behind the mercenaries. Sector 4 soldiers turn toward the sound and are met with a blanket of arrows piercing air - tearing through flesh. Nakano and her infantry take their positions behind the hills and rest until it is time to return to the fight.

After the fifth salvo Yver and his cavalry charge from the wood - lances forward - eyes locked ahead. The Sector 4 army is caught unprepared to meet Yver and his horsemen at their rear. They are easily run through one by one with lance and sword. Just as they bring Yver's onslaught to a stalemate, Nuriel and his force erupt out of the western forest and devastate the exposed enemy flank. Sector 4 militiamen and women are caught haplessly in between Nuriel and Yver. They wage a desperate fight for their survival on two fronts.

The southern flank of the Sector 4 battalion break off to attack Nuriel's exposed western flank. As they gain a formidable position against him Nakano returns from behind the hills and challenges their envelopment. With deadly accuracy Haddad's snipers pick off mercenary threats one by one. Firmly in the center of the eye of the cyclone, Sector 4 fighters are pummeled from every direction. They are bounced around like piñatas on a child's birthday. There is nowhere for them to go. Nowhere to hide. Nowhere to retreat. They are pressed in the vice of the Resistance.

Life is slowly squeezed out of them into lost eternity. The Sector 4 militia has been routed by Draden's forces. The militia captain breaks free from inside the carnage. He gallops full speed in the direction of Sector 4. Nuriel sees - whistles and clicks to his horse. She comes to him running over enemy soldiers. When she is near and harness is within reach he grabs a loose rein and flings himself atop her not missing a step. It is not long before Nuriel reaches full pursuit of the fleeing captain. Seizing upon the target, he puts away his Morningstar flail and draws out the bow that hangs from the saddle to his right. From quiver on the left he draws out a single arrow. Bow and arrow are firmly in hand – Nuriel squeezes his legs tightly around galloping torso - keeps himself steady - levels the point of his arrow just above the top of the fleeing captain's neck - aim is steadied - lets loose a deadly release. The captain's helmet clangs when struck and is thrust upward from the collision. It does not fly off. It is impaled to his skull. Almost as quickly as the arrow was flung the heavy body of the mercenary captain thumps lifelessly to the ground below. His horse rides adamantly on to Sector 4 leaving her riders corpse behind.

"Whoah there girl...whoah." Nuriel pulls back the reins steadily and pats his horse to a stop. "Well done Ameera." He says to her. She replies with a satisfied neigh followed by several grunts while she regains her breath.

CHAPTER 7

Kings

Alvarez and Maera sit to dine with Governor Sheldon, governor of Sector 7 in Moscow. Moscow is the capital of Sector 7. The tension in the room is heavy.

Sheldon breaks the silence nervously, "Draden and his force have quadrupled in number since obliterating the Chancellor's mercenaries. They have eliminated our outer defenses and are heading this way. My sources tell me that they will be at our walls by day's end tomorrow."

"We have six hundred thousand battle-ready fighters *and* you have me." Boasts Alvarez, "I will help you defend Moscow. Moscow will be yours as long as you want it."

"Did you not hear me?" says Sheldon, "Draden has almost one million people coming to destroy this city. How do you propose we remain standing against them?"

"Draden won't destroy anyone. If anything, he will ask you to turn me and the city over to him in exchange for your safe passage out of Sector 7." Calms Alvarez.

Maera interrupts with information that only she knew until this moment, "The Chancellor is on his way here personally at the head of one million of his own. General Alvarez need only hold off the attack until Darius arrives. Together they will eliminate this foolish Resistance once and for all."

"A toast then to General Alvarez and his companions," says Sheldon and clangs his glass uneasily with theirs. Alvarez and Maera toast. They have dinner together.

Governor Geoffrey Sheldon is the son of Lord Anthony Sheldon - an English Nobleman and businessman. The Sheldon's are a line of aristocracy that extend as far back as the 1800's. The family made their wealth through finance, textile, shipping, and industry ultimately reaching an apex in their family's fortune during the housing, high-tech and e-commerce explosions. To all who knew Geoffrey's ancestors, it was said, the Sheldon's were always one step ahead of the next bubble. Somehow, always positioned perfectly to make a brilliant profit. Rumors circulated of conspiracy that the Sheldon's along with other wealthy families around the world would collude in secret, closed, nefarious circles. In these meetings they would decide, as casually as ordering up dinner in a fine restaurant, which industry to inflate and when to cause the next bubble. They started them when they wanted and finished them when they felt they maxed out their return on investment. Then while it appeared to the world that they had impeccable timing, it was in fact a fabricated collusion of the ultra-wealthy to keep the population subdued and reliant on the goods and services they put out. It was Machiavelli's greatest hits set to repeat play on iTunes.

A shrewd man in all affairs not just his business, Lord Anthony regularly played the odds in the wars. He favored both sides at all times. Only when he felt that one side was about to topple the other would he throw the full weight of the Sheldon family dynasty behind the inevitable victor. This way the Sheldon's curried favor and longevity with anyone who was in power at any given time. This strategy continued to pay dividends when Darius assumed power.

Governor Geoffrey Sheldon was no businessman and he was no warrior. But he did have a way with words. More of a diplomat than a military man he aligned himself with friend and foe alike. Somehow he managed to find mutual interests in all his relations. And skillfully, he would maneuver his speech where his enemies would be left inexplicably with the conclusion that they were better off on his side than against him. A better wordsmith was not to be found in the whole of Sector 7. With diplomatic prowess he managed to convince Darius and Maera to let the excesses from Saint Petersburg freely spill over into Moscow. This included money, man-woman power, trade, goods, and even militia support. Half of the forces defending Moscow now are on loan from Maera and Saint Petersburg. Sheldon spoke with gentlemanly refinement and prided himself on his fashion sense. He is middle-aged and stands at an average height with a medium build. Dark brown hair is neatly swept to the left side of his head and his intelligent brown eyes put many around him at ease. Sheldon prefers to indulge himself in wine and women rather than sully his diplomatic station with soldiers and war. The notion that the resistance's greatest war general is set to sack Moscow makes him very uneasy despite Maera's revelations. Still he exhibits a very calm, measured countenance and manner.

He is not convinced that Alvarez can hold the city until Darius arrives. Present to who Maera actually is and to her ruse, Sheldon continues to refer to Maera as 'Susie' in front of Alvarez.

"I am sure you and Miss Blankenship would rather spend the evening in one another's company then with me here at dinner." He politely excuses himself leaving the couple alone.

⚊⚙⚊

Forces of the Seventh Resistance surround Moscow. Nesbit's contact near Saint Petersburg produced the promised results. Draden's army of two hundred twenty thousand has swelled to nearly eight hundred fifty thousand. The Sector 4 militia was decimated near Saint Petersburg. Draden lost thirty thousand in the clash. It is an astonishing and historic victory. A victory that Alvarez will not be remembered in. He will be remembered for having abandoned his post, deserting Draden and taking up with the enemy just prior.

Haddad positions his artillery around the city walls as he did when the Seventh faced off against Damascus before. Nearly one quarter of a million fresh and committed solders stand at every corner of the capital city. Draden walks to the front lines of each division. His great 6'5 frame dwarfs many of those lined up for the showdown. Yet, he feels as their equal. His first stop is to Nakano and her forces on the southern perimeter. He speaks to her but directs his question to the rest of the infantry so they can hear, "Lieutenant Commander Nakano," he starts, "our infantry has entrusted you with their lives. What say you to that honor?" Lieutenant Commander Nakano smiles. The rush of impending battle jumpstarts her heart racing. She fixes her gaze squarely into his eyes as she has done numerous time before and affirms, "as I have entrusted them with mine, General." Every infantry man and women listening is overcome with renewed passion and commitment to the fight and infused with loyalty to their commanders. Only a handful of footsoldiers present here now before the walls of Moscow were present back in Damascus nearly one year ago. A fresh era of Resistance has erupted from the silent catacombs of the earth. There is no turning back. No backing down. Nakano's infantry division clamor on their shield with spear and sword in honor of their general's question and their commander's reply.

Draden does the same with Yver in the east and Haddad in the west. Now in the north, he stands before his son. "My son, we have lost each other before, we may lose each other again. What say you to that possibility?" Nuriel pauses, looks to the heavens for guidance how to answer then into the faces of everyone standing before the city walls. There is silence as the eyes of every man and women is fixed on his reply. Many feel that Nuriel and Draden should not risk themselves in the battle. Their reunion is felt by all and they wish them to remain as far from harm as possible. Nevertheless, Nuriel answers drawing his sword and speaking to the entire army. His voice carries to the south, west and east. "In His infinite wisdom, Almighty God has pre-ordained our destinies. He has interwoven and connected us to each other so that here, today, now we will all be standing together united as one body under *His* banner. There is a possibility some of us may not leave these grounds, true." He maintains briefly before his voice booms with full conviction, "But for those who may perish today, know that an eternal spring awaits you. This eternal spring will replenish your souls if removed from this world and will replenish the souls of those who set aside their worldly fears and take up arms for a cause not of this earth. For we do not do battle solely with mere humans today, we, too, battle the demons and scourges of this universe who set these people to their derisions and delusions in the first place...and it is our duty..." his voice grows louder, "...it is our duty and our destiny to send these villains back to the hell from whence they came!" the warriors hussah and hoorah, shields clamor. The defenders of Moscow feel the sharp pang of fear set in on them. Shame envelops those who fled with Alvarez. Nuriel finishes, "That father," he says, "...that, is what I have to say to this possibility." Though it did not seem possible for the sound of the Resistance to grow louder, it did grow louder still to Nuriel's answer. Draden is moved by the gallantry, goodness, self-sacrifice and humility in the face of darkness. His stern face breaks into a subtle, understated but glowing smile. He nods proudly to his son.

Draden mounts his horse and gives the signal to commence bombardment of Moscow – "Release!" he booms.

Fire, flame, stone, wood, death and destruction rains down on the pulpits of the defending city. Defenders are hurled into the air or fall from the wall when the ground beneath them breaks apart and disintegrates upon impact of hard rock and metal. The smell of heavy smoke and smoldering wood enter the nose, mouth and lungs.

Sheldon takes for shelter in the inner keep. Alvarez climbs the stairs and stands upon battlements that have not yet crumbled. He reaches a point where he can be seen by all. Draden motions for the bombardment to stop. It stops. Soot and pieces of ash from the walls and bombs float around in the breeze.

"Alvarez," Draden shouts, "Alvarez, it is not too late. Let your people go and turn the city over to us. Nobody else has to die here today."

Alvarez scans the enormity of the force that stands eagerly to sack the city. "I loved you." He yells back. "I followed you. And you turned your back on me. On us." He says gesturing to those one hundred thousand that came with him.

"Alvarez, you're misguided my boy. A witch has played with your mind and tainted your thoughts. The woman whom you know as Susie belongs to Darius. Her name is Maera Lynx. She is a sorceress. She has been sired and trained by Darius himself. She does not love you. She cares nothing for you or for us. She serves Darius as a slave serves her master. And now she has made you Darius' slave too. Give up Moscow. I don't want to kill you." Pleads Draden.

"Lies! All lies!" Alvarez shouts back. Draden looks away and considers another means of action. He orders Haddad to fire off several canisters over the walls of Moscow into the citizenry. The canisters are not filled with boiling oil or rotten diseased animal corpses, rather, they are stuffed with words engraved on parchment. The parchment reads, *"Citizens of Moscow, surrender your city peacefully and every one of you will be secured safe passage out of Sector 7 to wherever you wish to go. You have 2 hours to give me your reply. After which time we will re-commence the systematic destruction of your city until there is nothing left. Your leaders have placed you at the brink of oblivion. Choose for yourselves. Spare those closest to you. Evacuate at once and surrender the city or perish along with them."*

After two hours Alvarez shoots his reply back into the ground below. An arrow runs through parchment. The paper reads simply, "No."

Draden sighs inwardly. With a heavy heart he orders the sack of the city. Within hours Moscow falls. Walls are torn asunder, blown through by incessant bombardment. One hundred thirty thousand defenders fall in the breach succumbing to the well-trained, well-disciplined and well-organized Resistance army. The remainder turn on Alvarez and surrender. They preferring the right of safe passage over last rites in life. Only twenty five thousand Resistance fighters met their end this day. True to his promise, Draden allowed those who wished to leave safe passage out of Moscow. A mass departure follows. Some returned to Saint Petersburg, some to Sector 4 while others have no idea where to go but leave. Those who defected with Alvarez from the Resistance beg forgiveness. Draden denies their request no longer able to trust them. He urges them to leave before further calamities befall them from angry Resistance fighters who would rather see them executed. They flee presently.

Yver brings Alvarez forward in chains. Nakano made the original capture and relied upon every ounce of restraint not to sever his head where he lay. If given another opportunity, Nakano would surely kill him. He takes custody of Alvarez instead. Nakano burns with disgust. Seething at Alvarez's sight she stands behind him raging within herself. Draden recognizes this and commands, "Katsumi, stand down. Please come over here next to me." Hoping that he can remain a human shield between her and Alvarez should Nakano lose her restraint. Sheldon is also in custody and ushered into the now tattered and crumbled outer keep. Draden's makeshift command room. Upon seeing Sheldon's entry, he orders him to be held in a different room until he has determined what he will do with Alvarez.

Draden looks at Alvarez, "Here we are Diego. What am I supposed to do with you?"

"Where is your witch?" rumbles Nakano.

Startled, the troop realize for the first time that Maera has indeed gone missing. The expression on Alvarez's face, the anger in his eyes and his disposition is different now than it was the last several days and atop the wall. He is in a daze. Somewhat of a stupor. Almost unsure of what transpired throughout the course of days. He is remorseful and ashamed. "I," he begins, "I deserve to be put to death general. I don't deserve your mercy." Answers Alvarez. Nakano jumps out from behind Draden eager to oblige and puts a blade to his neck ready to grant his wish.

"Katsumi, stand down." Orders Draden breaking her urge.

"He's lying." Screams Nakano. "Can't you see, he's a coward with no honor. Just playing games to buy time."

Draden not certain of the truth orders Alvarez held in the dungeons below until he determines what to do with him. "Where is Maera?" he asks of anyone who may have the answer. Nuriel shouts from the battlements through a pair of binoculars, "She's fled. She started running as soon as Alvarez took to the wall."

"Very well. Let her be. There is nothing we can do from here." Ascertains Draden. "I'm sure this is not the last we see of her. Bring me the governor, maybe he knows something that we need to know."

Yver brings Sheldon to Draden. Draden looks him over, "Governor Geoffrey Sheldon. I understand you are a man of reason and intellect above force and violence?"

Sheldon nods and cooperates as would be expected of a gentlemanly diplomat, "I hear the same about you General."

Draden is almost flattered and would be softened had he not known Sheldon's reputation for weaponizing words. "I really wish you would have peacefully turned over the city governor."

"I actually really wish I did too. But the lieutenant general fully believed his option of resisting was the better course of action." Answers the governor.

"Well he wasn't really thinking clearly now was he." Says Draden.

"I see now that Maera's pull over him was greater than I had originally thought." Offers Sheldon.

"Ah, so you knew." Presents Draden.

"Of course. There is more information that I am happy to offer you in exchange for a few comforts." Proposes Sheldon.

Draden asks Yver to give the governor a seat and remove his irons for the time-being. Yver does as ordered but keeps a close eye on his every movement. "Somebody please bring this man a cup of tea. He has had an exhausting few days." Sheldon smiles and understand that Draden is willing to barter comfort for information.

"My family has tended to the side of the victor in almost all conflicts ever waged as far back as the 1800's," begins Sheldon, "to be honest with you, I really don't know which side will win this war. Yours or the Chancellors. You are both kings worthy of your kingdoms."

Draden listens quietly.

"Whenever our side thinks you and your people are done, you bounce back and reverse the tables on us. And that surprise on Damascus last year, that, that was sheer brilliance. Truthfully, even the Chancellor was impressed with that maneuver. He was furious, sure enough, but he was completely impressed." Confesses Sheldon.

"Is there some information you have that will be of benefit to me and my people?" says Draden sternly.

Getting to the point, Sheldon answers, "He is on his way here now. The Chancellor at the head of one million is on his way here now. Those people you just let go, just now, they will likely be back here by mid-day tomorrow behind Darius."

"And how do you know this?" puzzles Draden hoping that information is not actually true.

"The sorceress," he says pointing in the direction she fled, "she told us last night. All Alvarez had to do was hold the city for a few days and Darius would be here to tip the scales."

Draden rubs then holds his unshaven chin. "Please see to it that the governor gets 3 cups of tea a day in his cell. He will not need to remain shackled while behind bars."

Sheldon nods gratefully, "I take 3 sugars with each cup please." He is escorted to his cell and locked up until further notice. Draden has decided to keep him there until Darius' forces arrive and leave the decision whether to set him free or not up to the Chancellor's discretion when he arrives.

Draden stands up and sighs, "Well, you heard the man. Prepare to move out. We have to accelerate our plans."

***

Global-imperial trumpets blare in the distance. Their every tune ushers in threatened annihilation. Draden rushes to the top of the walls for a better view of what he and his army are up against. With every step he wonders if the governor exaggerated their number or underrepresented the timing of their arrival or was intentionally given misleading information by Maera. Peering through his looking glass he sees the aged but daunting Chancellor riding at the front of an army greater than one million strong.

Draden is faced with an impossible choice. He can try to evacuate immediately and risk exposing his entire army to open terrain combat against a superior foe, or he can hole up in the city and wage a prolonged defense until a better strategy can be founded. If he stays too long in the city, he will miss his second contact in the mountains of Tbilisi. They have no supply lines arranged for a long-term defense. Reinforcements are not scheduled to arrive. To stay in Moscow would be to sentence everyone under his command to a slow and grueling death. He cannot do this. Tbilisi is the former capital city of Georgia and nearly intersects the former borders of Armenia and Azerbaijan. This contact point was chosen by Draden and Nesbit specifically for it's symbolic and geographic significance. A meeting with three emissaries from three bordering lands is intentional. This location and time was chosen in order to send a message that the resistance stands together with all God-fearing people from every faith and background united for one common purpose. To restore the rule of the earth to it's rightful heirs. He cannot miss this contact. He has to move out. He has to move fast.

Draden orders the evacuation of Moscow in the direction of Tbilisi, but not before a boulder crashes into its walls sending Draden and many others tumbling in different directions. Draden gets up and shakes off the shock. He is alright except for some ringing in his ears. "Move out! Move out!" he commands wiping the dust from his eyes. He coughs to clear out the speckled debris from his lungs. Draden intends to stay back to buy time for others to evacuate.

Nuriel is closest to him. "Father go! I will stay back and hold them off. You have to go."

With his son's pleadings he is taken back to that unforgivable moment in time that shattered his world. He is taken back to Nuriel's 16th birthday. When he was forced to leave his wife and son to their fate. An awful thought that tormented Draden for the balance of his days. His stomach still turns at the memory. He will not relive that experience again. He has lived his whole life with the belief that his son was meant to lead the resistance the last 20 years, not he. He lived his entire existence carrying the guilt and sorrow that came with that decision. No. He will not do that again. He was determined. His son will live. His son will be taken out of harms way. Not him. He looks upon his son with sad yet proud and grateful eyes. It is as if he knows now that his days are nearly at an end and it is time to turn over the fight. With a look that says goodbye, I love you, he says to his son, "Not this time Nuriel. Not this time. It's your turn now. Go. Lead them on. You know what you have to do." He smiles, turns and runs atop the pulpit. Nuriel knows there is nothing he can say or do this time to change his father's mind. Reluctantly but understandingly he obeys his father's wishes.

<hr/>

Waving his sword in a southward direction Nuriel cries out, "Come on! Come on! Follow me!" he screams. "Through the south wall, through the south wall! Move! Move! Quickly!"

Nakano hears Nuriel's orders and wonders why they are not being given by Draden. She looks to where the action is the thickest. Draden towers everyone atop the gable. Soldiers of the global-imperial army have begun to scale the walls and pour over the top and through the breeches made by the Seventh Resistance. She sees him fending off attackers and hacking down breechers. She moves as swiftly as her legs will carry. Painstakingly she fights through layers of human tissue to get to his side. With every effort she labors forward inching closer.

Out of the periphery Nakano sees a sight that drops her heart from her chest plunging it cruelly into the deepest corners of her soul. She is fully overtaken by the forceful pulse in her chest pounding violently as if the world at that very moment is set to slow motion. She watches helplessly in horror and disbelief as the tip of the spear flung from the far end of the wall pierces his armor and suspends itself from his side. Draden falls to the ground with a thud. His armor rattles as he slams into the ground. Before laying flatly on the stone-gravel stair he manages to remove the spear from his lacerated liver. The earth spins wildly around him. The ground is no longer firm below his body. It is a virtual teeter-tottering mass of dirt cycling his insides out. His blood spills fresh from the open wound onto the surface beneath him. Loose brown dirt gives way to his dark red blood. Faint hints of iron are taken in the nostrils from the heavy scent of blood in the air.

With a superhuman urgency Nakano closes the distance between them, "No! No!" she screams in terror, "This cannot be! This cannot be!" She hacks and slashes her way to him, "No! No! Nuriel! Yver! Haddad! Come quickly! Help me! Help me get him out of here!"

Now beside him she holds his unconscious head up from the earth. His thick brown hair is littered with dirt and wood and soaked in blood. "Godfather! Godfather!" she cries. Draden does not open his eyes but is still breathing. Barely. She stares vengefully at the one-eyed man who's spear struck Draden down. He eyes her back in a contest of wills. He is unphased by her chilling glare. His one brown eye peers behind an aged and sunken lid, the other half of his face nestled behind a black eye patch. He stands amidst the chaos as powerfully as ever. The brown inside his good eye radiates deep crimson as it captures the glint of blood pouring out of the dying all around him. With every step toward her, he reminds her that he is superior. He smiles at her hungrily and says to her, "So beautiful and so deadly. You will make a fine addition to my collection." He pulls a sword out of a fallen soldier's chest and approaches her unperturbed, almost invincible. He moves through the mayhem unaffected and disinterested in the fight that wages around him. He aches to add the famous Nakano to his body count. To make her suffer after he has done to her whatever else he wills upon her body. Having been pulled deeply into the psychological contest with Darius she is startled when Nuriel and Yver arrive to help her pull Draden from the battle.

Draden is pulled to just outside the gates of Moscow and placed on a stretcher made ready moments ago. Several resistance fighters scramble to carry him out of the chaos as fleetingly as possible. In a moment of consciousness Draden remembers Alvarez, he speaks at a barely audible level, "Alvarez, Alvarez, save Alvarez." Nakano does not understand why but complies while resisting the urge to kill the prisoner. She keeps him in chains and secured. Watched by two dozen fighters.

The race to evacuate Moscow is in full motion. The Seventh Resistance cannot cross through the mountains as they had done before. Their force is too large. They can only move one direction. South. They do so post-haste. Darius stays in Moscow to see to its proper recapture. Maera returns with him smiling at his side. Pleased at the outcome. After Moscow is returned firmly under the control of the globalists, half the global-imperial army splits away from the sieging force in pursuit of the evacuating Seventh.

The battle to retake Moscow bought Draden's army some time. In their flight, the Seventh Resistance have put about 2 miles of separation between them and their pursuers. They come upon a stream. It flows full enough and widely enough to give the escaping army a short but much needed respite. Wounds are cleansed and thirsts are quenched. Haddad reflects upon a possibility. He remembers from his mystical studies in the occult and arcane an enchantment that may give his fleeing army some additional time. While others are dressing their wounds and resting for a few moments in the shade, Haddad fumbles through his sack for a passage from the *Clavicula Salomonis [The Key of Solomon]*. It is said that the *Key of Solomon* is the lost manuscript that King Solomon passed on to his son

Roboam just before his death. In its pages are the secrets by which the wisest of Kings, Solomon, commanded humankind, nature, angels, demons and the Djinn.

Haddad quickly cycles through the aged, fragile and lightly discolored pages of the manuscript for references to the pentacles of the moon. He finds them. Putting the papers carefully on the ground to bookmark his spot he frantically searches his pockets and other panniers for the sterling silver pentacles he had engraved early in his studies. He looks for the first pentacle of the moon and the sixth pentacle of the moon specifically. He tried an experiment once before, many years ago with only one of the pentacles, it did not work. To add potency to his enchantment he must combine the first and the sixth to make the magical operation work as prescribed by King Solomon. "Aha!" he finds the sixth pentacle. After a moment's search, "Alhamdulilah [Praise be to God]!" he exclaims aloud in Arabic. He finds the first pentacle in his left pant pocket. He looks at them murmuring to himself, "the first pentacle of the moon serves to call forth and invoke the spirits of the moon. And it further serveth to…" his voice fades. Drowned out by his quiet thoughts. He is fully immersed in translating the hieroglyphics, symbols and inscriptions on the pure silver constructed plate. A skilled linguist and expert practitioner, he is able to make out the meaning in quick succession. He translates the names of four main guardians to the gates of the moon, Schioel, Vaol, Yashiel and Vehiel. On blank parchment he scribbles out a verse from Psalm 107:16, "For he shatters the doors of bronze and cuts in two the bars of iron." He puts the first pentacle aside briefly and picks up the sixth. He scratches his head trying to remember what he read…a lightbulb brightens in his head, "yes…if it be placed under water, the heavens will tear open the sky and send forth a crushing storm." As before he translates the symbols and engravings revealing a line from Genesis 7:11-12, "In the six hundredth year of Noah's life, in the second month, on the seventeenth day of the month, on that day all the fountains of the great deep burst forth, and the windows of the heavens were opened. And rain fell upon the earth forty days and forty nights." He scribbles it out and rushes to the stream with papers and pentacles. His hands shake nervously as he approaches the running water. Muttering quietly to himself his lips move almost in an anxious quiver but he is laser-focused. His intent and will are clear to God and the angels above. Kneeling beside the stream, Haddad raises the first pentacle of the moon up to the sky and utters a prayer in Hebrew, Aramaic, Arabic and Latin then repeats Psalm 107:16 aloud. He places it carefully on the ground to his right side. Then he raises the sixth pentacle up toward the clouds as if beckoning them to split open and bring forth the crushing rain. He repeats the prayer in reverse order, Latin, Arabic, Aramaic and Hebrew then speaks the words from Genesis 7 not as though it has happened in the past, but such that he is willing the fountains of heaven to burst forth now. He utters loudly enough for many along the stream to hear. Their heads turn toward the Sufi enchanter. They watch as Haddad submerges the pentacle under the water squeezing the plate tighter and tighter until the waves around his arm begin to stir.

Above head the sky darkens. Warm, moist air rises in a buoyant plume. The air begins to condense into a cumulus vapor. Rising and cooling temperatures interact violently. Warm air within the mist continues to rise, cooling and condensing rapidly. The condensation releases heat into the atmosphere, warming the wind. Heavy masses of fog rise diabolically up above. The hazy edges become sharp and distinct. Towering cumulus billows stir menacingly above head. Super-cooled water droplets and ice crystals form freely and coexist. Cloud to cloud lightning cracks the sky. Thunder shakes the earth. The cumulonimbus clouds flatten - blacking out the afternoon sunlight - extending as far as the eye can see. Strong, swirling winds usher in the smell of the soil from beneath the waves. Rich, heavy, full and wet is the air. The storm stirs overhead. It is a punishing anvil of epic proportions and stirs patiently awaiting Haddad's intent. He focuses harder. His eyes shut tighter. He squeezes the pentacle stronger. He commands nature north. North the storm surges.

After a few moments the skies directly above the Seventh clear again and return to calm. Northward however, nature's fury devastates the horizon slowing the pursuing army to a crawl. The global-imperial army is forced to stop their advance and seek shelter lest perish under the crushing weight of nature's anvil. Haddad pulls the pentacle from beneath the surface and puts his head to the banks of the stream in an exhausted and thankful prayer. Nobody utters a single word. All are in awe, stunned and in disbelief. Only the pounding sounds of the northern storm carry over from the distance. After a few moments, Haddad's own archer and artillery division break the amazement of the thunderstruck. They erupt in accolades. The chant of "Haddad! Haddad! Haddad!" is the order of the day.

Relieved that his operation actually worked, he puts his instruments away and goes to check on his fallen friend. Draden looks up from his stretcher and smiles weekly to Haddad and through labored breath he asks, "Why the hell didn't you do that earlier?"

Haddad shakes a friendly finger at Draden and clicks his tongue, "Why the heaven…why the heaven, didn't I do that earlier. Not why the hell. No hell here."

Draden answers with a quiet voice having trouble getting the words out, "yes, yes, heaven. I meant heaven. Forgive me old friend."

Haddad smiles and replies, "I tried to do it earlier. But it seems God did not will it then. But, He willed it now Alhamdulilah. Subhanullah [Praise be to God. All thanks to God]." He says expressing his extreme gratitude for God's assistance.

Laughing, though painfully, in quiet amusement, Draden answers, "Of course He didn't will it earlier," he says recalling a passage from scripture, "It wasn't quite the 11th hour yet." All those who heard the general's remark delight in his sharp humor, even during the bleakest of times.

Haddad looks at his friend with sad eyes but says reassuringly, "Rest now general, you must regain your strength for

Damascus." Haddad speaks only half-believingly. He knows Draden's recovery is likely a fantasy. His liver is too severely punctured for him to live much longer. The blood oozing from Draden's side is more black than red. A sign of inevitability. Draden knows it too - he swallows with difficulty and nods.

Before falling back into unconsciousness Draden motions for Nuriel to come closer. Nuriel has not left his father's side but gave Haddad ample space to have his conversation. Nuriel moves closer to hear his father's faintly audible words. When Nuriel's face is close enough, Draden lifts a weak arm and places his son's cheek in his left hand, "forgive him." Says Draden.

"Forgive who father?" asks Nuriel seeking clarification.

"Alv-..." he breathes arduously, "Alvarez." Nuriel nods. Draden continues, "He's a g-...", "..a gifted soldier. His knowledge..." Draden coughs, then finishes, "and skill will prove helpful. You will need him in coming days." He says as he struggles to take a deep breath and returns to sleep.

Nuriel understands that he is now the de-facto general in charge of the Resistance. While his troop's loyalty and commitment is unquestionable for the time-being, he knows that if he sides too quickly with someone who is believed to be a treasonous traitor he may lose the support he now commands very quickly. Many blame Alvarez for what happened to Draden. He does not share his father's request with anyone yet. Rather, he keeps the advice close to his chest for the best time to entertain such an action.

CHAPTER 8

Numbers

"Lift up your eyes on high and see who has created these stars, The One who leads forth their host by number. He calls them all by name; Because of the greatness of His might and the strength of His power, not one of them is missing."

ISAIAH 40:26

THE RAINSTORM HAS given the Seventh Resistance a full four days gain ahead of Darius' army. Back by Moscow the force of the tempest killed thousands of globalists, decimated supply lines and crippled movement. A few short miles ahead is Tbilisi. The city where the final contact is to take place. Nuriel stops the march and thinks for a moment.

"Up ahead is Tbilisi." Starts Nuriel. "Emissaries from Azerbaijan, Saudi Arabia and Armenia are expecting to see father. Not anyone else. I will take father. Haddad you come with me. I may need you to translate. Nakano stay here to keep an eye on Alvarez. Yver, keep an eye on Nakano. Make sure she doesn't kill Alvarez." All agree. Yver's advanced scout lead the way. Yver stays back to look after Alvarez's safety and to take command of the army should they be confronted by anything unexpected.

—※—

Nuriel, Haddad, and a handful of horsemen approach the gates of Tbilisi. A warning arrow is fired at the foot of Nuriel's horse, Ameera. Nuriel tugs her easily to a stop. Ameera descends from the powerful and exotic line of Arabian horse. Her name means "princess" in Arabic. Generations of exposure to harsh climates and constant guerilla and ambush-style warfare has made the Arabian horse virtually impossible to scare or intimidate. She grunts and protests the hostility from the gates. Defiantly she kicks at the arrow breaking it in two then lifts her head in three quick bursts up to the gate and grunts as if daring the shooter to fire again. Nuriel is ordered to give his credentials by the woman atop the gate and the purpose of his approach.

Nuriel waves to the soldier at the gate as if to beg an apology for his being there. He shouts up at her, "My name is Nuriel Draden, son of Samuel Draden, General of the Seventh Resistance armies. I am here on behalf of my father and Admiral Frederick Nesbit. We seek an audience with the emissaries who have just arrived to you from Mecca, Yerevan and Baku. I am here with my father who has been wounded in battle with Darius at Moscow." He points to Draden lying in a cold sweat on the stretcher, his bandages soak up remaining blood. The red spot of blood slowly increasing circumference as it continues to flow. "With your permission I would like care for my father and to send a message back to my army assuring them safe passage through your city on our way to Damascus. We lost many supplies when we retreated from Moscow and your generosity in helping us replenish them will be greatly appreciated." He concludes, wondering if he's said too much and if he has confused the guard rather than enlightened her of his purposes. Without saying a word she disappears down the stairs of the tower behind the city walls.

Several moment pass. Nuriel, and Haddad can hear Draden's labored breath in the silence. Finally after 10 minutes the guard reappears at the tower. Crunching gears pull back heavy chains. The pulleys clang and click as the steel and wood mechanisms creak and heave the thick iron bars of the gate off the ground. The gates open allowing Nuriel and his companions entry. Servants rush to Draden's aid and take him away to be granted the medical attention that Nuriel asked for. Relieved, Nuriel walks Ameera into the city. She casually trots inside the walls at his command. With a triumphant clip clap of her hooves she marches forward and grunts twice at the guard in the tower as if to say I told you so. Nuriel and Haddad dismount their horses to meet their contacts. Ameera and Haddad's horse are taken to the stables. There they will be looked after, groomed and fed.

At a large, round oaken conference table Nuriel and Haddad sit with the three emissaries. Fresh bread bakes in the kitchen.

It's aroma lingers at the table. Clear glasses of hot jasmine tea are brought in to be drank. The rich scent of the aromatic flower compels Haddad to reach for his glass first and take a sip. "Oh how I have missed you Jasmine tea," he confesses to the glass.

Nuriel and the rest smile. Nuriel starts the conversation, "Thank you all for meeting us. We haven't much time unfortunately. Our plans have changed since Darius took Moscow."

Ambassador Haitham Al-Qasem from Mecca responds first, "We understand. On behalf of the people of the former kingdom of Saudi Arabia we are humbled by the opportunity to be of service to the war effort's greatest general Draden and the ocean's most admired Admiral Nesbit. We grieve at your father's health and will pray for his recovery." Haddad apparently does not need to translate.

"Thank you for your prayers Ambassador Al-Qasem. He is in caring hands now. We can only hope for the best. Unfortunately we fear the worst." A moment of silent prayer follows in honor of Nuriel's father.

Haitham Al-Qasem is an original descendant from the companions of the Prophet Muhammad. His family is one of the dozens of Saudi families tasked with preserving the oral tradition of passing down by memory the Qur'an and Hadeeth from one generation to the next. He, just like his ancestors, take great care and pride in having been able to successfully do this for over a thousand years. He is not a boastful man. His clothes are very simple and plain. His beard is short and neatly groomed upon his weather-worn face. His hair is thick and black on his head. He does not wear the traditional Saudi headdress. He gets too hot too fast when he wears it. His eyes are big and black, but kind and refined. He speaks eloquently and concisely. His hands are large, rough and callused. They are the hands of a stone mason despite his gentle upbringing. He is also a free and accepted mason from Mecca lodge. A lodge that has operated in secret for centuries for fear of reprisal from royal instigators and opposition decadents. He is a devout and spiritual Muslim.

"The free men and women of Mecca and the warriors of the former kingdom of Saudi Arabia pledge our forces to your father's cause. If it pleases God Almighty, may your father's strength pass on to you, his beloved son, should your father not make it to the final day of reckoning." Al-Qasem wishes sincerely.

"Thank you Ambassador. May God bless you and those closest to you for many years to come." Responds Nuriel.

Haddad speaks in Arabic to Al-Qasem, "May God bless you and empower you and grant you and your family good health and luck in abundance."

Sahag Hakobyan, the emissary from Armenia extends his well-wishes to Nuriel for Draden's recovery. "The Templars and peoples of Armenia region stand behind your father and you." Nuriel looks appreciatively over to Hakobyan.

Hakobyan has gentle and caring blue eyes. He speaks with the authority of a knight and with the wisdom of a scholar. His right ring finger bears a large and heavy gold ring with the insignia of the Knights Templar etched upon it. It is a family heirloom passed down from the eldest son to the next since the inception of the Templars. He is broad and muscular and carries himself with compassion and empathy for the meek and powerless. If one would hear him speak without seeing him in physical form one would picture him wearing the brown robes of a cleric copying pages of scripture to scrolls by candlelight instead of the herculean warrior he is - replete in heavy plate mail - wielding a great and massive broadsword. Across his chair is flung the red cape of the cross. His family blade rests formidably against the thick oak table leg to his left. His family crest on the hilt of his sword glimmers brilliantly amidst the torchlight flickering along the walls. Sparks crackle from the flames. His face is strong and square, jawline is angled and sharp. He is not clean shaven. He is also not scruffy.

Like the descendants of Al-Qasem, the Hakobyan family are sworn protectors of the gospels of Jesus Christ. Originally his family walked with Jesus during his lifetime and over generations kept the promises of his teachings alive to pass down through generations. During the early crusades, Hakobyan's ancestor's were among the first Knights Templar who crossed the lands and seas to protect Christian pilgrims on their migration from Europe to the holy city of Jerusalem. Because of their dedication to the word of God and living in authenticity with the main tenet in all scriptures – tolerance of our neighbors – the Hakobyan family was allowed to remain under the protection of Muslims in Jerusalem during King Philip's inquisition of the Knights Templar. Many Knights sought safety behind the walls of Jerusalem but mostly, they were corrupt and self-preserving. The Hakobyan's were among the few who were afforded this protection because of their pious reputation and adherence to Jesus's teachings. During Philips inquisition, the Knights Templar went underground only to re-emerge several hundred years later as one of the highest honors one could achieve as an active designate in freemasonry.

"Thank you Ambassador Hakobyan. Your aid and your wisdom are most welcome in our fight to come." Assures Nuriel.

Emissary Levi Cohen was one of the first Israeli expatriates to settle outside of Israel in the mountains of Azerbaijan at the start of the war of the hemispheres. When Israel was destroyed, hundreds of thousands of Jews followed him and emigrated to Azerbaijan. They sought shelter and refuge in the mountains. Cohen was able to give it. His care and attention to the fleeing peoples of Israel added to his unchallenged influence in the region. He is a devout and holy man who leads first by the old testament then by contemporary rules. Cohen represents the body politic of the Azerbaijani Jews. While not from among them, he is the head of a large subgroup of Jewish people who migrated to the mountains during the Sovietization of Zionism in the early 1920's. At one point in time, the capital city of Baku had the largest population of Jews in one capital city outside the state of Israel. That is, before Israel was devastated in the war of the hemispheres. Baku is still home to the largest synagogue of what was once considered Europe. He is average height with a lean and muscular physique. Many years of mountain life have honed his senses and given him a thorough understanding of how to survive amidst arid rugged terrain. His eyes are dark green and his hair is a wavy sandy brown curling at his temples around his ears. His voice is especially deep when compared to his build. He is thoughtful and complete with his thoughts.

"The mountain Jews of Azerbaijan region will support you Nuriel. Your father is a great man. We are honored to stand beside you both." Cohen speaks directly and with conviction.

The counsel of emissaries discuss their plans and formulate their strategies through to completion. Their meeting is adjourned.

The Seventh Resistance arrives. They are granted safe passage through Tbilisi and have been reprovisioned enough to continue their advance. With Yver at the head, the Seventh has formed up in orderly military fashion on the south gate of the city. They pass through the narrow valley between the walls of mountains and stand ready to continue their march to Damascus.

Nuriel receives a letter from Admiral Nesbit. Nuriel tears it open quickly. It reads, *"Nuriel, I received news of your father with great sadness. Thank God you are okay. I have just completed my business in India. Stay the course. I remain sincerely yours, Fred."* Nuriel puts the letter away neatly in his pocket.

After a half day's march, advanced scouts from the south return with news of an approaching army of unknown origins. The count is two hundred thousand in number. At the front rides a gleaming golden scythed chariot pulled by three horse. Its rider is fully plated in golden armor. She flies a light blue cape. It flaps in the wind as she accelerates toward the Seventh. Her helmet is open faced in a T, showing only her eyes. Horns rise on either side. Her thick honey-gold hair flows freely behind her in the wind. The army resembles Norsemen on the march behind the mythological Queen Freya, wife of the all-powerful Oden, father of the mighty Thor.

Half the force is comprised of cavalry, half of light infantry. No archers or artillery are present. No archers or artillery gives Nuriel a certain comfort. His force exceeds hers in number but he cannot afford to lose anyone to long ranged skirmishes and prolonged engagements. Nuriel signals the order to form up in preparation to outflank and surround. If he is to engage her, he must make sure there is no route of escape otherwise he could be drawn into a rolling guerilla battle which he hopes to avoid at all costs. He hasn't the time nor the mobility to win such a scuffle. The Seventh moves south preparing to engage. The south moves north quickly closing the distance between them. The armies halt less than a quarter mile from one another and face-off. The leader comes to a poised, controlled rolling stop. Nuriel's cavalry has taken positions on every flank. A company of one hundred thousand has looped around the southern army and now stand behind prepared to tighten the snare should Nuriel give the order. Hostilities do not commence.

A cold, quiet calm descends on the field. The sun is setting behind the mountains at back of the golden chariotress. A soft mountain breeze brings with it mixed scent of sweating horse, cured leather and sweet floral mountain hydrangea overpowering them both. Nuriel looks on. He does not draw his sword. The leader steps off her rolling fortress and without hesitation walks boldly toward Nuriel. Her arms fall relaxed at her side as she approaches. She is unarmed and non-adversarial. Moving closer she walks tall with straightened posture and commands an air of royalty. Nuriel is unsure how to respond. He dismounts - remaining armed – keeps a hand on his blade and waits for her to arrive.

She is directly in front of Nuriel and stands much shorter than he. After some examination of his face and stature, her icy, piercing blue eyes soften and relax into a mystical blend of turquoise, sage, azure and gray. "Look at you, my baby boy all grown up." She removes her helmet and reaches up to kiss his exposed face several times on each cheek. Aurelia does not look a day over forty years, though she has just entered her sixtieth year.

"Mother!" he exclaims. His eyes widen. He is not sure if he is in trouble with her for something he did when he was 16 and is overdue now for a scolding. No chastisement comes. He is overjoyed to see her. With her arms already clutched tightly around him, she draws him nearer still. Nuriel returns her affections warmly. The Seventh Resistance looks on with mixed emotion. Mother and son are reunited while Draden holds on to life. He hangs helplessly on the brink of life. Aurelia is not a sentimental woman. She has a warrior's heart through and through. But their reunion gladdens her heart and fills her with joy. A mother's love for her son, no matter her statuesque outward appearance, is enough to melt glaciers and pour emotion into the souls of the sea. A single tear rolls down her cheek for her joy is mixed with pain. She easily maintains composure, doing so with calm and dignified grace. She sniffles a single sniffle then asks, "Is it true about your father?"

Nuriel returns a solemn expression, he curls his lips together and nods his head. "Yes, let me take you to him." He takes her to his side. Draden is halfway in this world and halfway out of it. His eyes occasionally roll to the back of his head showing only their lower whites. He lets out troubled breaths and groans intermittently with fever and sweats. Aurelia kneels at Draden's side. He is clutching something metal in his hand. Aurelia does not pay immediate attention to it.

"Sam...Sam," she whispers softly to him.

The fading general thinks he is dreaming. Without opening his eyes, he grunts and moans in an attempt to usher the dream away. Aurelia takes his free hand. It is cold and clammy in hers. She warms his hand in between both of hers. "Sam... wake up. Wake up darling...it's me. Aurelia."

Draden knows he is no longer dreaming now, he opens his eyes. They roll back to their regular position and lock onto hers for a moment. He does not speak but looks to the object in his hand. He breathes something out that sounds like Aurelia. He looks up at her and breaks a weak smile. He struggles to lift his free arm around her and tries to draw her in for a kiss. He presses cracked, dried lips to her mouth. Looking to the silver and stone object in Draden's hand, Aurelia recognizes it instantly. It is the silver and moonstone bracelet she lost when they were separated. He kept it with him for over 20 years. It is in immaculate condition. Just as it was the day he gave it to her. A rush of emotions swell inside her. The steady calm of Aurelia begins to wear on her, she cries but resists the urge to break down. She feels her pain fully, but does not let it drive itself to the surface. Her tears moisten Draden's chapped mouth. She presses her cheek against his - wetting his weathered face. She lifts her head off his and with a look that beams with the purest love urges him to will himself back to life.

Aurelia looks at her husband deeply – her mystical blue eyes shine with celestial light though they are slightly reddened from behind her tears. The contrast of light red, blue, green, azure and gray combine to give her eyes a magical quality "You have to live. You have to live," she pleads with him to fight for life tightening her hands around his. His hand shakes as he extends to give his wife her bracelet. She accepts it readily. Draden's smile widens when she takes it back and returns it to her wrist once more.

"It still fits nicely." Aurelia says with breaking tear.

Nakano comes to her with a flask of water and hands it to her. Gently Aurelia lifts his head from off the soaked pillow and guides the water into his mouth. Some spills from the sides of his lips. When he's finished drinking she lays his head tenderly back onto the pillow and delicately rubs the dirt from his hair. "Rest now my love," she says to Draden, "I'll be back to check on you again soon."

Urgently Aurelia gathers Nuriel and the other commanders to deliver the information her scouts have picked up. "Not far from us, about a days march south," she explains, "a globalist army from Kabul moves to block your escape and pin you in between them and the marauders from Moscow."

"How many?" asks Nuriel.

"One million." She exclaims.

After Aurelia's separation from Draden and Nuriel 20 years ago she found her way to Perth Australia in Sector 8. From there she snuck through enemy lines posing as a harmless gypsy beggar woman. She would sing and read people tarot cards and Nordic runes for food and supplies. By hopping methodically along the islands of Indonesia and the Philippines she was able to remain undiscovered. Along the journey she remained open for any signs of allies to the Resistance. She found sympathizers aboard a merchant vessel trading along channels in the Indian ocean. During her employ aboard the ship, Aurelia cooked, cleaned, repaired what needed repairing and fought off pirate raids alongside the merchant captain. In exchange for her service she was delivered to Yemen at the foot of Sector 1. The merchant captain gave her the name and location of a family who needed her help and particular skills. This family was very well off, but suffered from looting and bandit brigades that regularly extorted them and plundered their business whenever they needed extra rations or supplies. In addition to caring for their children and home, Aurelia organized her own militia to fight off and dispatch the bandit brigades once and for all. So grateful for her aid but no longer requiring her services, the family arranged for her employment with the royal family of Jerusalem. The royal family had no heirs. All their children had died in wars or were taken by ill-health. Their eldest daughter would have been Aurelia's age by the time she started working for them. Aurelia undertook arranging the royal family's domestic affairs and fighting off looters, gangsters and extortionists. By the time the matriarch of Jerusalem died, Aurelia had gained their complete and unbridled trust and loyalty. It was the wish of the royal matriarch that Aurelia assume her title and position as the Queen of Jerusalem when she died without being obligated to fulfill all the wifely duties expected of the Queen. Perhaps, not shockingly the patriarch did not object to this arrangement. An aged man in his 90's he was grateful to have her aid. When the patriarch died, Aurelia inherited full power and control over royal Jerusalem, its finances, forces and spiritual affairs. Because of its important symbolism to all the peoples of the world, it was largely left alone in order to avoid further insurrection that would stem from sacking the revered city. As such, Darius allowed Jerusalem to remain an independent city within the borders of Sector 1. The Chancellor even visited with the new Queen of Jerusalem on a couple of occasions. Aurelia was a gracious hostess and played her part as a loyal subject of the global-imperial cause so well that Darius did not suspect her of being anyone other than who she said she was.

⚜

"So, a million to the south, half a million to the north and we with a little under nine hundred and ninety thousand now with the inclusion of Aurelia's forces. This could work. I have an idea," says Yver. All listen in.

"They want to confine us inside a pincer movement. But you know what that maneuver needs in order to work? I mean, to really work?" They look on.

"Surprise. It is missing the element of surprise. Being cutoff and knowing we're cut off gives us tactical advantage. I'm certain they did not expect us to know." Everyone agrees. "The pincer is simple. Put pressure on the army from one side and push them into a killing wall on the other." Yver shows crushing walls with his hands. "If we know the wall is killing, we can sever the killing mechanism before it kills us." Yver tells and begins to draw the scenario into the dirt floor with one of his daggers. He goes through the formations and division strength, movements and expectations. He looks at his diagram and is puzzled at how to fill a missing piece.

"What is it?" Asks Nuriel.

Yver sighs inwardly, "We need cavalry support here on the fourth corner." He points to the top left of his diagram. "I can lead the eastern surge, you can lead the southern surge and your mother can lead the western surge, but our north needs a cavalry pincer of our own in order to seal the walls." He says figuratively.

Alvarez comes to Nuriel's mind immediately, though he is not certain how to present that possibility to those present. Perhaps more importantly, how to make that option okay to the near million men and women who see Alvarez as a traitorous coward. News of his release and trusting him to ensure their safety may be objected to disquietingly. Aurelia feels the discontent in her son's thinking. "Son? Out with it?" She says.

"Alvarez," says Nuriel.

Immediately upon uttering his name, Nakano protests sharply, "No way in hell!"

"Here me out Katsumi," he pleads.

Nakano stands aggressively with her arms crossed and suggests to him that he has only one shot for an explanation and it better be damned good.

"We will have a gaping hole in our defenses if we don't seal off the northern pass with cavalry. If we put Haddad's people there, they will get one or two shots off before being run down and pushed outward into the mountains. If we put you there," Nuriel points to the northern pass, "we will have no one to break them in the middle. Essentially what we are doing is driving a superior force into our barrel to be picked off en masse. Haddad's people will literally pin them down in the center. Without you here ensuring that they stay here," Nuriel points to the center of the diagram, "there is no picking. The picking is the whole strategy. And you are at the center of it." Explains Nuriel.

Nakano puts her hands on her hips in upset that Nuriel's explanation made a solid case for letting Alvarez go. "Unbelievable shit." She says before storming off to prepare for battle.

"I don't think she expected you to come up with a good explanation." Shares Haddad before smacking Nuriel affectionately on the shoulder. "Let's get to work." He goes to prepare.

"You should inform your people that you are letting Alvarez go and explain to them why. You don't want them finding out about it on the battle field." Insists Aurelia. Nuriel nods and begins explaining to the other officers to explain to their companies. Murmurs and objections rise to a peak briefly then settle down as they understand it is a military decision made under difficult circumstances.

Nuriel stops by his father's makeshift bed before the armies of the Seventh ride into battle. "Father?" he urges.

Though still very weak and ill, Draden is more conscious since Aurelia's arrival. The medical attention he has received has reduced his pain and brought down his fever. The infection in his liver still spreads however. He is alert when he receives his son. "Alvarez will not betray you. He is a good soldier and knows how to adapt effectively to the field and flow. I would have made the same choice." He tells Nuriel in hopes of comforting him in his decision.

⚊⚌⚊

"You look well," says Aurelia arriving at Draden's bedside. A 9 year old girl runs out from behind her clutching a doll in her tiny fingers, "somebody wants to say hi." Aurelia tells Draden.

Draden looks at the little girl through straining eyes, "Amalee?" he says brightly.

The little girl runs to Draden and hugs as much of him as she can, pressing accidently on Draden's bandage. She is overjoyed to see him. Draden whinces in pain briefly and returns her hug with as much strength as he has available to him. Draden looks to Aurelia, widens his eyes and with a tilt of his head asks the question, what's she doing here? Aurelia explains how Amalee came under her protection.

On the road to Hanover, a band of hungry, unsavory thugs jumped the trio and their escort. Thanks to the protection Draden provided them for their journey, Rebecca and Amalee survived the attack. Dalia was not so lucky and was taken by the bandits as they fled. Her body was found later in the woods tattered and ravaged. After the incident, the only safe place Amalee and her mother could be taken was Jerusalem. Draden understands. The wife, daughter, and sister of a former Resistance fighter who turned globalist spy is known to the masters he served. It was a reasonable insurance measure the globalists took to ensure that the spy they turned to work for them isn't also working as a double agent against them. If he was in fact a double agent, his family would not survive to hear about it. At the moment Cooper accepted the globalist offer to betray Draden, he wittingly or unwittingly also placed his wife, sister and daughter at their mercy. Jerusalem was an independent city. One of the few known places remaining on earth that they could find safety. It made sense that the escort Draden provided would take them there. But Draden does not yet know how Rebecca and Amalee came under Aurelia's protection. He is still unaware that she is the Queen of Jerusalem. Aurelia smiles at her husband and sits by his side and rubs his forehead. Draden notices that the bracelet he returned to her shines brilliantly on her wrist. "I have so much to tell you." She says and provides the abbreviated version of her journey before she rides off into combat.

Draden grins as bigly as he can, "So, does that mean I'm like the King of Jerusalem?"

"Maybe." She says playfully, "but you'll have to live long enough to find out." She smiles. "Rest darling. Your son and I have some global-imperialists to kill. See you in a bit." She walks off. Amalee stays protectively at his side. Draden rubs the top of her head with the closest hand.

⚜

Alvarez lines up in position to the northwest. The head of one hundred thousand horse. Precautionary measures are taken to make sure he does not betray them once again. Alvarez will lead the northern cavalry seal but his company contains officers from Yver's brigade, Nuriel's company and Aurelia's norsemen. If there is any sign of deceit or treachery, the officers are given orders to kill Alvarez on the spot and the senior most of them would take command and finish the charge. Nakano's suggestion. She didn't really leave much room for argument or negotiation on the subject. Basically she insisted that everyone agree to those conditions or they could do the 'barrel picking' themselves. "I like this girl." Aurelia says about Nakano.

The Last Days of Draden

Nuriel pulls the muscles in his left cheek back contorting his mouth in the process, as if to roll his eyes and say, mom you're not helping. Instead of saying that, he settles for "Let's move out."

※

The earth starts to rumble beneath the heavy hooves of the Seventh Resistance and the steady turn of the wheels of Jerusalem's chariots. Yver surges to the east. His company rides closely along the shores of the Caspian Sea at the head of one hundred thousand cavalry. He is careful to leave enough distance between his force and the enemy force to complete a full loop around when the time comes.

Nuriel and his division of two hundred thousand heavy horse start into a southeasternly dash that will eventually hook upward to catch the global-imperialists from behind. Their job - drive them to the center of their lines as if sheep being herded by the shepherd. Speed and precision in timing between Nuriel, Yver and Aurelia is essential in order to maintain the façade that the resistance force is superior to their own and they have caught the global-imperialists unsuspecting.

Aurelia awaits on the western front with one hundred thousand heavy chariot. She will advance slowly - applying pressure on the herded global-imperial force. Once the bulk of the opposing force is within range she will pounce on them with all rights. Her attacks will resemble a lightning storm that draws forth Thor's hammer with every strike. Each chariot is equipped with lance and spear, shield, bow and scythe. The riders of these deadly rolling fortresses are skilled horseman as well as lethal infantry. The global-imperial army has not prepared for chariots and will be caught off-guard. They will not be able to reconcile their strategy with this new, unaccounted for mobile threat. Nakano will handle the enemy cavalry once they are herded to her.

Alvarez stirs at the ready with one eye over his shoulder. His task will be to limit how many of the Moscow force get through the narrow mountain pass at any one time. He is well up to the task and without a doubt the best man for the job. Eventually he will let small numbers of Moscow marauders through so they may be decimated along with their colleagues in the deadly barrel.

⚜

Nuriel and his force accelerate their charge. Yver is surely near his mark by now. In a rounded, looping movement, Nuriel's two hundred thousand start to hook upward. Dust swirls behind their advance. Heart rates hasten, muscles clench. In the distance Nuriel sees clouds of dirt kicked up by Yver's cavalry. The moment is exact. The marching army from Kabul is caught completely by surprise. The pincer wall is ordered pressed. As riders of the Seventh Resistance arrive at this fateful moment, animal and rider alike know each other's moods and movements. They respond to one another instantaneously. The nudge of a knee the flex of a hip, a forward lean to intimate power, a subtle tug to a burst of speed. In nature's perfect harmony, they work as one.

The Last Days of Draden

From the northeast and southeast, riders of the Seventh resistance race forward and slam their wall into the rear of the Kabulian formation. Disoriented and in disarray the rear of the Kabul lines have no choice but to try and repel the attack. As anticipated, the forward lines continue to move on toward the last known location of the Seventh Resistance at the Tbilisi mountain pass. Nuriel and Yver have not been identified as part of the Resistance. Instead, the global-imperial officers think they have been ambushed by a completely random foe. Nuriel whirs his Morningstar in the air. The whistle of the spiked-iron ball grows louder as he increases the velocity of the spin. One after another Kabul soldiers are struck down by his hand. Ameera tramples and thrashes incoming foot-soldiers. Her battle armor sharp with death - slices, cuts and stabs. Screams of the dying resonate. The salty scent of the sea is soon overpowered by the stench of death in the sky. Yver and Nuriel press their wall west as designed.

The forward positions of the Kabulian army are funneled into the center of the barrel. Nakano meets the rush of their cavalry with sturdy spear and lighting-fast side assault. With every collision she and her infantry knock riders from the safety of their saddle to be cut down swiftly on their backs. Aurelia presses east to cut-off the ground support of the Kabulian infantry. Her chariots roll and rumble over the earth sending rock and wood flying from beneath their wheels. The razor sharp blades of the wheel scythes mow down enemy infantry cutting through tissue, cartilage and bone as easily as if she were riding through a field of paper soldiers. The confusion of the Kabulian army enters new heights some already begin to flee.

Up along the northern pass, Alvarez continues to cut down Moscow militia limiting entry into the field of battle. The army from Kabul has lost tens of thousands to the blades of the Seventh while in their disorientation and disorganization many other thousands have fled. Remaining soldiers in the main battlefield on either side are now near equal in number. Momentum continues to mount on Nuriel's side. Soon, Aurelia's chariots can see the pressing walls of Nuriel and Yver's cavalry inching closer west. The pincer is working.

Alvarez now bears the worst of the brunt. The Moscow forces have begun to catch on to what is happening and have modified their strategy to break his seal. Before each rush of militia through the mountain pass, a flurry of arrows and artillery thins out the blockade. More and more of the Moscow militia men and women are getting past his line. Alvarez refuses to concede their advance and rushes head long into the carnage. His action inspires others around him. They join him in the melee. Alvarez and his force fight on. They fight while moving backwards on their heels. Still they hold. They will hold as long as they can until there is enough devastation of the Kabul army that their position can be reinforced.

Alvarez is knocked off his horse. His sharp instincts deflect a deadly blow to his head. The angle of his defense was not sharp enough to come away from the blow unscathed. The heavy axe that befell him cuts through his armor and tears into the back of his right shoulder. He wreathes in agony

and falls to the ground. His shoulder sears hot with pain. The
musty smell of the ground mixes in his nose with the smell of
blood. He has broken his nose in the fall. Blood rushes down
his nostrils into his mouth. He spits and desperately grabs for
his sword with his good arm. In anticipation of another strike
he raises his sword to block, the power of the slash knocks
Alvarez's sword back onto his chest. The blade of the axe is
buried into the soil only inches away from his head. He can
smell the raw steel and wood from the weapon next to his
face. The axe is hoisted up again for a deadly final blow and
the clang of crossbow missile into standing armor instantly
sends his assailant toppling to the ground. Axe and marauder
fall together. His leather and scale jerkin rattles on the dirt,
the axe blade chimes and wooden handle thuds against the
rock and gravel as it lands. Alvarez looks in the direction of
the missile to see a 9 year old girl standing over a crossbow.
Amalee did not even think, she saw Alvarez in trouble and
an abandoned crossbow, closed her eyes and pulled the trig-
ger. She did not know what she was aiming at only that it was
pointing generally at Alvarez's attacker. Alvarez picks himself
up and hurries to her protection, dragging his sword in his left
hand and wiping the blood from his nose away with the back
of his injured right. It occurs to him that his forces have been
pushed very far back from his original line. As far back as the
medical tents. It seems Amalee was hiding out inside the tent
next to Draden when the sounds of battle got too close for her
to ignore. In an attempt to protect Draden she went outside to
ward off any attackers.

When Alvarez reaches her he instructs her to remain hidden for the rest of the fray and promises her that he will come back for her after it's all over. A sudden memory returns to Alvarez. He recognizes this girl. She's Cooper's daughter. The spy that was executed in Hanover. He then shamefully recalls protesting Draden's order for an escort and actually arguing for leaving her, her mother and her aunt to their fates. He is overcome with enormous guilt for having had such a thought. A change begins to swell inside him. A transformation is occurring within his core. Suddenly, he remembers Draden's voice clearly in his mind as if the general were speaking these words to him now just before Amalee's father was executed for treason, "We have a duty - to every soul on this planet – to save any and all who can be saved." He recalls with absolute clarity. Not only clarity of thought but also with clarity of purpose. He accepts now that this war effort is not about individual glory or being remembered as a war hero. It is about every man, woman…and 9 year old child… doing their part no matter how large or small. With zeal and fervor standing united in common purpose. A purpose far greater than themselves. In his stream of thought, Alvarez forgets his pain and is carried back to the field with a fire and vigor he has never felt before. Lieutenant General Alvarez has finally transcended himself.

⚊

Nuriel, Yver, Aurelia, Haddad and Nakano survey the field. They can still see the dust clouds in the distance kicked up by the retreating Kabul force. Bodies in the mountain pass to the north are piled so high that it is impossible to see over them. The ground is red with blood, the earth is moist beneath their feet. The stench of blood and death lingers heavily in the air. Once in a while, a clean mountain breeze carries with it the purifying scent of mountain Hydrangea and Jasmine breaking the monotony of the decay. Nuriel has heard that Alvarez has fallen and searches for his body. He is unable to find him amidst the carnage.

"Maybe he left." Suggests Nakano. "He did his part and left."

Nuriel thinks her suggestion over. "Maybe," he says dolefully, not convinced that Alvarez would just up and leave if he were still alive. Nuriel never wanted Alvarez to die. He respected him, his abilities on the battlefield and for the devotion he had given to his father for so many years.

"Let's go check on your father," recommends Aurelia placing a caring hand on her son's back.

⁂

Nuriel and Aurelia enter Draden's medical tent. They are followed by Yver, Haddad, and Nakano. Inside, Amalee runs to throw her arms around Aurelia in a tender welcoming embrace. "Mama Aurelia!" exclaims Amalee happy to see her adopted mother.

"Hey there little warrior." Greets Aurelia.

"You're not kidding," affirms Alvarez.

211

Alvarez is seated unassumingly next to Draden's bed. Nakano grabs for her katana. Draden is awake and lifts an unsteady hand to stand her down. The lieutenant general rises from Draden's side and picks up the doll that Amalee dropped in her excitement to see Aurelia. Grimacing in pain and favoring his injured shoulder, he brings it to her - kneels tenderly at the young girls side, hands her doll back to her, smiles at her and gently kisses her head. "This little warrior saved my life." Having said that, in soldierly fashion he stands and waits for anyone else to speak. He is ready to accept whatever punishment he must face. Whether he is to be locked up again or is to be executed now after his usefulness has been spent.

As he stands, there is a different glow about Alvarez. He is soft-spoken, modest, and laden with humility. The pompous, arrogant, prima-donna, glory seeking, reputation obsessed Alvarez has been broken away from his true self. His authentic self is now strongly present. He no longer cares about how the Resistance will reflect on his legacy. His only wish. His sincere, solemn commitment is only to victory over global-imperialist oppression and injustice. He does not care how large or how small his role will be in this fight. He only knows that he will do whatever he needs to make things right. His duty as far as he is concerned is to live with Draden's words etched into his mind for as long as he lives. He has a duty - to every soul on this planet – to save *any and all* who can be saved. It's not about himself any longer.

"You look like shit." Breaks Nakano, "but I no longer want to kill you." She says.

"Well, that's very good news Lieutenant Commander. And I am very happy to hear it." Alvarez breathes in relief.

"We are just about to plan our attack on Damascus Lieutenant General, your insights will be most welcome." Invites Nuriel.

Alvarez smiles and accepts graciously. "May I propose something General?" he asks Nuriel, referring to him for the first time by his rank without contempt.

"Of course," replies Nuriel.

"May I propose that Lieutenant Commander Nakano drop the Lieutenant from her name and just be referred to as Commander? I can't think of anyone else more worthy of it." Alvarez request sincerely.

"I think that's a wonderful idea Lieutenant General. Thank you for proposing it." Acknowledges Nuriel.

"Masha'Allah," exclaims Haddad expressing his vast wonder and amazement at God's hidden workings and secret designs.

Nuriel requests a few moments alone with his mother, father and Amalee. Alvarez, Yver, Haddad and Nakano acquiesce obligingly. "We will see you over there when you're ready." Yver says referring to the war room.

⊰⊱

"Mother?" Nuriel asks, "Do I have a little sister?"

Aurelia nods her head, "I legally adopted her in accordance with the laws of the independent royal city of Jerusalem. It was her mother's wish before she died. It was Amalee's wish and frankly, it was my wish too."

"Okay then. That is good to know." He looks over at Amalee, "Nice to meet you little sister." He says to her and waves a few fingers. Amalee runs over to him and squeezes him tight. Then she hurries to Draden and gives him a kiss on the head forcing his smile. "Papa Draden saved my mother and me's life. Mama Aurelia took care of us when we had nowhere else to go. And now I'm going to look after all of you." She says innocently but at the same time earnestly.

Draden puffs his lips in astonishment and tells his son, "Oh, and, ah, by the way, Did you know that you're the prince of Jerusalem too?"

Nuriel is confused, "Huh? What are you talking about?"

"I'll let your mother explain," smiles Draden.

CHAPTER 9

Samuel

*"Blessed is he who reads and those who hear the
words of the prophecy, and heed the things which
are written in it; for the time is near."*

REVELATION 1:3

ADMIRAL NESBIT ANCHORS off the coast of Gibraltar just on
the border of Sector 5 and Sector 2 between Morocco and
Spain. His 3 level Trireme warship guards the channel into
the Mediterranean sea and Syria with 125 ships. Fifty ships
span the length of the Mediterranean at strategic guard-points
that stretch to the coasts of the Levant and Sector 1. Seventy
four ships provide immediate support to the Admiral in the
water against incoming global-imperialists naval vessels. 525
other vessels guard channels into Sector 1 along the Indian
Ocean from points in Sectors 9, 1 and 5. Battle ready galleys
are anchored in the Black Sea above Turkey and in the Caspian
Sea above Iran. Several longboats are moored in the Baltic
Sea to deny land access to Sector 1 via route of Sector 7. The

remaining 100 vessels are arranged in five squadrons consisting of 20 vessels each. They have orders to sweep and patrol Sectors 8, 3, 5, 6, and 0, harass any vessels launched from those sectors, and sink or damage them until they reach the blockaded access points in Sectors 1, 9, 2, and 7. With a force of 800 vessel brought together from every watery chasm in the earth, Admiral Nesbit has cut off all major water ways into and out of the capital city of Damascus. The strategy he explains in simple terms is, stop the blood flow into the heart and brain of the global-imperialist body and they will die a quick death.

Months ago in the war-room of Mount Torghatten Nesbit and Draden chose the Admirals blockade at Gibraltar by assessing military capabilities and possibilities as well as their studies of various sources of scripture. One particular vague passage in the Qu'ran caught their eye. The eighteenth chapter called 'The Cave,' verses 94-99 reads, *"They said, 'Oh Dhu'l-Qarnayn! Truly Gog and Magog are workers of corruption in the land. Shall we assign thee a tribute, that though mightest set a barrier between them and us?' He said, 'That wherewith my Lord has established me is better; so aid me with strength. I shall set a rampart between you and them. Bring me pieces of Iron.' Then, when he had leveled the two cliffs, he said, 'Blow!' till when he had made it fire, he said, 'bring me molten copper to pour over it.' Thus they were not able to surmount it, nor could they pierce it. He said, 'This is a mercy from my Lord. And when the promise of my Lord comes, He will crumble it to dust. And the promise of my Lord is true.' And we shall leave them, on that day, to surge against one another like waves. And the trumpet shall be blown and we shall gather them together."*

At their initial reading of it, the passage made little sense. However, the words "barrier," "iron," "two cliffs," "fire," and "waves" kept nagging at Nesbit. He insisted they review the passage one more time. When the two war chiefs cross-referenced the Qur'anic passage with the bible, Hebrew scripture and other scriptures, they were able to pinpoint the location of "the two cliffs" to the cliffs of Spain and of Morocco which border the Strait of Gibraltar just at the mouth of the Mediterranean Sea where it meets the Atlantic Ocean. It was this passageway that Alexander the Great or his father, Philip II of Macedon, were urged to seal off at the behest of their subjects to stop the incessant destruction and catastrophes that plagued the entire coastline of the sea as far east as Egypt, Israel, Syria, Turkey and Persia. Gog and Magog may be actual people that roamed the coasts of the Mediterranean wreaking havoc and wanton destruction on a peoples, or, Nesbit and Draden thought they could be something else. They may be descriptions for forces of destruction known by other names and that were not human at all. In all historical references, Gog and Magog are depicted as forces of nature, both of which have highly destructive capabilities. It was assumed they were human. Gog and Magog are mentioned in the Hebrew scriptures and in the New Testament as forces of destruction. In Ezekiel 38:2, the prophet Ezekiel is told to prophesy against Gog of the land of Magog who would attack Israel. In Revelation 20:8, Gog and Magog refer to the nations that Satan will rouse to fight with him in the end times. A Muslim Hadeeth describes Gog and Magog as huge in size, while other accounts describe them as very small. The word Gog is translated by some ancient civilizations as a derivation of the word A'*Juj* or *Ya'juj*. To make a *Ta'ajjuj* is a verb of *Ya'Juj*, which literally means to "ignite a fire." The word Magog stems from the roots of *Mawj* or *Majuj* and refers to destructive waves of the sea. Both forces are destructive and each force descends from opposite poles of nature. In some historical parables Gog and Magog are always destructors of a people that arrive to the purpose of destruction via opposites poles of the earth. Throughout the history of the earth, fire and water have caused destruction of biblical proportions time and again. Fire and water could not be more far apart yet so closely related. A comparison that the Admiral and General will use to their advantage in coming clashes with global-imperial forces.

Admiral Nesbit's entire global fleet consists of 200 heavy Trireme's one of which he is standing atop as the flagship of the Resistance navy. The others are 150 light trireme, 300 medium galley, and 150 small galley. By contrast, the global-imperial navy is mostly made up of heavy frigates and warships designed to overwhelm small groups of pirate vessels, traverse large bodies of water for cargo, deploy troops on foreign lands, patrol large sections of ocean, and survive constant exposure to storms and the elements. They are ill equipped for large scale, quick attacks from multiple smaller, faster vessels. Nesbit and Draden know this and thus is how they selected the elements of their fleet. Through Nesbit's vast network the fleet of the Seventh Resistance was especially created for this single, epic, fateful time.

Nesbit's trireme carries 200 battle-hardened men and women. 170 control the oars, direction and speed. Working in near perfect synchronization the oarspersons maneuver the ship with Rolex precision. When not navigating the ship, each are fearsome and deadly infantry in their own right that serve the fleet the same way the Marine's had in years gone by. Thirty officers command small platoons of five people each. The captain is in charge of twenty. There are two decks of oars for maximum speed and agility. The third deck is the ship's main. Two masts rise several feet into the air to provide additional power and speed when ramming, maneuvering or escaping. His immediate ships, and many of the ships deployed around the world are equipped with catapults, ballistae, grappling hooks, battering rams, archer towers, flame throwers and canisters of coal and pitch polymers.

Looking through his spyglass from the crow's nest Nesbit sees the first wave of attack by the global-imperial navy. The heavy smell of the beach and sea fills his lungs with every breath. Seagulls squawk above head. Nesbit relishes in the scent. Adrenaline begins to course through his aged veins reinvigorating his heart and pumping new life into his body. 150 large, well-manned frigates approach the mouth of the Mediterranean. They are followed and harassed by twenty smaller ships of the Resistance fleet. On Nesbit's command a light blue flag is hoisted on one mast, and a black flag hoisted on the second signaling the smaller vessels to disengage and return to their patrol in the North Atlantic. Once disengaged, the flags are lowered and one much larger flag replaces two smaller ones. The new flag is freshly sewn for this very occasion. A light blue, solid black flag is raised on the taller mast with a distinct white border extending its length from bottom left to top right. This border divides darkness and light into separate and distinguishable quadrants. The colors of the original Resistance, the Resistance before Darius, are soon hoisted atop every ship in Nesbit's formation. All personnel take their general quarters in preparation for battle.

Nesbit's fleet keeps steady in formation and watch patiently while the global-imperial navy lumbers closer. The globalist navy starts to bend formation in a peripious flank. The globalists aim to push Nesbit backward into the coastline for easy ramming against the rocky and jagged shoreline rising behind him. Once sufficiently battered, the imperialists will attempt to grapple the broken barges, board, burn and annihilate everyone on board. Nesbit waits patiently at the head of his 75 craft.

Once close enough, Admiral Nesbit gives the order for the first 75 to form behind him in a wooden wedge to breakthrough the center of the widening gap in the global-imperial formation. In perfect time, 74 triremes turn and glide atop the water's surface. A powerful diekplous ram made up of Nesbit's navy punch a hole in the center of the globalist fleet battering enemy walls and slicing through hulls with brass blades bearding top levels and hidden just below the ocean's surface. The sound of crashing vessels pounds in the ears. Global-imperial vessels in their path are ripped asunder, pulverized. Their timbers decimated and torn to shreds. Twenty global-imperial ships have started to sink. Bodies splash into the sea, thrown overboard by the powerful jamming force of the wedge. The ram works as one. Many ships of the Resistance focus brute strength on few global-imperial targets pummeling and crushing them to bits. The smell of broken wood and ravenous sharks beneath the waves permeate the senses.

Just behind Nesbit's advance, in the mouth of the strait, Resistance ships from the Mediterranean fill the channel, squeezing through the narrow pass to block imperialist entry and escape. They create an impervious battering wall that cuts-off almost all remaining 100 ships of the global-imperial navy from forward action.

Many of Nesbit's ships are now behind the globalist formation. "Turn!" orders Nesbit. With rhythmic chant every floating fortress moves in choreographed brilliance. Bag pipes whistle tunes in tandem guiding the powerful oarsperson strokes into motion. The entire fleet turns as one and looks down their decks at their enemy with battering rams, grappling hooks and ballista missiles facing forward.

"Move!" Shouts Nesbit. Again by perfect uniformity of cadence and song Nesbit's fleet pushes forward to smash the ships in front of them. They drive them back toward the coastline and into the awaiting ships in front of the channel.

In a second collision, more bodies are thrown overboard, Resistance and Imperialist alike. Nesbit's Mediterranean fleet has begun battering and shattering global-imperial vessels that have drifted too far inward to the coastline of the strait. The global-imperial sailors, soldiers and mariners try desperately to grapple to pull Nesbit's vessels closer on their own terms. But it will not be so. Nesbit's forces are too well-disciplined, too fast and too nimble. Once they collide with an enemy hull in synchronized cadence they pull back with just the same ardor. Imperialists grappling hooks are mostly ineffective against Nesbit's well-trained, organized Resistance armada.

"Circle fire!" orders Nesbit. In harmony the squadron encircles the global-imperial ships and prepare for broadside attack.

In position the Seventh Resistance ships fire away mercilessly. The first wave of attack is ballista. The large wood and iron arrows skewer dozens of sailors as they crash and bounce across the surface of the ships out the other side propelling them into a watery grave. Next, catapulted stones fired from the coastline sail through the air and tumble devastatingly on the global-imperial decks below. Some ships take surface damage, others fill with foam and water from the sea when the stones travel clean through the boat's spine. Global-imperial vessels fire back with flaming arrow, boulder shot, and tar. The Resistance take damage. Several ships are lost. They react quickly halting much more destruction. Oarspersons have stopped rowing and ascended to the main deck with shield and plate. On command they lock shield across the entire surface of the ship deflecting burning arrow and flaming tar harmlessly into the ocean. The Resistance answers with a counter.

Rock, metal and stone are replaced by heated coal and pitch. "Ignite!" yells Nesbit. In one coordinated salvo, the admiral's fifty seven ships remaining in the Atlantic and the fifteen from the coastline raindown fire and smoke upon the enemy. Sixty global-imperial ships begin to smolder, forty of those catch full fire and turn to ash. Imperial ships are trapped. They are pressed on one another. When one vessel ignites, it acts as a natural ember fueling destruction onto neighboring boats. Any ship that tries to escape the furious incendiary is forcefully rammed back into the fire bomb. They signal the retreat. But on this day, Nesbit will not let them go. Today is the day of reckoning. The day that the global-imperialist fleet crumbles under the Resistance's might.

"Harpax!" orders Nesbit!

In an instant every Resistance vessel within range of an enemy boat launches a mechanized grappling harpoon into the nearest enemy warship. The tethered spear punches into the hull and locks itself into place. A series of metal winches and cranks are pulled and activated by Resistance hand. The global-imperial ships cannot escape. They are pulled back into the fight. A violent hand-to-hand, deck to deck melee ensues. The seas turn red. Sharks circle voraciously below in anticipation of their next meal. They devour anyone knocked into their midst.

The total annihilation of the North Atlantic Global-Imperial Fleet is complete. The last vessel bannered by Darius' flag disappears in a whirlpool beneath the waves. The sea opens and closes its swirling jaws swallowing its final morsel and pushing it into the depths below.

A victorious Nesbit strides along deck to the Captain's pulpit. Cheers of triumph settle down as the Admiral prepares to speak.

Nesbit stands atop the pulpit, dignified, tall and proud. He takes a moment to gather his thoughts. He speaks with the authenticity in his heart. He is moved by the gallantry and bravery of his men and women. "History has been written today! Each of you has inscribed your name into the halls of eternity. Those who are still here with us, breathing this salty air and those of you who have just given their lives so the rest of us may live. Every one of you shall be remembered for your role here today no matter how large or how small. You were once pirates, you were once officers, you were fisherman, farmers, deckhands, husbands, wives, sons, daughters, fathers and mothers. Some of you were lost, others could not be found. But here, today, we all stand as one! We stand together without title or badge, or class or occupation. We stand as one for freedom. We stand together for hope. We share each other's pains. We feel our neighbor's loss. Together...make no mistake...together, we are free and together our destinies cannot be denied! The age of the final reckoning has come."

Triumphant applause explodes on the sea. Nesbit stands commandingly but with total humility. His clothes are splattered with blood. His forehead is covered in sweat. His tunic is torn where enemy blades nearly cut into him but missed. Resting his hand upon his sword he regains his breath. With compassion and grace, he looks into the eyes of as many as look back.

⌗

Nuriel visits with his father in the medical tent before examining the front lines like his father used to do over his legendary career. The medical tents are set up on the hills overlooking the capital. From here, Draden and Amalee have a bird's eye view of the battle and can see for miles around the city. Nearby guards are posted as well as officers who will signal from the position tactical opportunities that are not readily visible from the ground amidst the frenzy that is sure to come.

When Nuriel enters, he notices that Draden's condition has significantly worsened. Pus mixes with blood. His bandages stick tightly to his wound. They are removed with great difficulty. Every change of cloth brings with it grueling pain as skin is torn from torso with every pull. His fever has returned and is the highest it has been since he was struck by spear. He is unable to drink much or keep any food down and has lost 50 pounds. His once powerful and commanding frame is reduced to a frail skeletal representation of himself. He is conscious and alert and in great discomfort. His skin is pale and cold, his eyes are sunken and tired. Breathing is labored.

Aurelia and Amalee are also by his side. Nakano, Yver, and Alvarez have just left. Haddad lingers for a bit trying all manner of mystical herbal remedy in a last ditch effort to return vitality back into his friend's deteriorating body. When he sees Nuriel enter, he says his farewell to his friend.

Haddad believes that he has done all he can to restore Draden to health. He is not optimistic about his recovery and does not know if he will ever see him alive again. Haddad shares heartfelt words before he departs. "Sidiqi, you are my truest and best friend. I ran away from life into the mountains and Allah sent you to find me. You returned to me hope. You gave my life meaning once more. Because of you, I realized that my parent's death did not have to be for nothing. I am eternally grateful to you for showing me that. I am eternally grateful for your friendship. You will be forever missed and never forgotten." He kisses Draden's hand noticeably grieving. Haddad leaves to take position on the field surrounding Damascus.

When all are gone but Aurelia and Amalee, Nuriel shares, "Father, I bring news from our fleet in the west." Nuriel sits by this father's side. Draden looks at his son feeling his time is very near. "Nesbit has won. He has destroyed the North Atlantic Global-Imperial Fleet." The news livens Draden. His face breaks into a wide and pleasant smile. For a moment he has forgotten his own discomfort. He knows that with the water channels secure Nuriel can command freely in accordance with their plan. He will be safer now that reinforcements cannot come infinitely from every direction. He is more happy for Nuriel's increase in odds of success than in the news of victory. Though the news of the triumph gladdens him greatly.

Draden speaks weakly with a last bit of advice, "When making deals with pirates, always make sure that your own booty is not exposed."

Nuriel smiles, "Of course father. Nesbit and I will see to it." Draden nods in acknowledgement. Nuriel leaves.

Aurelia kneels beside her husband. The moonstone and silver of her bracelet glisten in the light. This may be the last time she sees her husband alive. "Samuel, my dear wonderful Samuel," she says, "you have reshaped history and given us all a chance at a better life. A powerful life. A life free from tyranny. A life for all to re-shape and re-create their own destinies and fortunes. I am indebted to you. The world is indebted to you. We will carry your legacy forward for as long as we live. I promise you my love. I promise you. I love you." She remains strong on the surface but mourns silently inside. A single tear manages to break through her wall. It falls tenderly on Draden's cheek. He pulls her in close to him, kisses her mouth and top of her head. "You make sure our son stays alive." He beckons her.

"Of course I will." She smiles and gets up to go.

As Aurelia nears the exit, Draden says, "He moves just like you, you know?" he looks gently upon her.

"He thinks just like you." She returns.

"In that case, he'll be fine." He smiles. She returns a grin of her own and takes her place on the field.

He pats the open space beside him on his bed and requests that Amalee sit next to him. She obliges happily.

—※—

Damascus is surrounded by two million of the Seventh Resistance. Among them are the Jewish warriors from Baku, the Christian forces from Yerevan, the Muslim soldiers from Mecca and thousands of other faithful who do not subscribe to any one house of worship over another but believe in one supreme Lord who embraces all who embrace Him. Standing together shoulder to shoulder, spear to spear, horse to horse. They are supported by dozens of trebuchet's, catapults, mangonels, siege towers, ladders, battering rams, bores and a few thousand engineers who will dig beneath the walls breaking their foundations loose from below. Since Draden's last invasion exactly one year ago Damascus has made strong improvements and modifications to the weak points in their defenses. Because of Draden, the global-imperialist forces have learned how to better defend themselves against a Seventh Resistance siege. At the same time, because of Draden, The Seventh Resistance has learned how to better take the city.

Nuriel does have more time than Draden did to take Damascus. The time is not indefinite however. Darius is on his way from Moscow with millions of his own and will arrive in a few days time. The battle for the control of Damascus must be measured and sustained, while at the same time be fast and overwhelming. The Seventh must capture the city and quickly turn their attentions to defending it before Darius arrives. Two distinctly different strategies – offensive and defensive - will need to be employed and executed with masterful precision. They have had practice in attack, but have had no practice in defense. Will they be able to hold? Many wonder but don't care. They will take the city the rest will fall into place they conclude.

To compensate for the speed required to take the walls and then reverse tactics to defend the walls, several more siege apparatus' and engineers have been commissioned than would typically be needed to break through the city's defenses. Once taken, Nesbit and his fleet will move their ships closer into land so as to be able to deploy reinforcements as needed and fend off global-imperial relief and supply from the sea.

In planning for their assault at Mount Tor, Nesbit and Draden had placed Darius in the capital city for the siege. Due to Darius' absence, Nuriel and Draden with correspondence from Nesbit have modified it in recent weeks to accommodate their change in plan. Nuriel reassures himself that no mistakes have been made in his understanding of the adjustments. Time will soon determine if he has correctly understood their renewed plans.

⚓

The siege of Damascus is just about to commence. Nuriel moves to atop a rising where he can look upon the sea of troops and siege engines that span miles around the capital city. A scene that is only rivaled by an onlooker's account of witnessing the pilgrimage of millions of faithful into their holy city.

"My father dedicated his life so that we may all have a chance to live free. His blood, and the blood of millions cover these grounds. Those who came before you, stood on the very same earth you stand upon today. Look around you. They are among you. My father is not with us on the field today but he is with us still. From those hills...," Nuriel points to his father's tent. The figure of Draden on stretcher looking down upon them burns itself into their eyes and etches into their minds. Draden's image looking on fills their hearts with courage and ignites their blades with fury.

Nuriel continues, "From those hills he watches us. His spirit protects us. He believes in all of you. And his legacy will live on through us all. We do not take Damascus for my father nor do we take Damascus for ourselves." Nuriel's voice rises, "Nay, we take Damascus for our children and for the future of humankind. We take Damascus to purify our lands from the scourge of hell that has reigned upon us for more than fifty years. We take Damascus to return the world to the hands of the kind, noble and just. We take Damascus to return our homes to the guidance of the wise. We take Damascus in service of liberty! My father did not allow us to bow down to tyranny and you shall not allow each other to be denied our freedom!" The roar of 2 million emblazoned warriors echoes into the clouds and sends chills down the globalist spine.

Impassioned and ordained, Nuriel commands the artillery with the words, "Let us finish what we started! Fire!"

What follows is nothing short of epic devastation.

—※—

Hundreds of missiles are unleashed and pulverize the fresh stone into grains of dust and sand. Wood beams and panels are reduced to cinder. They crackle and blaze into ash. Defenders are thrown several feet into the air with almost every collision of rock, metal, stone and spear into the walls. Smoke rises from the towers. The scent of burning embers carries into the wind. Screams of the dying resonate in the ears. The smell of burning flesh penetrates the senses.

"Fire!" orders Nuriel ushering in the second wave of blasts.

The thrashing continues at an accelerated and compounded rate. Towers crumble. Debris tears through tissue and brings the icy grip of death with every burst. The jeweled city of Damascus is on fire. Nearly every corner explodes. The burning city reflects brightly in Draden's eyes. His earth colored pupils are ablaze with scenes from below. The traces of the sea around their rims glow orange with flame.

Not to be denied a defense, Damascus answers the assault with a devastation of its own. The large, massive wooden and iron spears of the ballista rip through Resistance lines. Barrels of burning tar and oil are sent hurling through the air and collide with masses of the Seventh huddled close together. They are set aflame and scrap in agony for relief. Some are put out of flame when doused by water. Still they suffer from their burns. Others are turned to char and die. Arrows upon arrows are slung into the ranks of the sieging army. Hundreds of arrows find their marks.

"Come together!" cries Nuriel. "Shield wall." On command the Seventh defend the assaults from the walls.

"Towers to the wall!" Nuriel commands.

Massive, lumbering towers from every side of the city are pushed to the wall. They are steered forward and helped along with systems of winches and pulleys to settle in just the right position upon the ramparts. The treated animal hides reduce the effects of fire on the frame. Scores of soldiers form behind the gargantuan structures prepare to scale the ladders inside to the drawbridge above and across the enemy wall. Ladders are carried from behind. The towers reach the fortifications and attach. Warriors surge through the roof. Ladders set, men and women climb on to meet their fates.

"Battering rams!" shouts Nuriel.

Beneath a protective covering of hide and repellant, the Seventh push and heave the rectangular and triangular shaped mobile fortresses forward. Levers, ropes, rollers, pulleys, and winches guide their movements to the gates. The heads of the ram's hammer incessantly at the hinges of the gates grinding away stone, iron and wood. One hundred soldiers beneath every ram move in rhythm to swing the bronzed spear head of tree-trunk back and forth. Every pounding crushes away more mortar and stone.

Engineers are hard at work removing the earth from beneath the walls. Many are taken from life. Undaunted by their losses they bravely measure, calculate and dig on.

"Breach, Breach!" cries someone from the front.

"Into the walls! Into the walls!" orders Nuriel, sword held high, Ameera on hind legs, her front legs balance in the wind.

Seventh Resistance fighters surge into the opening in the walls. A second yell comes from across the city, "Breach! Breach!" The heavy crack of splintering wood and crumbling stone gives way to a gate ripping off the wall on the opposite side of the breach.

Alvarez grips the reins tightly, "Into the breach! Into the breach!" he yells. Thousands of foot soldiers lead the way with spear and shield. Hundreds of horses follow behind. On approach, riders of the cavalry throw themselves off their horses and take flight. They crash atop defending infantry breaking imperialist necks and crushing globalist spine.

From the front, the main gate comes crashing down. It falls forward crushing many under the battering ram below but forms a natural bridge across the moat supplementing Resistance siegeworks and constructions.

Nakano yells, "Follow me!" her detachment rushes after her like water bursting from a chasm ten thousand feet deep.

In the rear of the city, to the north, another shouts, "The walls have fallen! The walls have fallen!"

Yver storms through the north. Aurelia and Haddad's divisions lend support along the fringe. Aurelia's forces hack and slice global-imperialist that squirt out from the melee. Their powerful chariots run down any in their path. Haddad's snipers pick off imperialist support from the walls and his artillery focuses fire on city defenses.

Atop the hill Draden looks on, his condition forgotten while his heart swells with possibility. Can it be? Can Nuriel take Damascus? Is victory so near?

Advanced Resistance scouts yell from the northwest. "Incoming! From the mountains. Incoming!"

The Resistance has prepared for this possibility. Aurelia moves half her force to secure the mountain pass. Alvarez joins her on the western flank with one third of his detachment. Nuriel looks up from hacking sword to ensure his army is deployed as scripted. Seeing his mother and Alvarez charging into the direction of the threat he returns to the melee in which he is entrenched.

Draden looks nervously in the direction of his wife and Lieutenant General. He knows they are the most capable for the task but he fears for their fates still. He returns his attention to the flaming capital. The Resistance has begun to fight inside its walls. They have moved the battle into the city. Victory is near at hand.

Nuriel breaks through the gauntlet of wielding sword and flying arrow. He charges headlong to the head of his interior force. The city's gates and city walls are now firmly under Seventh control. Danger has receded to the inner keep. The tower that shelters Darius' throne.

Nuriel whirls his sword after the retreating army and orders bombardment of the inner keep. Battering rams are brought in to pound through the inner gates. Stone crashes with stone, the top of the inner tower tumbles to the ground below. Battering rams and engineers hasten their work. The inner gates fall.

"Into the keep! Onward!" declares Nuriel. Cavalry dismount. A vicious hand to hand melee crowds the inner walls.

⚜

Over in the mountain pass, Aurelia and Alvarez have put up a formidable wall. Their brigades begin to wane - forced to fall back. Desperately they plot their movements to give Nuriel the precious time he needs to take the city. Their numbers start to fail at an accelerated rate. Haddad sees the threat and declares his intent to the heavens. "Subhanullah, al-Aziz, Al-Hakeem. [Glory to God, the Wise, the Just]. Grant me the necessary strength I need to complete this operation." He says and rushes to the only tower that remains standing.

From the hills, Draden eyes a figure in white robes ascend the eastern tower. Somehow miraculously, the easternmost minaret of a ruined mosque in Damascus is the only tower left unmolested by the havoc and devastation. It remains structurally in-tact. Draden's attention is split between the mountain pass, the burning city and the minaret.

Haddad pulls the lost *Key of Solomon* from his hipsack once more along with the 7th Pentacle of Saturn. Fastening the parchment to his waist, he raises the lead pentacle plate on high then nestles it securely on the railing below. The pentacle is engraved with ordinary Hebrew characters and where incomplete was made complete with symbols known as *The Passing of the River*, a lost language of angels. Nine orders of angels are engraved on the plate. Haddad grips the Saturnian portal tightly in his right hand and calls upon each of the nine orders one by one pleading with them for their intervention and imploring God to allow their aid. He calls for Chaioth Ha Qadesh – Holy Living Creatures; Auphanim – Wheels; Aralim – Thrones; Chashmalim – The Brilliant Ones; Seraphim – The Fiery Ones; Melakhim – Kings; Elohim – God; Beni Elohim – Sons of God; Cherubim – Protectors. After having called upon each order in succession he recites aloud in Latin Psalm 18:7 "Then the earth shook and trembled; the foundations also of the hills moved and were shaken, because he was wroth." Instantaneously at the moment Haddad uttered the final letters of the word "wroth" the mountains to the northwest shake and tremble, quake and rattle. The earth beneath them reels and rocks tumbles and heaves. A mighty earthquake is unleashed. Astonished at the event, and not believing his own good fortunes, Haddad remembers and recites to himself a passage from the Qur'an chapter 56 verse 5, "and the mountains are pulverized to powder."

Falling stones crush the skulls of the crossing global-imperialist soldiers. Many are sent hurtling to their death when the ground below their feet is torn asunder and made to give way. Attempting to be saved, they latch on to their compatriots for life, but rather than be saved, they pull the other to their death along with them. Legs are broken, bones are smashed. The weight of the rock suffocates some who are not lucky enough to be killed on impact. The northwest mountain pass into and from Syria, the pass that Draden used exactly one year ago to escape and save thousands of his people, is sealed for all time. It will forever be recorded in the annals of history. Haddad prays gratefully, "Bismillah, Mash'Allah, Subhanullah [In the name of God, Glory be to God, God has willed!]." He quickly packs his stuff and descends the tower.

Aurelia and Alvarez were spared the earthen devastation. They were pushed far enough away from the upheaval by the fighting that not a single one of their troop was killed. In amazement, they freeze in awe for a time before turning direction and riding back to the walls of the capital. The look to each other and ask at the same time, "Haddad?" They both agree simultaneously, "Haddad."

Draden cannot believe what he sees, but accepts it for what it is. Amalee is elated that Aurelia and Alvarez are still alive. Draden focuses his full attention back on Damascus. As far as his eye can see, there are only Resistance fighters inside the city walls. Suddenly, the midnight blue, black crimson flag of the global-imperial army is pulled down vigorously from mast. Celebrations of the Seventh Resistance erupt in the firmament.

Draden's heart leaps joyously at the sight of his son emerging from the carnage alive and not too seriously harmed. He watches as Nuriel triumphantly begins to raise the new flag of a free world over the capital city. Nuriel and several others heave and pull. With every tug, the flag of the Seventh Resistance is hoisted higher and higher for all to see. Until finally it is waving freely and triumphantly above the land. It floats and snaps majestically in the wind signaling to all that a new age of the earth has been brought forth.

Draden feels his pulse starting to fade, his eye lids get heavy - the cold of the atmosphere embraces his body. Before he can no longer move he pats the head of the young Amalee sitting dutifully at his side. He cannot move again. With his last breaths a subtle smile breaks on his lips then disappears in a final exhale. His breathing stops. His eyes close slowly last. With his gaze affixed proudly on his son inside the new capital of the new world, Draden dies.

CHAPTER 0

Revelation

> *"A river of fire was flowing, coming out from before him. Thousands upon thousands attended him; ten thousand times ten thousand stood before him. The court was seated, and the books were opened."*

DANIEL 7:10

"Papa Draden, Papa Draden..." shouts Amalee excitedly, "We won! We won!" She turns to give her adoptive father a warm and enormous hug only to realize he is not moving and does not breathe.

She shakes him a few times before she understands, "Papa Draden? Papa Draden? Are you asleep?" She gets no response from his expired body. She is frightened and in disbelief. "Papa Draden, please wake up. Papa Draden!" She realizes her efforts are futile. She weeps next to him.

The guards rush over to see what has happened. With one look at the body of their general, they know that death has come. One puts his arms around the distraught 9 year old and tries hard to comfort her knowing full well there are no words. They must find the words when Nuriel and Aurelia come for a report.

⁂

Nuriel and Aurelia arrive to sad and terrible news. Samuel Draden has died. A father, a husband, a fighter, a war general, a hero, a legend. He is gone. Ripped from this world by the spear throw of a vile tyrant. A liar, a murderer, a thug, a villain, a false prophet.

Nuriel and Aurelia grieve at their loss, but they are not shaken nor surprised. They both knew when they left him early yesterday morning, he would likely not be alive to greet them when they returned. Amalee desperately clutches at Aurelia's leg, distraught and crestfallen.

"It's okay little one," assures Aurelia, "It's okay. You still have us." Referring to herself and Nuriel. Amalee sniffles and tries hard to understand why she has to suffer so much death around her. So much dying of the people she loves. She is comforted by Aurelia's words.

Nuriel looks to the sky with vengeance in his heart and hatred in his eyes. Darius will arrive soon for a final reckoning. Arrangements need to be made to lay his father's soul peacefully to rest and defend the city. Nuriel kisses his father's cold forehead and returns to the capital to break the news of his death. Before he leaves, he orders that his father's body be properly washed and prepared for burial in accordance with his father's wishes. Aurelia stays behind to see that his wishes are kept.

⊶

Nuriel stands mournfully on the steps of the capital and prepares to address the new nation. "We have won a great victory here today!" the crowd thunders. Then they notice that the victory is not the subject of his address. There is something more solemn behind his words. The onlookers quiet down. Some knowing in their hearts what they are about to hear.

He continues, "We are the pillars of a new nation. The pioneers of a new, powerful, noble and just way of life and being." Heads in the crowd motion in agreement. "Sadly, I must announce that the father of this movement, my father, General Samuel Draden will not be with us to see our movement through." Some sound off with audible heartbreak, others murmur and gasp in grief. Others stand proud that they have recognized at least one part of his dream - the capture of the capital city and the return of the free world to the hands of the free.

Nuriel goes on, "For only a few short hours ago, my father was pronounced dead." Even though many in the audience already knew this, when Nuriel actually utters the word "Dead" Draden's passing becomes real. People react.

"My little sister told me," he starts, "for the brave little girl never left his side..." he smiles at her a gentle smile. Nuriel's words give her comfort, the droplets in her eyes slowly recede

"...she stood beside him to protect him from the evils of this world...she told me that he did live long enough to see our flag hoisted free and full above our capital." Some in the gathering chuckle at the picture of a tiny 9-year old girl protecting their 6 foot 5 general. Others find contentment and solace in the testimony that Draden did live long enough to see the beginnings of his dream for a free and united world realized.

"Tonight we shall put his body to rest within these walls, beneath this earth. He will be buried in the exact mid-point between the three most time-honored and holy sites in this city. The mosque in the east, the church in the north and the synagogue in the west. It was his wish and his solitary vision that every member of every religion of this world would one day gather peacefully in honor of each other's beliefs and not stand bitterly at the other's toes. For we know all too well, history has made all too clear, that fractures between our sisters and brethren whether in faith or politics, if risen to levels unchecked, will lead to a world where no one is free and tyranny and oppression become the law of the land. Please join me tonight for a bitter sweet celebration of our victory over tyranny and to remember all who have fallen in its wake." Sadness and joy exist simultaneously. Funeral arrangements begin.

Draden's body is carried to the burial point between the 3 ancient buildings. A procession follows. Aurelia is first. She holds a candle and says a silent prayer for God to protect his soul in death and shares her gratitude with the Lord for having given him life. Amalee walks next to her. She is still teary-eyed and downcast. Nuriel is next. He does not carry a candle. He walks forward behind his mother. His head is down in prayer and his hands are clasped loosely at his front. Cohen, Hakobyan and Al-Qasem stand somberly and patiently before the fresh hole in the ground just dug to receive Draden's body. Nakano, Haddad, Yver, and Alvarez bow their heads dolefully. Their hearts ache. Yet they are able to find solace, even glimpses of happiness in the memory of his life. The crown of his head will be positioned facing southeast. His feet will extend northwest.

Draden is wrapped plainly in a simple white cotton sheet. Otherwise naked underneath. He is freshly bathed and most of the hair from his body removed. His signature around the clock 5-o'clock shadow and thick, wavy dark brown hair remain on his face and head. His expression is peaceful and serene.

As his body is lowered into the ground, Nuriel shares a quote that his father had shared numerous times *"How wonderful are the affairs of our lives, for all that happens to us is good. If something good happens to me, I am thankful for it. If something bad happens to me, I shall bear it with patience. God knows what is best for me better than I know myself."* Indeed these words summarize the doctrine by which Draden lived. Nuriel speaks them as if Draden is speaking from his grave.

Hakobyan follows with a prayer, "The Lord is my Shepard, I shall not want. He makes me lie down in green pastures; He leads me beside quiet waters. He restores my soul; He guides me in the paths of righteousness for His name's sake. Even though I walk through the valley of the shadow of death, I fear no evil, for You are with me; Your rod and Your staff, they comfort me. You prepare a table before me in the presence of my enemies; You have anointed my head with oil; my cup overflows. Surely goodness and lovingkindness will follow me all the days of my life, And I will dwell in the house of the Lord forever." Hakobyan's words echo Draden's life.

Al-Qasem quietly recites the opening passage of the Qur'an called, 'The Opening,' as is customary among Muslims. He follows with two supplications, the first, "O Allah, Samuel Draden is under Your care and protection so protect him from the trial of the grave and torment of the Fire. Indeed You are faithful and truthful. Forgive him his sins and have mercy upon him, surely You are The Oft-Forgiving, The Most-Merciful." The second supplication, "O Allah, give him a preceding reward, a stored treasure, and an answered intercessor. O Allah, unite him with the righteous believers, place him among Abraham, and protect him by Your mercy from the torment of Hell." Al-Qasem captures the supplications of the many impacted by the great general.

Cohen recites a Hebrew meditation, "May God remember the soul of Samuel Draden who has passed to his eternal rest. I pledge charity on his behalf and pray that his soul be kept among the immortal souls of Abraham, Isaac, Jacob, Sarah, Rebekah, Rachel, Leah, and all the righteous men and women in paradise. Our God and God of our fathers, may the memories of those whom we lovingly recall as we say Yizkor this day influence our lives for good and direct our thoughts away from the vain and fleeting toward that which is eternal. Teach us to emulate the virtues of our dear ones so that we too may be inspired to devote ourselves to Thee, the source of all our aspirations. Our departed mothers and fathers and all our loved ones be united with us. They live in us, in our hopes, and shall their influence continue in our children. In Thee, O Lord, they and we are one. `When I stray far from Thee, O God, my life is as death; but when I cleave unto Thee, even in death I have life.' With Thee are the souls of the living and the dead. Teach us to live wisely and unselfishly in truth and understanding, in love and peace, so that those who come after us may likewise remember us for good, as we this day affectionately remember them who were unto us a blessing. Amen." So it is how Draden will be remembered.

And thus is the manner by which General Samuel Draden is laid to rest.

⚬⚬⚬

Before Nuriel attends to the pressing matter of repelling Darius' attack, he has decided to let all of the prisoners of the city go free without reprisal or retribution. Those who wished to stay and fight could but those who wanted to leave were let go. An exit tax was exchanged for freedom. The tax was minor. A tribute equal to 10% of all they owned was to be left behind. The tribute could come in any form – weapons, food, clothes, medicines – so long as it equaled 10% of all they owned. If it was given, they were released. Hundreds gave it and were granted safe passage out of the city. Many of the Resistance were outraged by Nuriel's leniency. When asked why he did not execute the prisoners or put them to labor repairing the city, Nuriel answered with his father's words, "We have a duty - to every soul on this planet – to save any and all who can be saved." Arguments against his decision to let them go were soon halted by the memory of this legacy.

Nuriel turns his attention to the religious sites that were put out of commission under Darius' reign. Rather than functioning as houses of worship, the synagogues, churches and mosques of the city were decommissioned as such and used as brothels, gambling dens and opium houses. A direct slight to their intended purposes. Nuriel orders that all the sites be cleaned up and restored to their original uses. Certainly he understands that this task will not be completed before Darius arrives in 2 nights time, but he does order that plans begin being made for their restoration and recommission.

Next he gets to putting together the capital counsel. An impromptu collection of a single selected representative from each body represented on the field is hastily formed. Their immediate focus will be on how to see to the effective defense of their new capital. Nuriel, Cohen, Hakobyan and Al-Qasem form the base of the counsel. Afterwards the counsel will decide on the principles of a new constitution. The American constitution will be considered among others. Mostly, it is conceded however that rather than create a constitution simply on logical and rational laws as so many countries have tried in the past and that are subject to pressure, corruption and alteration from self-interested groups, a seraphic code of unalterable beatific tenets must remain at the new constitution's core. These tenets will remain unsullied by human thought or hand and are non-negotiable.

—※—

The city parapets are too damaged from the Resistance assault to provide any real protection from a well prepared siege. Where the ramparts were destroyed, wooden barricades have been erected in their place. A cover of fire retardant hide is fastened and stuck securely on them in defense of flame. Working with what was available, the Resistance has done its utmost to seal the city off from any uncontested entry. Troop engagement in the open is unavoidable.

Much of the fighting will have to take place on open land, in the mountains and sunken knee-deep in the marsh. The battle cannot be waged and won from within the capital. Cohen's contingent will take position on the mountains west and north of Damascus. They will halt any global-imperial advance to take high ground advantage. Hakobyan's knights and horseman will join Aurelia, Alvarez and Yver outside the walls of the capital taking formation on the field.

Al-Qasem's mostly infantry squadron will join Nakano in the swamp and along terrains that are too muddy to give the horse much advantage. Half the infantry will remain within the walls, mostly the spearmen and shield legions. The other half will be with Nakano spread out across the land. The battlefield will stretch for miles. Some of the Resistance detachments will actually be deployed too far away from the capital to see what transpires along the ramparts of the jeweled metropolis.

Haddad's archers will form up on the remnants of the Damascene wall and the artillery will be protected behind the fortifications of the city. Throughout the fight, Nesbit will trickle in reinforcements to give the impression that the combined Resistance forces are much larger than they are. Also to provide real Resistance support.

On the latest reports, Darius marches to retake the capital with four million men and women-at-arms, artillery, cavalry, and missile. The Resistance strength as of this morning is two million and three hundred thousand. This enumerates all combined forces, including the ones that Nesbit provides from the seas. The siege to take Damascus yielded a heavy toll on their number. The men and women of the Seventh Resistance are in for the fight of their lives.

⚔

The hour of reckoning has come. Darius' banner waves balefully in the wind less than 2 miles away. Trumpets blare. The war hammer of the drums pounds thunderously in the distance. The seemingly endless landscape of the desert disappears behind global-imperial lines. Siege engines rise like skyscrapers above them. Battering rams, belfries, ladders, ballistas, mangonels and trebuchets inch closer to the capital and are towed along by the massive military corps. 1.5 miles outside the city walls, the attackers stop their advance. There is silence. The drums cease. Trumpets stop.

The sounds of battle-march are replaced by the grunting, breathing, spitting and the grinding of teeth milling together in indignation. Thumping of beating hearts is raised to a level of urgency. Beads of sweat drip from foreheads of heavily armored militia. Horses are wet with perspiration after the arduous crossing through unforgiving desert sands. The global-imperial army is wrought with madness, enraged by the impetuous conduct of the Resistance. Many stand wrathfully and crack their necks together from side-to-side staring hungrily forward at the live bodies along the Damascene wall and across the Damascus terrain. They stand ready to rain death upon the land.

The Resistance waits impotently before the global-imperialist army. The Seventh artillery cannot reach the imperial lines from this distance. They are a quarter of a mile too far. The barrage engines heaved into the hills are further away still. Launching now would likely fall short of their intended targets and reveal the location of the arsenal. They cannot do that. They cannot take that chance. They must rely on surprise so the enemy does not know in which direction to advance. Darius has his own plans this day.

The sky is set ablaze with flaming global-imperial artillery. Rock, metal, stone and wood are smashed into the Resistance walls as fireballs hurtle people to their deaths in burning flight. A firestorm of artillery rains down from all directions like death's hammer. Fortifications are pulverized. Black smoke rises once more from the city ramparts. Wooden beams and dry straw are set alight. Inside the city, the defenders are gasping and struggling for breath. They flee the flames. Burning flesh pervades rhinal passage. Screams of the dead and dying echo in the atmosphere. Chaos and disarray spreads as wildly as the blaze. The Resistance has no answer from behind their walls.

Outside, soldiers of the Resistance perish under the assault. Only light field fortifications protect them. Interlocking shields and tactical maneuvering keep them alive. Alvarez, Yver, Aurelia, Nakano and Al-Qasem are forced to spread out and thin their lines under the invasion. They keep a steady will and disperse from the danger but do not buckle under the onslaught. This is the last reckoning and there will be no quarter. So, there shall be no surrender.

Nuriel climbs to the eastern minaret and waves a signal. Like an atomic bomb exploding from its epicenter, the cavalry corps of Yver and Alvarez burst into a mushroom cloud around the enemy. Riders on horses lean forward on steeds. Their eyes glow red with rage. Hands clench tightly on reins and legs stiffen firmly around saddle. Hearts race to provide breath. Chests expand and collapse in determination. Adrenaline fuels the veins. The collision is colossal. Lances crash mightily with armor and shield. The clang shatters the ears. Bodies bash violently into one another. Masses of lifeless corpses thump steadily onto the ground. In a few moments, the brown dry sand dunes run red with the fresh stain of blood. The pungent stench of death feeds the fury. The clash is swift and severe. They disengage.

Overcome with frenzy, the global-imperial lines have pursued Resistance horse for over a mile and crossed unwittingly into range of aerial death. Haddad's artillery fires. A deadly barrage rains down on the global-imperialist troops. Boulders slam incessantly on to the field crushing any beneath. The ensuing tumble tears through the lines flattening skeleton into pulp, breaking bones, ripping away limbs. Tar laced fireballs explode on sand. Black resin sticks mercilessly onto leather, metal armor and skin. Deadly snakes, poisonous scorpions and searing sand pour overhead then crash into the ground below. Life is extricated by venom and sand. The globalists are prepared. Shield walls rise in unison. They cannot deflect the boulder but survive poison and tar. Darius has prepared his army well.

The Chancellor rides to his front lines and taunts at the minaret in booming voice, "Nuriel, son of Draden, I expected something more original from you. You're still up to your father's old tricks I see. If this is the best you can do, your precious *Resistance* will be annihilated by days end. All will die a slow and grisly death. I will see to it. Just as I saw to your father. I will feast on your liver tonight Nuriel, son of Draden. Pity, I didn't have the chance to tear your father's out and dine

251

on his just the same. Speaking of which, where is that pretty little officer Nakano? She will make an excellent addition to my concubines." Darius spits and orders continued assault. His army advances steadily in slow cadence. His artillery gives them cover. And so it is. Walls on all sides crumble under the weight of the bombardment. Nuriel and Damascus brace for survival.

⚬

The sound of elephants rumbling forward rises from the east. The horn of their trunks are melodious with war cries. India has arrived! The letter Nuriel received outside of Tbilisi. Nesbit's work in India. That's what he was talking about. The Indian Resistance was not crushed as Darius had thought. He was lured into a decoy war with a decoy leader who willingly sacrificed her life in the name of the Resistance in order to make the ruse work. The armies of India had remained alive through underground channels. Now they answer destiny's call. One million of some of the most formidable and lethal combatants to ever walk the face of the earth pour into Damascus now during darkest hours. War elephant, assassin, foot-soldier, and longbow charge and shoot decisively into the rear of Darius' army. Darius is surprised but undaunted. The global-imperial army takes many losses. The Chancellor assumes command of the defense.

Atop his red horse, Darius blasts into the melee. Even in advanced age, he is invincible to mortal blade it seems. His mere presence on the field in the midst of battle is enough to make the most formidable warriors shudder in doubt.

Nuriel had heard stories of Darius' supposed invincibility but to see it played out in front of him with his own eyes is unnerving. Not one that faces him lives he observes wearily. Nevertheless, India has bought him time to adapt his tactics. Sending signals to the front and to the warriors in the capital, the final confrontation is delayed no longer.

Nuriel orders full attack from all sides while India has them engaged. Devastation spans as far as the eye can see. Hakobyan and Al-Qasem launch their forces into the heart of the melee.

The struggle that follows is monumental, epic, savage, barbaric, gruesome and macabre. From the capital walls the artillery of the Seventh launch grapples into the siege towers and pull them down. Flaming tar is poured below and glues itself to unlucky assailant and incinerates wooden machine. The grounds are once more lit ablaze by pig's grease. Ballista on both sides tear through anyone and anything in their path. Tons of stone and debris crush and rip apart tissue, cartilage, bone and organ. Burning swine, boiling flesh, blood and excrement overpower the senses. The stench of death consumes the nose and lungs. Soldiers on both sides vomit from the smell and devastation of the reckoning. The air reeks of bile. Nesbit's forces fill the perimeters as planned, but soon they too succumb to the horrors of the befallen. Cohen descends from the mountains to halt the advance. They are beaten back. Aurelia presses through with chariot and spear. Her division is decimated by iron and ox. Wheels are broken off platform. Riders are flung from frame and are made to stumble into death. Nakano cannot move fast enough to break their flow. She loses many to the afterlife. Alvarez and Yver suffer heavy losses and fight moving backwards. Much of Haddad's artillery has been destroyed. Many of his archers burned alive, hurtled to their deaths or pounded out of existence.

"Fall back! Fall back!" Nuriel orders.

His armies are being torn to shreds. Not much of the fortifications are left. Having little alternative, all who will fit into the city fall back. Those who cannot are slaughtered outside what remains of the gates. Nuriel stands ready for a last stand. Darius breaks through the front. Fire swirls all around the city, he is unscathed. He draws sword and axe then focuses a deadly eye on Nuriel.

"Nuriel, son of Draden, it's time to die." Darius attacks.

Nuriel fights back with Morningstar and blade. The battle is tilted. Darius quickly establishes the upper hand. With swift forward kick, Darius knocks Nuriel to the ground. The young Draden rolls away from downward slash and gets up quickly. Darius' sword and axe sink into the sand where Nuriel was. Darius slashes again with axe. Nuriel deflects a steady blow and answers with a flurry of strikes. His attacks are expertly placed. Darius defends skillfully. Seeing an opening Nuriel hacks at Darius' torso cutting through leather and flesh. Darius is stunned that he's been bled. He looks back at him with a depraved smile as if he enjoyed the pain. It only emboldens him. His brown left eye is now fully red stained with the reflection of blood. He comes at Nuriel with a flurry of his own. Nuriel is forced backward. Morningstar is knocked out of hand and sent flying out of reach. Darius approaches one last time to pass final judgement on his rival. Nuriel steadies a shaken sword and prepares to defend.

A golden sphere streaks through the sky. Its trajectory is to the easternmost minaret of the eastern mosque. Miraculously, it still stands. Nuriel looks up to the sound of sound being broken. Darius is agitated by the distraction but the sphere is too radiant to ignore. Clutching a golden scepter upon the backs of two creatures with four wings rides what looks to be the figure of a gray-haired man with hair flowing to just beyond his shoulders and is parted down the middle. His golden armor shines with light from the sun. It is hard to determine if panicked eyes are playing tricks on the mind. Or if what appears to be is actually what one sees. All remain captivated by the sight. The glowing orb races speedily through the air. It crosses between double archway pillars on the minaret. Suddenly it is catapulted into Darius' chest as if lightning had struck him square. There is a magnificent explosion. In an instant, the flash is gone.

On the ground lies Darius' lifeless body. His face is frozen in a twisted expression of horror. The eye patch over his right eye has been incinerated revealing the empty black hole in his head that once held his eye. Smoke rises faintly from his face and body. There are signs of a mighty struggle in the dirt around him. As if a supernatural battle unfolded so fast that for an instant the world seemed frozen in time. The faint scent of jasmine, myrrh, cinnamon, and ferula is left behind and swirls softly in the air. The sphere is gone.

Haddad marvels. He thinks he knows what happened, but stands enchanted and in disbelief just the same, "Subhanullah ammaa yushrikoon, la howla wa la quwatah ilah bilah [Glory be to God who is free from that which they associate with him, there is no power except with God]."

The echo of battle departs from the battlefield. All that is left from the global-imperial siege is smoldering wood, rubble, smoke and mountains of carnage. The fires engulfing Damascus are doused. Remaining global-imperial soldiers flee at the sight of their vanquished leader. The light blue black flag of the Resistance still rises atop the capital dome snapping smartly in the desert wind.

Lifting himself up from one knee Yver asks anyone who is listening, "What the...?"

Nuriel looks at him and shares a possibility, "My father once told me that, in their truest form, the three great religions of the world agree on more than what we think they do. And they deserve more credit than what we give them credit for."

Everyone looks to him for further explanation. Nuriel paraphrases what every revelation of every religion foretells, "I can't say for sure that this is what just happened, but among all the great religions, one revelation is constant and identical... *When all else is lost and the earth is in its darkest hour, a Messiah will be sent from above to set it free. He will restore the earth to the faithful, noble and just. And he will be the one who saves humanity from itself.* Maybe, perhaps, he just did. Are we not – at least for the moment - free?"

Peace descends upon the earth...for a time.

Made in the USA
Columbia, SC
21 September 2018